D1714601

Two's Enough
Three's A Crowd

by

Brenda M. Hampton

authorHOUSE™

1663 LIBERTY DRIVE, SUITE 200
BLOOMINGTON, INDIANA 47403
(800) 839-8640
WWW.AUTHORHOUSE.COM

First published by AuthorHouse 01/31/05

ISBN: 1-4033-9472-5 (e)
ISBN: 1-4033-9473-3 (sc)

Printed in the United States of America
Bloomington, Indiana

This book is printed on acid-free paper.

ACKNOWLEDGEMENTS

Special thanks to the following, whose faith in me, belief in me, and/or critical responses enabled me to create such a fun-filled novel:

Jarina M. Ball, Debbie Davis, Deandra Furlow, Phyllis M. Payne, Carmen Y. Turner, Cleveland B. Walton III, and Regina M. Walton.

An Extended thanks go out to:

Joyce M. Hampton, for your endless support, your helpful criticisms, your generous love and for listening to my imaginary dreams while we were children.

My children: Monique, Monica & Aaron, for not complaining when I stayed in front of the computer for days, for allowing me to miss dinners, for forgiving me when you were ignored, for listening, as I read to you and offering your honest opinion, and for giving me a reason to keep on writing.
Aaron Littlejohn, for your patience, your support when I needed it the most, your encouraging words, for allowing me to be me, and for bringing out the best in me.

Finally, a more extended thanks to the Lord Jesus Christ, for with Him in my life all things are possible.

JAYLIN

Eeny, Meeny, Miney, and Moe. I got Eeny and Meeny, now all I need is Miney and Moe. I love women. They're what make the world go round, so the more of them I have, the better off I am. Settling down is out of the question. There's enough of me to share with as many women as I want—as long as they meet my standards, of course. And those, I do have. Any woman who wants to be considered, must be not only bodacious, but must have a degree, be able to cook, have a job, drive a nice car, be African American, have no kids, and most important, must be willing to cater to my every need. If not, then she ain't worth my time.

I'm dealing with two sistas right now who meet most of the above but slack on a few, here and there. So, I'm getting bored.

Nokea is the kind of woman you definitely can take home to Mama, but since Mama ain't around anymore there's no need for that. She's a pretty petite thing with curves in all the right places. Her skin is so smooth sometimes I call her Silk. She's got beautiful big round eyes that go well with her lucious soft lips. Her hair is shiny black and just long enough for me to run my fingers through. But my true attraction to her is her brains. She's a smart woman, knows her shit. Most of all, knows what she wants in life. Since she's been with me, I've only accented her life. I've shown her what a real man is like. I don't play games with her and have never lied to her about my situation. When she's needed me, I've been there. When she's lonely, I hold her. When she calls, I'm there to talk.

However, the problem I have with Nokea is she ain't upping no booty. She firmly believes a woman shouldn't give herself to a man unless she's married to him. And even though I respect her needs, I got needs too. And I need to fuck. Minimum of, at least, three times a week. I expressed my concerns to her but she insists on depriving me.

So, that's where Felicia comes in. Felicia's bad. She gives it to a brotha when, where, and however he wants it. Lay it smack dead on the table and pow-dow, brotha be all up in it. She's got a smooth soft round juicy dark-brown ass and nice firm breasts to match. Her long braids that roll down her back go well with her pretty round face. And her smile is to die for. All she gotta do is lay one on me and I melt. She got a good-ass job and her salary could only enhance mine.

The only thing with her is she's fucking cheap. She never spends a lot of money on me. The only time she does is when it's a special occasion like my birthday or something. Or, if the day before I've fucked her brains out and she wants to be generous. Now Nokea, she buys me everything. Sends me encouraging cards when I'm feeling down. Takes me to dinner and pays. Even buys me clothes when she thinks it's something I might like.

I just can't decide which one of them accents me better. That's why I don't. No one woman can give me everything I want, and for that matter, no two. So, now I'm on the prowl again. Looking for somebody to fill up some of this emptiness I've been feeling lately. Looking for somebody I can add to my collection. More realistically, I need some more pussy. Getting sort of tired of the same stuff. Felicia's good but I want better. And lately I've been trying to ease myself up in Nokea but she's still tripping. So, a brotha gotta do what he gotta do to make sure his needs are being met. If I ain't happy nobody's happy. And one thing Mama always taught me is to make myself happy before I make anybody else happy.

I miss Mama. A mugger robbed her as she walked home from work one day and killed her. I was only nine years old and had to go live in an orphanage until my Aunt Betty came to get me damn near two years later. Living with her was hell. She was a dope addict and treated her kids and me like shit. I moved out at sixteen. By the time I turned eighteen, my grandfather died and left me part of his estate. I found a job and used that money, along with the money my grandfather left me, to pay for my education and to buy a house. Been doing well ever since. Never looked back.

Got a call a few months ago from Aunt Betty begging for some money. She claimed she had kicked her habit and needed a new start, but I ain't no fool. The money I work hard for ain't never gonna be used for smoking no crack. I told her I was on my way but never showed. I guess she got the picture.

Now, I do keep in touch with my cousin Stephon. He's like a brother to me. He turned out pretty cool after being raised by her. Got his own barbershop and makes decent money. To me, he's the only family I got. As for my father, who knows where he is? The last time I saw him was at Mama's funeral. I was sure he would come for me but he didn't.

So, now, I'm doing shit my way. Being very limited about who I let be a part of my life and only keeping positive people in my company. If I feel some bullshit about to go down, I jet. Ain't got time for it. My main focus is my career, my body—I work out every single day—and the ladies in my life. Those things are what make me a confident, well-respected Black man.

NOKEA

I've known Jaylin Jerome Rogers since we were kids. His mama worked with mine at a cookie factory in South St. Louis. He finally noticed me at twenty-one, and we've been an item ever since. He has everything I want in a man. Only thing, he insists he's not ready for a commitment. And since I was with a no-good brotha before Jaylin and I got together, I'm not quite ready for one either. Whenever Jaylin isn't too busy, he finds time to make me smile, to make me laugh, and to just plain ole comfort me. I can ask him for just about anything, and without hesitation he delivers. I think he's going to settle down eventually and when he does, I'll be waiting. I have a special bond with him more than any woman he's been with does. And he told me, when the time came, I would be the One.

So, my future is already in the making. Brotha got a good job as an investment broker and makes about $500,000 a year. That doesn't even include the money he inherited from his grandfather's estate. He needs a beautiful educated woman like me in his life, and if he thinks he can make it without me, he's crazy. I was there when his mama died and when his baby's mama, Simone, took off with his daughter to live in another state. He cried on my shoulder. I promised to always be there for him, even when we were kids. To this day, I've never let him down and I'm not going anywhere.

I'm well aware of his relationship with Felicia but she doesn't have what it takes to keep him. I, on the other hand, do. She doesn't realize a piece of booty isn't all Jaylin's looking for. Hell, he probably doesn't even know it yet. But, I've had years to observe him. I know what he needs, and I know what he wants. In the end, I'll be the one to give it to him. She's only temporary and I'll still be there once she's gone, just like all the others.

See, while Jaylin makes it clear that he doesn't want a commitment, I make it clear that I'm saving myself for my husband. We've come close many times but he knows I stand my ground. He respects me for not giving my body to anyone but my future husband. He also knows Daddy taught me well and I wouldn't do anything to dishonor his wishes. I know he's got needs; that's why I don't care about his other relationships. As long as I hold the most important thing on him, that's all I care about. And that, of course, is his heart. No woman will be woman enough to take that from me. And deep down, even he knows it.

As kids, our parents said we were destined to be together, and there's no way he's going to forget what his mama told him. So, some day—hopefully soon—I'll be Mrs. Nokea Rogers and having the time of my life.

FELICIA

The first time I saw Jaylin, I knew he was the one for me. He stepped out of his black SL 500 Roadster Convertible Mercedes Benz at Tony's Restaurant on Market Street and asked for my digits. Even though he was entertaining someone else that night, I didn't care and neither did he. His dark Armani suit and his curly black hair are what attracted me to him instantly. When he removed his tinted round glasses and I got a glimpse of his bedroom light-gray eyes, I was hooked. I ain't never been excited about no light-skinned brotha but Jaylin had it going on.

After one day of talking, we were rolling in the sack. I held his broad shoulders and damn near broke my back trying to make sure this brotha called me the next day. And that he did. Been calling me ever since. Mostly, late nights after he's exhausted from all the ups and downs of the stock market—which, by the way, can be a pain. His mood swings be killing me; but every time he puts one on, I get up and go.

I know Jaylin loves me but he has a funny way of showing it. This homely bitch, Nokea, thinks he's so deeply in love with her that he can't let her go. But, I got news for her. He could care less about a woman trying to caterer to him like his mama. He already told me I'm the true happiness in his life.

When we get our shit together, our salaries combined will speak for it self. Ain't a damn thing we're gonna want for. We've been to Jamaica, to Paris, and even to Hawaii together. He does nothing like that with Nokea. I'm the one who holds the key to his heart and if he lets me go for her, he'd be a fool. Hell, from what he told me, she ain't even giving him no ass. Now, what kind of woman play that shit in this day and age? How can you be foolish enough to even step to a brotha like Jaylin Rogers and play that "I'm saving myself" bullshit? All she's doing is saving herself for a big fucking disappointment, cause I'm working him and working him good. I'm the only pussy he's laying into right now, and hopefully forever.

He stressed that as long as I continue to give him what he wants, he'll continue to make sure I play a big part in his life. So big, that one day, hopefully soon, I'll be the future Mrs. Jaylin Jerome Rogers.

1 FELICIA

Dinner was spectacular last night. Jaylin didn't seem to be his usual self but work always seems to have his mind occupied. No matter how tired he is, he still finds time to make us dinner on Friday nights. I offered to help but he always gotta have his way. He wanted the credit for such a scrumptious dinner and didn't want me to have anything to do with it. I cleaned off the table and piled the dishes in the sink so I could wash them later. Jaylin went into his room to lie down because he insisted his head was banging. I peeked into his room to check on him a couple of times, and he was on the phone. I knew he was probably talking to that bitch Nokea. He always acts like she's his mama or something. Every time something bad goes down, he calls to cry on her shoulder. It bothers me a bit but I ain't no fucking psychiatrist. I don't have time to listen to his drama, and that's definitely what it is. My job is to only satisfy his physical needs and that's what I intend to do.

I went back into the kitchen and started on the dishes. Jaylin has a dishwasher but he was a particular brotha. Real tidy. Clean as a pin and according to him, a dishwasher doesn't do the job he wants it to do. He had to scrub the dishes himself to make sure they were sparkling clean. Then why buy a fucking dishwasher if you ain't gonna use it? Didn't make sense to me. He said it was bought just to blend in with his other stainless steel appliances in his kitchen. He had to have everything even if he didn't use it. Like his silver pots that dangled from the ceiling right above the black marble-topped island that sit in the middle of the kitchen floor. Never been cooked in at all. He even flew to Paris just to find a European dinette set that's never been sat in or dined on. When we eat, we eat in his bonus room, designed specifically for his guest. It has a theatre-size TV, a pool table and a cocktail bar with every kind of alcohol you can think of behind it. There's also a mustard-colored leather sofa that surrounds the room. We use it for fucking when we can't make it to his bedroom.

I dried the last plate and laid it neatly on the shelf. Soft music played on the intercom throughout the house and I heard Jaylin open the kitchen door. When I turned around, he stood naked, and looked at me like something was wrong. The sight of his muscular body always

1

weakens me, so I laid the towel on the counter to see what was on his mind.

"Jaylin, baby, are you okay?"

"I'm fine. I just came down to see what was taking you so long. My dick don't stay hard all night, you know," he said, smiling, rolling it around in his hand from side to side.

"I was just finishing up, if you don't mind. Besides, I didn't think you were ready yet. The last time I checked, you were still on the phone."

"Well, I'm off now. So, when you get finished in here I got something waiting for you up there," he said, pointing in the direction of his bedroom.

"I'll be up in a minute. Keep my spot warm for just a few more minutes."

Jaylin grinned and walked out of the kitchen. I took a look at his tight muscular ass and rushed myself. Wasn't no sense in me tidying; if he'd come down later and seen something out of place, he'd throw a fucking fit. And I wasn't in no mood to hear his mouth.

I slid out of my sexy red dress in the kitchen and dropped it on the floor. Then I left my black bra on the banister at the bottom of the staircase, and tied my lace black panties around the rail when I reached the top of the stairs. I removed my hair clip and let my braids fall down my back. I followed Jaylin's scent to his room and I quietly opened the double glass tinted doors to his bedroom.

He lay there asleep. Looked so handsome and peaceful, I didn't even want to wake him. I eased into his California style king-sized bed and lay next to him. I rubbed my fingers across his thick plush eyebrows to straighten them and kissed his cheek.

He slowly opened his eyes. "What took you so long?" he mumbled.

"I came right up but you had already fallen asleep." By the time I finished talking, he had already fallen back to sleep.

Friday nights just aren't the same. Jaylin and I didn't used to miss a beat when it came to sex. He'd even wake up just to lay it on me. Something was wrong tonight but I just couldn't put my finger on it. I fell asleep thinking about what was troubling him, only to wake up later by the sound of his loud voice.

"Felicia!" I heard him yell from downstairs. "Felicia! Why is your dress in the middle of my damn kitchen floor? You of all people know I don't like that shit!" He walked up the steps with my dress in his hand.

"Damn, I'm sorry. But you ain't gotta get all upset about it at three in the morning," I said, standing at the top of the stairs, naked. "It wouldn't have stayed there all day because you know I gotta wear something home, don't I? So, what's the big fuss?" He didn't say a word. Tossed my dress to me and gave me a look like he wanted to tear me apart.

I wrapped my dress around my naked body and walked back into his bedroom where I could see him bending over, running some water in his Jacuzzi tub. I stood in the doorway and watched. Hot steam filled the bathroom as he stepped in and laid his head back on a pillow.

"So," I said, removing my dress from around me. "Would you like some company in there?"

"No, not right now." He closed his eyes like he was in deep thought.

"And why not?" I asked with a slight attitude.

"Because, right now, I want to be alone. And before you get started, Felicia, I ain't up for a bunch of questions. So, either go to bed, or leave. Preferably, the door awaits you."

"Jaylin, look, I'm confused. Did I do something to you tonight? I know the stock market is down but I don't want to be dumped on because you're losing your fucking money."

He ignored me. Got out of the tub, poured himself a glass of Moet, and got right back in. As much as he probably wanted me to, I wasn't leaving. I jumped my ass right back in bed and turned on the flat-screen TV on the wall in front of me.

As I slowly nodded off, I heard him on the phone again. Sounded like it was one of his boys this time, because I heard him say, "Man, she be tripping." Since he was all laughs and seemed to pick up a new attitude, I figured it had to be Stephon on the phone. Stephon is cool. He ain't as devious and arrogant as Jaylin is but they do have a lot in common. They resemble each other in so many ways that I started to get with Stephon when I first saw him. By then, Jaylin had me hooked. The only thing different was Stephon was a dark-chocolate brotha. He had light brown hazel eyes and was bald. Everything else about him

3

matched Jaylin to a tee. Even their bodies—I couldn't tell which one was in better shape. Jaylin treats Stephon like a brother. Bought him a barbershop in the Central West End, gave him half on the white 500-series BMW he drives, and recently, gave him five grand to take this bitch he had only known for two weeks on a cruise. Hell, if I can't use him, I guess another motherfucker might as well.

Jaylin got the nerve to always call me cheap, but every time we go out, he be talking that "split the bill" bullshit. We can go through the drive-thru at McDonalds and he be having his hand out asking for half.

Didn't used to be like that. I guess in the beginning he did what he had to do to keep me; but now, if it wasn't for his good loving he be putting down, I would have been gone. I've had plenty of brothas but nobody set me out like he does. Especially if the stock market is booming and he's making money. Brotha be working this ass all night long. Sucking me dry. And then, wound the night down with a bottle of chardonnay. That's the Jaylin I fell in love with. He'd better come out of this fucking shell, because if not, I'll be looking for another brotha to give it to me like he does. It'll be tough but sista gotta do what a sista gotta do.

I could hear the water running down the drain and watched Jaylin as he dried off. When he came into the bedroom, I pretended to be asleep. He lifted the covers from the bottom of the bed and crawled up right between my legs. I felt his soft thick lips kiss my thighs and trembled as his tongue lightly touched them. I quickly interrupted him.

I lifted his head from between my legs. "Jaylin, I thought you wanted me to leave."

"Felicia, why don't you just go? You've messed up my mood twice tonight, so I think it's best that you leave." He moved over next to me in bed.

"Before I go, do you want to talk about what's troubling you?"

"Nope. I told you once I ain't got time to talk. If you want to talk, call one of your girlfriends up. They'll listen to you. All I was trying to do is get my fuck on. And since I can't do that, see ya." He turned over and pulled the covers over his head.

I put my dress back on, grabbed my bra from the bottom handrail and jetted. I left my panties on the top for memories, wasn't no telling when I was coming back. I'd have to try him another day. A day when he wasn't clowning like he was tonight, which, knowing him would probably be tomorrow.

2 JAYLIN

Felicia know she be bullshitting. If I can just get that woman to pick up after herself, she'd be all right with me. She left me horny as hell at five in the morning with a hard-ass dick. So, I called Nokea to come over and keep me company. I might as well had gone ahead and played with it my damn self because she ain't about to get it down for me. I slid in a porn movie and went to work on myself before she came. Didn't make no sense for a brotha to have to get off like that, but when a woman gets in her fucked-up mood, a brotha gotta do what a brotha gotta do to get his.

The doorbell rang and I ran downstairs to get it. My baby was nice enough to come all the way over to keep me company. She knows how much I hate being alone and would always come when I need her to. The smell of her perfume hit me as I opened the door. After she walked in, I gave her a tight hug.

"Thanks for coming baby," I said.

"You sounded like something was wrong. Are you okay?"

"Yeah. I had a bad dream and I wanted you to come hold me."

"Well, I'm here. Do you want me to make you a drink or something?" she asked, walking upstairs to my bedroom. My mind left me for a minute as I visualized myself pounding the sweet little ass that walked up the steps in front of me.

"Naw, I'm cool. I just had one before you came."

"That's not all you had before I came," she said, picking up Felicia's panties from the top handrail where she had purposely left them. "So, who's been over here Jaylin?"

"Baby, you know I ain't gonna lie to you; Felicia left not too long ago. She got upset with me because I didn't feel like having sex and left. Don't be mad. It ain't nothing but a fuck thang," I explained.

"Must you keep this trifling woman in your life? You act like you can't go without sex. If I can go without, I know you can. I'm just not sure how much more of this I can take."

"Don't go giving up on me now. I got needs baby. And since you don't want to fulfil them, I gotta do what I gotta do." Nokea walked into my bedroom and pulled my Gucci sheets off my bed.

"Get me some clean sheets, Jaylin. I'm not going to lay my head on some sheets I know for a fact she laid her butt on tonight."

I went to the linen closet and got some clean sheets so I didn't have to hear Nokea's mouth for the rest of the night. She lay next to me and didn't say anything else about it. As a matter of fact, she ended up falling asleep in my arms. I held her instead of her holding me but I didn't mind. I knew what I put her through was wrong but I needed more than just Nokea.

The next day I found it. I was going through my normal Saturday-morning workout lifting weights at the gym, and she walked in. She asked if I was using a towel that was neatly folded on the rail beside me.

"No," I said, checking out her smooth sweaty breasts as I handed the towel to her. "This towel is for anyone who needs to use it."

"Then I guess that's me. I'm so exhausted from my new aerobics class that I don't think I'm going to be able to keep up." She wiped the sweat from her body "So, what's your name?"

"It's, Jaylin...Jaylin Rogers. And yours?"

"Scorpio Valentino."

"Scorpio what?"

"Valentino. My mother is Black and my father is Italian."

"Oh, I see. Well, ah, Scorpio, would it be too much trouble if I asked you out some time?"

"No, of course not. But let me get your phone number. I'll call you."

I watched her wipe around her belly ring right above the good stuff, then wrote my number down on a Post-it notepad and gave it to her.

As she walked away, I watched her long bouncing curly hair move from side to side and her ass jiggle like it loudly called my name. Now, that there was my kind of woman. She could definitely become number three in my life. And I know she liked what she saw because she couldn't keep her eyes off my chest and this big bulge in my pants.

As I was in deep thought about making love to this woman, Stephon stepped up and smacked me on the back of my neck.

"Man, what the fuck you doing? That shit hurt," I yelled.

"Nigga, I saw you checking out that fine-ass woman with that bodacious body. I tried to grab her myself, but when I seen her step to

7

you, I backed off. While you were lifting weights, I saw her staring at your ass like she wanted to come eat you alive."

"She was pretty nice looking, wasn't she? I gave her my digits and I hope she calls me tonight. I'd love to add those panties to my collection. If not, I'm gonna call and apologize to Felicia for last night and see if she'll come shake a brotha down."

"You know damn well she'll come. That pussy got your name written all over it. She hooked, and I mean bad. Shit...sometimes I wish I had it like that. These knuckleheads I be going out with just be looking for a damn handout. When a motherfucker gonna start handing me some shit? That's what I wanna know."

"What happened to that chick you took on that cruise? I thought shit was cool with y'all?"

"Please. I fucked her on the ship and that was it. When we came back, I had to let that ass go. Wasn't worth my money or my time. Besides, she was married. Her husband came to my shop and tried to start some shit. I had to call the police to get his crazy ass out of there. Wasn't my fault he wasn't sticking it to her like I was."

"Damn, dog, that's messed up. You be careful messing with those scantless-ass women. What you need to do is step up to my zone. Start having qualifications and setting rules when it comes to your women. Don't just give your dick and trust to anybody."

"Nigga, I thought one of your rules was to only date Black women. That cutie who stepped out of here just a minute ago wasn't Black. She looked like she was mixed with something—if not, damn near white."

"Yeah, I know. But this time, exceptions are going to be made. There has to be an exception when it comes to a woman that fine."

"I hear you, my brotha, but don't go breaking all the rules unless you wanna wound up like my Black ass."

"Naw, dog...never."

Stephon headed off to work and I headed to Victoria's Secret at the Galleria to find Felicia something nice to make up for last night. I also picked up a dozen red roses at Schnucks in Ladue just to make her feel extra special. Since I was already in her hood, I decided to pay her a visit. Her gray GS 300 Lexus was in the driveway so I knew she was home. After I rang the doorbell, I leaned against the screen door. I held the roses behind my back with one hand and held the bag from Victoria's

Secret up with my finger so she could see it. She opened the door and looked shocked to see me. But when she saw what I had for her, she was all over me.

"Damn, woman, don't get close because I'm still sweaty from my workout."

"I can't help it baby. Is this for me?" she asked, taking the Victoria's Secret bag out of my hand.

"Yes. I want you to go put this on for me. NOW."

She pulled the pink tissue paper out of the bag and looked inside. Then she turned in upside down and shook it.

"Jaylin, there's nothing inside of this bag," she said, standing there with her hands on her hips.

"I know. That's what I want you to go put on for me. Nothing."

"Cute. Really cute."

Felicia took the roses out of my hand and went into the kitchen to put them in a vase she already had from my previous flowers. I stood there and watched, as I thought about my plans with Nokea tonight.

"I just wanted to tell you I'm sorry for the way I behaved last night. I'm losing money every day and it's killing me. I don't mean to shut you out but the less I talk about it, the better," I said.

"Jaylin, I understand." She wrapped her arms around my neck. "That's why I don't bother you about anything. I don't want my man stressing all the time because you ain't no good to me if you're stressed."

"Well, I ain't stressing now." I rubbed my hands on her fat juicy chocolate ass.

"And I ain't stressing either so you know what that means."

"It means, I gotta go jump in the shower so I can get myself ready for some of your sweetness."

"Well, you know where to go, and after you finish, this here will be waiting for you over there," she said, taking her clothes off and pointing to her room down the hall.

I smiled and watched her prance her sexy ass to the bedroom. I had to be out of my mind tripping with a woman like her; sista couldn't give more than she was already giving. But there was no way I could forget about that sweet little piece of ass I saw today. Couldn't stop thinking about how fine that woman was, but I was dealing with Felicia right now.

Brenda M. Hampton

I hopped in the shower, and afterwards, made my way to the bedroom to let Felicia help me release the tension I'd been feeling lately. No problem there. She rode me like a jockey trying to win a race. And then placed those soft little lips on my goodness to finish the job.

3 NOKEA

I waited and waited for Jaylin to come home, but it was near six o'clock in the evening and he still wasn't there. I hoped he didn't forget about our plans tonight. Every Saturday we go catch a movie or go to dinner. Sometimes we go see a play depending on what's at the Fox Theatre. Wasn't like him not to call me all day, but since I had a key to his place, I decided I'd just go there and wait for him.

After watching *Wheel of Fortune*, I decided to rummage through his belongings. I always do that when I'm alone at his house because it's the only way I can keep up with what's really going on with him. Now, if I ask, he'll tell me; but I have to pretend like I don't care all the time. I had already seen some naked pictures of Felicia and some of his ex-girlfriends in a shoebox at the top of his closet. For whatever reason, there seemed to be some new ones. I don't understand how women could stoop so low by flaunting around naked pictures of themselves. Wasn't no telling what Jaylin did with these pictures. I know his boys had probably seen them, and there's no way I'm going to let his friends know what my goods looks like. Hell, Jaylin barely knows. Well, he knows what it looks like but he doesn't know what it feels like.

I checked out this one picture of this chick with her leg wrapped around her neck, and I was disgusted. Then, I heard the front door shut, so I quickly threw it in the box and put the box back in the closet where it belonged. Jaylin jogged up the steps and I walked out of his bedroom to meet him.

"Hey baby," he said. He looked startled to see me. "How long have you been here?"

"Uh...maybe just a few hours waiting on you to come. Why didn't you call? And why are you so late?"

"I got caught up at the gym earlier, then I went to apologize to Felicia for last night."

"Apologize for what? You said she was the one who left you."

"She did but I wanted to apologize for my bad attitude, that's all. I don't like anybody leaving my house upset with me about my mood swings."

"And I'm sure you made it up to her. Just in case you didn't notice, it's Saturday. And according to you, this is our day. So, what are

11

you doing spending time with her? You could have called and apologized to her over the phone."

"Nokea, what's been up with you lately? You know this ain't nothing new I'm dishing out. I don't like nobody mad at me, that's all. Now, you know that. So, let me get out of these clothes, and take a shower so we can go," he said, taking off his sweaty pussy-smelling clothes. I furiously walked back downstairs and waited on the couch until he got ready.

Jaylin hurried down the steps with his silk off-white shirt on and his black wide-legged pants that fitted him nicely around the waist. His shirt had a few buttons undone so you could get a glimpse at his sexy chest. He'd trimmed his beard so thin on the sides you could barely see it, and his gray eyes shone as he walked into the living room and asked if I was ready to go.

"Yes, I'm ready. Been ready for quite a while now," I griped.

"So, what's the plan for tonight? If you don't know, I got a place in mind."

"Oh, yeah, and where might that be?"

"There's this restaurant downtown, The Hampshire, where we can sit on the terrace and overlook downtown St. Louis. The scenery is off the chain and I want to share a lovely dinner with you this evening."

"What's the special occasion?"

"The special occasion is to show you how much I appreciate you being there for me. How much I know you want to kick my ass to the curb but you don't. Also, to show you how much I enjoy being with you."

"Jaylin, I already know that. It's just sometimes my jealousy gets the best of me. Felicia doesn't threaten me in any way. I, of course, don't like the idea of you being with her." I placed my hand on the side of his face. He kissed it, and then held it in his.

"Sex, baby, that's all it is. No feelings no nothing. My true feelings shine when I'm with you." He gave me a quick kiss on the lips and all was forgotten. He grabbed his keys, and as we got ready to walk out of the door, the phone rang.

"Wait a minute, baby, let me see who that is." He walked over to the phone. "Jaylin," he answered. "No," he said smiling. "I mean, yes I...I was on my way out the door. Why don't you give me a call

12

tomorrow?" He paused…"Hey, no bother. Just call me tomorrow and we'll talk."

Jaylin hung up and gave me a funny look. I knew him too well. *That* was a new bitch. I didn't even have to ask him. But I wasn't tripping, because if anything she'd replace Felicia, not me.

Dinner was fabulous. Jaylin was right: The Hampshire had it going on. The staff waited on us hand and foot like we were celebrities or something. As soon as our wineglasses were empty, they'd rush over to fill them. Jaylin ordered the filet mignon and I had a juicy New York Strip steak. The food was to die for. And when the organist played a soothing slow song on the piano, Jaylin asked me to dance. There were only white people who surrounded us and they smiled as we slow danced across the floor.

"Nokea, you feel so good in my arms," Jaylin whispered, and held me closely to him.

"So do you baby. I love you so much and the thought of us being like this forever is what keeps me going."

"Yeah, me to. Promise me something though?"

"What's that?"

"Promise me no matter how rough things might get for you and I, promise me you'll always be there. I know it's asking a lot, but you're the only good thing I got in my life. I thank God for you and if I didn't have you in my corner for all these years, I don't know where I would be."

"That's an easy promise for me. I know it's going to get rough. It's already rough allowing you to do some of the things you do. But I have a purpose for putting up with you. You are mine. You were made for me. As our parents always said, we were destined to be together. So, I'll wait. You'll come around…sooner than you think." I rubbed my hands up and down his back, as he squeezed me tighter.

"Woman, that's why I care about you so much. Ain't nobody like you, and one day, I'm gonna make sure you have everything you need."

We continued to dance and then went back to his place for a nightcap. I wanted to give in that night, but I couldn't. I didn't want to be on the other side with Felicia and the rest of his female companions. I wanted to continue to stay in a category all by myself. I seem to get more respect from him by being that way, and he loves me more than anybody.

4 JAYLIN

Damn, she called and I didn't even get a chance to talk to her last night. I was glad when Nokea left. She hung around all day today and I waited for Scorpio to call back. It really didn't matter because I would have talked to her anyway, but I didn't want to disrespect Nokea.

Stephon and Ray-Ray came over to watch the football game with me so that preoccupied my mind for a while. However, the sound of her soft sexy voice stayed on it most of the time.

"Nigga, are you going against the Rams or what?" Ray-Ray said as we debated who'd go to the Super Bowl.

"You know ain't nobody in the league better than them right now. As long as we got Marshall Faulk running the ball and Isaac Bruce receiving it, the Super Bowl is well within our reach, " Stephon said, agreeing with Ray-Ray.

"All I'm saying is we need to quit with the turnovers and get back to business. Now, ain't nobody gonna beat us, I just think we got some work to do," I said.

"Well, then stop talking that bullshit. You gotta have a little confidence in them, that's all. And I don't care how many damn turnovers they make, no other team in the league can beat them..."

As Stephon continued to rant, I walked over to the bar and poured another glass of Courvoisier. Then the phone rang. I knew it wasn't Felicia because I fucked her so good yesterday, she didn't have a reason to call. I knew it wasn't Nokea because she had just left this morning on cloud nine. I knew it wasn't any of my clients because they knew better than to call me over the weekend. And my boys were here. I knew who it had to be so I rushed to answer it.

"Jaylin," I said sounding aggressive.

"Hi, Jaylin. Hope I didn't catch you at a bad time again."

"No, you didn't. As a matter of fact, I wondered when you were going to call." I walked off into the other room so my boys couldn't hear me.

"I would have called you earlier but I took my daughter to Forest Park. We usually go there to spend a little quiet time together." Damn, I thought, she's got a kid. I particularly didn't want a woman with kids, but maybe this would have to be exception number two. If I have to make anymore, she's history, I decided.

"To Forest Park, huh? That's cool. Gotta take time out for the kids."

"So, do you feel like company tonight? I've been kind of thinking about you and would like to see you." Now, she was really rushing things. I thought it was my job to ask her out, but wasn't nothing wrong with persistence.

"Sure, Scorpio, I would love some company tonight. What time should I expect you?"

"Is eight o'clock okay with you? All I need to do is find a sitter and I'll be there by eight."

I gave Scorpio directions to my crib. I wanted to screen her a little more before inviting her over but her kid was bugging her in the background. I had my doubts about this one. But what the hell, if anything I'd just get a good fuck and call it a day.

Ray-Ray and Stephon weren't budging. They hung around all day just so they could check out Scorpio when she came. I went upstairs and changed into something comfortable—my silk burgundy pajamas—and turned on a song by Frank Sinatra that played on the intercom throughout the house.

"Man, what the fuck is that?" Stephon said, laughing at the song.

"Nigga, it's my 'let me come make love to you' song that be having women jumping out of their panties, that's what it is."

"Sounds more like it'll have their asses jumping out of the window to me," Ray-Ray said, giving Stephon five.

"You know, y'all really be playa hating. I got this nice-ass woman coming over here and you two insist on cock blocking. Then when I put on something romantic, y'all dissing my song. I tell you what, why don't both of y'all get to stepping? I'll share the gory details of tonight's events with y'all later."

Just then, we heard something that sounded like a loud truck with a rattling engine.

"What the fuck is that?" Stephon said, looking out of the upstairs window.

"I don't know. I hope it ain't nobody's car," I said.

"It is a car," Stephon said, laughing. "And it's in your driveway. That pretty little thing from yesterday seems to be the owner."

"Man, what kind of fucking car is she driving?" I rushed over to the window to see for myself. This bitch had a raggedy-ass 1977 get-out-and-push Cadillac that I knew was probably dripping oil in my damn driveway. "Fuck that! This is it for her. I'm going right downstairs to tell her I got plans tonight and made a mistake inviting her ass over here."

"Man, now you know you be too hard on the sistas. Everybody ain't got it like you, my brotha. Give the lady a chance. She might have just borrowed a car from a friend," Ray-Ray said.

"Which probably means she don't have a car at all. Man, I ain't even wasting my time."

I ran downstairs to open the door because she rang the damn doorbell like she was out of her mind. Ray-Ray and Stephon followed. I quickly pulled the door open and couldn't say shit. Woman looked and smelled eatable. She made me briefly reminisce about my baby Nokea.

I moved aside and let her come in, and when she did, I couldn't tell whose lip hung down the most—Stephon's, Ray-Ray's, or mine. She had on a white linen jumpsuit that criss crossed in the back and tied around her neck. It draped in the front where I could see just a sliver of her cleavage, and her long curly black hair hung on both sides of her shoulders. The bottom half of the jumper was kind of see-through. I noticed she wore a thong because of the string line on her upper hip. Her white-strapped sandals accented the outfit and so did the red fingernail polish on both her hands and toes.

"Hey, uh...Scorpio," I said, clearing my throat. "This is my cousin Stephon and one of my friends Ray-Ray."

"Hey," both of them said. They stood there and looked stupid. I nudged Stephon in the side to get his attention.

"Aw, wha...what's up, Scorpio? Nice to meet you." He reached his hand out to shake hers. She smiled and shook his hand. Stephon didn't let go. He held it and rubbed it with his other hand. "Smooth. Sweetie, you got some smooth-ass skin. What you putting on yourself these days to keep yourself so smooth like that?"

"Nothing," she said, laughing. "I always bathe in baby oil. That's all."

"Hey, Scorpio. Why don't you go ahead and have a seat. I'm gonna walk my cousin to his car."

"Okay, Jaylin, take your time."

Stephon and Ray-Ray waved goodbye to Scorpio and we walked to Stephon's car.

"Man, man, man. What you gone do with all that in there?" Stephon said. "Sista might have a fucked-up car, but a woman like that—I'd buy her a new one. She is fineeeee. And if you think she doesn't meet your expectations, then pass her to me. She definitely meets mine."

"Nigga, please. I'm gonna try to tap that ass tonight and afterwards, you can have it. I ain't buying nobody shit. And when she leaves, there better not be no oil stains in my driveway from that fucked-up car. If there is, I'm gonna ask your ass to correct it since she'll be kicking it with you."

"That's alright with me. I'll correct anything she wants me to. But you'd better watch out. She got a devious look about her. I think she's gonna give you a run for your money."

"Please. I've had finer women than her chasing after my ass. Trust me, she'll be calling you tomorrow."

"Alright, my nigga. Don't say I didn't warn you. Something about that woman just doesn't sit right with me. And brotha, please strap one on tonight. I don't want you around here burning and all. You catch my drift?"

"Always, my brotha, always."

"Well, Ray and me gonna go get our skate on at Skate King in Pine Lawn. Are you sure you and Miss Sexy don't wanna come along?"

"Naw, man, I'm staying right here tonight. I'll roll with y'all some other time. Besides, I ain't in no mood to see you bust your damn head open tonight. Them Cats be rolling down there, and personally, I don't think you can hang."

"Hang on this," Stephon said, grabbing his shit. "I'll holla at your ass tomorrow."

We laughed and Ray-Ray and Stephon jetted.

I walked back into the house and Scorpio stood in the living room, while looking at a picture of Mama on the fireplace mantel.

"Is this your mother?" she asked.

"Yes, it is," I said, taking the picture out of her hand. "She's dead though. I like to keep her memory around, you know what I mean?"

"Yeah, I sure do. My mother died of cancer when I was nineteen and I still haven't been able to part with her pictures yet."

"So, can I get you something to drink? I haven't had time to cook any dinner because my boys had me tied up all day with the football games. Or, if you'd like, we can order some Chinese."

"Well, what do you have to eat? If you have something to cook, I'll be more than happy to throw us a little something together." I took Scorpio's hand and walked her into my kitchen. Her eyes wandered. "Jaylin, this kitchen is immaculate. It's a woman's dream to have a kitchen this beautiful and clean. Are you sure you live here alone?"

"Of course I do. I used to have a maid but I got a few good friends who help me keep it clean every once in a while."

"Oh...I see. So, what do you have in the fridge?" She opened it up.

"I picked up some ground chuck, steaks, and chicken from Straub's last week but the ground chuck is the only thing that's thawed. How about some simple ole Hambuger Helper? I got a box of cheeseburger macaroni on the shelf and it shouldn't take long at all."

I put everything on the counter for Scorpio and told her I would be back. I went to my bedroom to call Nokea back because I saw her number on the caller ID. She must have called when I was outside and I didn't want her to come over tonight and mess up my groove with Scorpio.

"Hey baby, you call?" I asked.

"Yes. I just wanted to tell you what a wonderful time I had last night. It kind of got me thinking more about our relationship. How much you and I are meant for each other. How much I know you love me and I know some day you'll be my husband. So, baby, I think I'm ready."

"Ready for what?"

"I'm ready to give myself to you. I want to make love to you. Tonight. I started to come over but I wanted to be sure I was ready to do this." After all this time, and tonight she decides she's ready. I knew I was anxious to get inside Nokea, but tonight wasn't the time.

"Baby, listen. I know how strongly you feel about saving yourself and I want you to continue to stand your ground. If you're ready, I'm not. You're special to me and I don't want you to be a part of this mess I'm in with these other females." I couldn't believe that bunch of bullshit had come out of my mouth.

"But, Jaylin, I…I thought you wanted to make love to me."

"I do, baby, but not while I'm having sex with other people. Tell you what, we'll sit down tomorrow and make sure it's the right thing to do. Then, if we decide it's time, we'll do it. Until then, let's wait," I said.

"But…"

"But nothing, Nokea. Let me get off the phone and stop listening to this nonsense you're talking. I'll call you tomorrow when I get off work. You can come by then."

"Alright, Jaylin, but…do you have company? You seem to be rushing me off the phone." I've never lied to Nokea but if I told her the truth she'd have more questions for me, and I was trying to work on getting my thang wet.

"No. I'm just tired baby. That's all. I promise, I'll call you tomorrow."

She gave me a kiss over the phone and hung up. Damn, I hated to lie to her like that, but I guess there's a first time for everything. I just hoped she believed me and wasn't in the mood for one of her unexpected visits.

By the time I got to the kitchen, I could have died. Scorpio had burned the hamburger meat and had fucking grease everywhere. This was it for me. Bitch couldn't even cook? I didn't give a fuck how fine she was, she had to go.

"Say," I said, trying to be nice. "Why don't you go in the living room and have a seat. Let me clean things up in here and I'll call and order us some Chinese."

"Jaylin, I'm so sorry. I searched for some seasoning salt in your pantry and when I turned around, the meat had burned. Let me make it up to you. I'll pay for the Chinese if you call it in."

"Okay, that's fine. Just go have a seat in the living room and I'll be out in a minute."

She walked her sexy ass into the living room and out of my presence. As I cleaned up, I tried to come up with a good reason for her to leave so I could call Nokea back and tell her I changed my mind about waiting. Right about now, I'd rather be up in Nokea than with this dizzy-ass broad.

I turned off the kitchen light and walked into the living room. Scorpio was leaned back on the sofa with her arms folded and her legs crossed, while listening to the music on the intercom. I sat next to her.

"Scorpio, look. I think it was a big mistake asking you to come here tonight. I uh…have a woman and right now we're having a difficult time in our relationship. I thought inviting you here would ease my pain," I said.

"Well, how did you intend for me to ease your pain, Jaylin?"

"I don't know. Sex, probably, but I don't think it's in my best interest to sleep with you. If she finds out, we'll probably never be able to work things out."

"I see. So, what makes you think she's going to find out?"

"You know how y'all women are. Sooner or later, the truth always comes out." She leaned over to whisper in my ear.

"If you won't tell, then I won't tell." Now she really had me wanting to fuck her. Just that fast.

"So, are you saying if you let me hit that, I don't have to call you tomorrow?"

"All I'm saying is I live for today and not for tomorrow. And right now, today, I want to see what this big bulge I saw in your pants is all about. Not only that, I want to feel it inside of me. I want to get to know you, just for the night. And if you want to come back again, we'll have to take care of that when the time comes."

Sounded like a motherfucking plan to me. Scorpio stood up and removed her white sandals. I scooted back on the couch, stretched my arms out and watched her. She stood right in front of me and untied her white linen jumper and eased it down past her hips until it hit the floor. When she turned around to walk over to my furry black floor rug I noticed a tattoo of a red rose smack on the right cheek of her fat juicy ass. She lay on the floor with her breasts facing me and her legs opened so I could see the neatly trimmed hairs that covered her pussy. My dick throbbed and I was about to explode. I stood up and got ready to remove my pajama pants.

"Jaylin, no," she said seductively. "Stay right there, baby. When I need you, I'll ask for you." She inserted her finger into her goodness as I watched. She moved her finger in and out and licked it with her tongue as I sat filled with excitement. Slowly, she rolled her finger over her clitoris and I could see her juices starting to flow. "Now, it's your turn." She opened her legs wider so I could come in.

I rose up and removed my pajamas slowly so I could tease her as she awaited me on the floor. When she got a glimpse of my nine-plus inches, she smiled. I wanted to go for the good stuff first, but I also wanted to tease her ass like she had done to me so well. She held her finger out and I licked it to get a quick taste of her. I eased my body between her legs and placed my lips on her breasts. She sat up on her elbows and watched to make sure I did a good job. As I teased her nipples with the tip of my tongue, she closed her pretty eyes and leaned her head back. I licked my way down her chest and rolled my tongue inside her belly button. As she laid back and closed her eyes tighter, I went for it all. My face brushed up against her soft pillowy hairs. I took a few light licks up and down then stuck my tongue deep within her. She moaned and I could feel her body tremble. I rolled my tongue around her clitoris and sucked the juices as they rolled down my lips. Nothing but the taste of sweet cherry lemonade hit me. When I finished, I found her lips and shared the taste with her.

"Fuck me Jaylin," she whispered in my ear. "Fuck me good baby." She didn't have to ask because that's what I intended to do.

I stretched her legs out in the air and held them with my hands as she laid back. I rubbed myself up against her to make sure she was soak and wet. As I entered, I damn near lost control. I dropped her legs and leaned down to catch myself for a minute. Pussy felt so warm and good on my dick, I thought it had melted. I closed my eyes and tried to think about the St. Louis Ram's football game today. About my job—anything to prevent myself from coming inside of this woman so fast. After a few more seconds I was able to maintain my composure and get back to work. I worked her insides better than I had ever done before. Turned her over and pounded her ass like a piece of meat. And just when she thought I was finished, I bent her body over my leather sofa, held her tiny waistline and gently stroked her from behind. After all, she was the one who said, "fuck me."

Scorpio and I were exhausted. I lay on the couch with my legs open and she had her slim sexy body on top of mine with her head on my chest. I rubbed my hands on her soft ass as she started to talk.

"Jaylin, I haven't been sexed up like that in a long time. It was so good to release all that energy with you."

"Same here. I haven't felt like that in a long time myself."

"So...where do we go from here? I know you said you already had somebody in your life but I kind of felt a connection between us. Tell me if I'm wrong."

"I don't know, Scorpio. All I can say is we need to take it one day at a time. First, let me tell you I ain't for just being with one woman. I have a lot of friends—good friends—whose company I enjoy a lot. If you don't mind being a part of my world, then sure, I'd love to keep you around."

"So, what's the need for so many women in your life? Can't you get everything you want from just one?"

"Honestly, no. Everybody in my life accentuates it in a different way. I need to have all these different flavors to keep myself motivated. That way if somebody decides to leave, I won't be left without."

"Oh, I see. So you're afraid of being left alone?"

"Somewhat...yes, I am. But at the same time, I don't want nobody in my life around the clock."

Scorpio continued to lay her head on my chest. I got sleepy so I suggested we go to my room for a drink. I took her hand and we moseyed up the steps.

"Jaylin?" she said, stopping me in the middle of the steps.

"Yes."

"I forgot something."

"Forgot what?"

"Sit and I'll show you."

I sat on the steps and she sucked her lips into mine. She took my hand and put it between her legs so I could wet her up again. Then, as soon as my dick gave her some attention, she swallowed it like no other sista had done before. I leaned and enjoyed the sensation of the back of her throat. No doubt, she put it on me. Stroked me so good, I couldn't think about anything else but being inside of her.

"Scorpio, damn, baby, please. Brotha tired," I said, suddenly feeling drained, which was quite unusual for me.

"Jaylin, you ain't fucking me," she whispered in my ear. "I need a man to fuck me."

I couldn't sit there like no punk who couldn't hang so I turned her ass over and stroked her gently from behind. She held on to the banister to keep still, and her long beautiful hair dripped with sweat. I

23

moved it over to the side to kiss her neck as I felt myself about to explode. By the time I did, I was hanging onto the banister as well.

"Woman, what in the hell is you trying to do to me?" I whispered, while still laying on her ass from behind.

"I'm not trying to do anything. When I got something as good as you to work with, the best of me comes out. But, Jaylin?"

"What's up?"

"You're heavy. Do you mind getting up?" She pushed me back with her body.

"Aw, I'm sorry. I was just caught up in the moment." I stood up and reached down to help her up.

We went into my bedroom and she seemed amazed as she looked up at the high vaulted ceiling.

"You really have a beautiful home. Did you have someone design everything for you?"

"Yes, I did. I hired an interior decorator and she basically told me what would look good. I told her to go for what she knew and when she was finished, I couldn't complain."

"Well, she did a phenomenal job. I'm sure you rewarded her well."

"I sure did. Paid her well and gave her some of this good loving," I laughed.

"You probably did knowing you." She hit me lightly in my arm. She climbed in the bed and got her little sexy self under my covers.

Thinking about the mess we left downstairs, I went down there to pick up our shoes and clothes and brought them back up to my room. Just the thought of my place being junky upset me. I laid her outfit on my chaise and put her shoes under it. I hung my pajamas up in the closet and got in bed next to her.

She lay on her stomach, and soon after a short conversation between us, she fell asleep. Some of her hair covered her face and I moved it over to the side so I could look at her. She was an amazingly beautiful woman but I didn't know much about her. Couldn't decide if I wanted to keep her in my life or not. Then I lifted the cover and looked at her well-shaped naked body. I decided she was a keeper. She needed some work but that wouldn't be a problem for me. I'd just have to do what I had to do to make her fit into my circle.

5 FELICIA

Jaylin didn't even call last night. I called his house all night but he didn't answer. I started to pay him a visit, but I was sure Miss Homebody was probably over there. But even if she was, he usually still answered the phone, so I guess something really must have been up.

Today, I went to the Galleria at lunch to buy myself something nice. After all the bullshit I put up with from Jaylin, the least I could do is take good care of myself. As I walked into Dillard's, Nokea was on her way out with a shopping bag, which looked to be filled with men's clothing.

"So, I see Jaylin's got his mother going shopping for him again," I said.

"Felicia, give me a break. You know I'm not trying to be anything like Jaylin's mother. Just in case you didn't notice, he is my man and I like to take good care of him."

"Well, you go right ahead and spend your little money on him. If you think buying him clothes is going to keep him, my dear, you got another think coming."

"And Felicia, if you think screwing his brains out is going to keep him, then *you* got another think coming."

"Bitch, when are you going to wake up and smell the coffee? All Jaylin wants is a good woman who can fuck him like I can. You are sadly mistaken if you think he's going to settle down with you and you ain't upping no ass. That just don't keep a man in this day and age."

"In case you want to know, I'm meeting with Jaylin today. And we're going to talk this sex issue over. As soon as I decide to give myself to him, you are gone. So, please, enjoy it while it lasts because your days are numbered."

"If that's the case, you should have talked to him about that last night when you were there. If it didn't make a difference then, then today definitely ain't going to."

"I wasn't at his place last night. When I spoke to him, he was tired. Tired of your mess and all these other females' mess. So, as I said before, after tonight, you are history." She turned and walked away.

I hated that little preppy bitch. Maybe because deep down I knew Jaylin cared about her a little more than he did me. But I didn't have time for the dumb shit. It was time to face reality. What if Jaylin decided to get with her ass tonight? Where would that leave me? I had too much class to be caught up in this kind of bullshit. There were more fine brothas who had it going on like Jaylin and were interested in me. Especially, where I work. I just didn't want to go there because relationships in the workplace just didn't seem to mix well with one another.

I flew down Brentwood Boulevard in my Lexus and thought hard about what Nokea said. When I got back to work, I asked my secretary to get Jaylin on the phone. When she told me he didn't go to work today, I tried him at home and got his voice mail. Damn, where is he? I thought. I hadn't talked to him since Saturday morning. Normally, he would call to say hello by now. Then it hit me. Nokea said she wasn't over there last night so, that probably meant somebody else was. He wasn't calling because he had a NEW BITCH. Every time somebody new came along, he acted funny. And when he realized nobody could give it to him like I can, he dismissed them. So, here we go again. I'm gonna have to go over there tonight and fuck his brains out so he can get his mind back on the right track. As a matter of fact, since Nokea would be there, we'd have a good ole time. We hadn't had one of our deep arguments in a long time and it was well over due. I needed to know where things stood between us. If Jaylin all of a sudden wanted to settle down, then I'm going to let him. I'll take my walking paper tonight with pride. But knowing him, he's gonna say the same thing he does every time we confront him together: *Y'all know my situation. I can't be with one woman. If you don't like it, then you know what you can do.* I'll continue to go with the flow as long as it takes. But I'd be damn if I let him tell me after all this time he wants to be with Nokea.

6 NOKEA

Jaylin is ending it with Felicia tonight. This is the last straw. After seeing her at the Galleria, I stopped at the Saint Louis Bread Company on Carondelet Avenue when I saw an old girlfriend of mine, Mona, from college. She sat down to have a cup of coffee and Danish with me.

"So, how's everything going Nokea? I haven't seen you in a long time."

"It's going fine, Mona. I just got a promotion and things are going swell. How about you? I heard you and Carlos tied the knot."

"Yeah, we finally got married a little over a year ago. I have a little girl; her name is Jasmine Marie, and she's a beauty." Mona reached in her wallet to show me a picture of her baby.

"Mona, she's beautiful. You are so lucky." I gave the picture back to her.

"So, Nokea, you haven't tied the knot yet? I know the last time we talked, you were dating that fine-ass investment broker. Whatever happened to him?"

"He's still around. We haven't decided to walk down the aisle yet but it's coming. Probably sooner than I think."

"Well, don't wait too long. You know we aren't getting any younger. I had to lay it on the line for Carlos. We'd been together since college and he still wanted to play the field. I took him to dinner one night and said look brotha—it's either the streets or me. Two weeks later, he proposed. Sometimes a man needs a little help. He doesn't realize a good thing until it's gone and I made it perfectly clear to him when I'm gone, I'm not coming back. And even though he was somewhat pressured, we have a good life together. He thanks me every day for getting him on the right track."

"I'm sure everything will work out for Jaylin and I. We've known each other a long time—and you're right, we're not getting any younger. I can't wait to have beautiful babies with him like you have with Carlos. Are you planning to have any more?"

"I sure am. Carlos wants to wait but he doesn't know I stopped taking my birth control pills. So, I'll have another surprise for him very soon, I hope."

"Girl, you crazy. But it's good to see things are going well for you."

"Same here, Nokea. But you get that handsome man to marry you so y'all can start making those beautiful babies." She looked down at her watch. "Look, I gotta go. I have a hair appointment at three, and since I know I probably won't get out until late, I'd better get on my way. It was good seeing you Nokea. Call me some time." She handed me her phone number.

I watched Mona get into a brand new Jaguar. She really seemed to have it going on. Carlos had a good job and she didn't even have to work unless she wanted to. If she did, she had her marketing degree to fall back on. I knew what she said was right. I couldn't put this off with Jaylin anymore. My birthday was just two weeks away and I'd be thirty years old. I had given Jaylin nine years of my life and things had never changed since day one. He's been with other women and insists some day soon all of it will end. I thought, How stupid can I be? I must be out of my mind to put all this into a relationship and not get anything in return but some "quality time." Which had to be on specific days because he had to make time for his other women.

I got so mad thinking about it that I called him on my cell phone to make sure we were still on for tonight. His secretary, Angela, said that he worked from home today, but when I called, he didn't answer. I supposed he had to run an errand or something, so I got in my car and went home to find something nice to wear for tonight. When I got home, there was no message from him. I called his house again and left a message for him to call me back.

7 JAYLIN

"Um...Um...Um...Scorpio you sure know how to fuck up a brotha's mind," I said, lying next to her in bed.

"I told you I can go forever as long as I'm with someone like you."

"Well, you just keep on going." I rolled on top of her to kiss her again.

We had been at it all day long. On the floor, in the tub, on the chaise in my room, and of course, in my bed. Time flew by. I didn't even have enough strength to get my ass up and go to work. I called Angela and told her to take messages for me today and if anybody important called to hit me on my private line at home. The only people who had that number were she and Stephon. Since that didn't ring, I spent the entire day fucking Scorpio. She just couldn't get enough of me and I couldn't get enough of her. This woman was mine. I didn't care what anybody said. She wasn't leaving my life any time soon.

Scorpio got up and took a shower. I watched as she stood in the glass shower with soap and water dripping down her naked body. My dick got hard again but I was too tired to go at it. I picked up the phone and called Angela to see if anybody had called.

"Jaylin, where have you been? Are you coming in at all today?" she said anxiously.

"Hold on, what's the problem? I told you earlier I wasn't coming in. I also told you if it was important to call me on my private line."

"Well, it's nothing important but your friends—I mean your girlfriends, whoever the hell they are—been calling here like crazy looking for you. I can't get anything done because they won't stop calling."

"Sorry, Angela. I'll call them in a minute. How's the market doing today?"

"Actually, it's up. The DOW's up and your other individual stocks are looking pretty good—with the exception of one."

"That's cool. I knew today would be a good day. That's why I stayed my ass at home."

"Negro, please. You know you stayed at home because you got some female over there. But that's your business, not mine."

"That's right, Angela, it is my business. When I was at home banging your ass you didn't seem to have a problem with it."

She laughed. "You know I'm just messing with you. But it would be nice to get things going again."

"Angela, transfer me to my voice mail so I can check my messages. I'll talk to you about your offer when I get to work tomorrow," I said, smiling.

Angela transferred me to my voice mail and Felicia and Nokea blew the damn thing up. One of my most important clients called and said he wanted to buy some more shares of this company that was booming on the West Coast. That meant more money for me so I went downstairs to my office to call him.

"Mr. Higgins, how are you sir? I just got your message. What deed can I do you today?"

"Jaylin, I think this fucking company is going to explode. I want to buy more shares now because when it does, buddy, I'm going to take my family and move my ass to a different country. Maybe even Africa," he said, laughing.

Ha, Ha, Ha, motherfucker, I thought. Africa would turn your white ass around at the door. Pissed me off. Didn't know shit about Africa. "Sounds like a plan Mr. Higgins," I said, laughing back. "I'll write your ticket up for you today and when I get to the office in the morning, I'll be sure to take care of that for you. So how many additional shares do you want to buy?" Higgins gave me a figure that could help set my ass out even more. I continued sucking up to him and laughed at his corny ass jokes.

After fifteen minutes into our conversation, the door to my office squeaked open and Scorpio stood naked with a towel wrapped around her. I put my finger on my lips for her to be quiet. She smiled and walked over to my desk, pushing my papers aside so she could sit on it. I leaned back in my leather chair and watched as she removed the towel. I closed my eyes and tried to focus on my conversation with Higgins. She took my hand and made me feel her insides. Getting excited, I tried to end my conversation with Higgins but he just kept on talking. I stood up and slid my boxers down with the phone rested on my shoulder. Quickly, I inserted myself. We rocked back and forth for a while and then Scorpio loudly said her famous words: "Fuck me Jaylin."

"Jaylin, buddy. Am I interrupting something?" Higgins asked, sounding like he tried to listen in.

"No, not at all." I placed my hand over Scorpio's mouth. "That was just a friend of mine playing around with me, that's all."

"Sounds like she's doing more than just playing around with you buddy. Sounds like she's fucking the shit out of you, or you her," he laughed.

"Well, you know how it is." I laughed back.

"Why don't I just call you tomorrow? Hey, I got a better idea. Why don't we get together for a game of golf on Friday? The last time, you beat my white ass and I owe you one."

"That's fine, Mr. Higgins. I'll see you Friday."

"Hey, Jaylin, suck on those tits for me," he said, laughing and finally hanging up.

Scorpio and I continued fucking on my desk. It took a while for me to come because she had damn near dried my ass out for the day. Then when she gave me a little love and tender care with her mouth, I let go.

"Baby, that's it for the day. Don't you ever get tired?" I wrapped my arms around her waist as she sat on my lap.

"Not really. I thought you were going to join me in the shower, but when you didn't, I came looking for you."

"That's cool and all, but you can't be messing with me like that when I'm talking to my clients. Luckily, he's cool like that. Some of them be tripping when it comes to their money. They want a broker who sits in front of the monitor all day long and does nothing but watch the market as it goes up and down."

"Sorry, baby, I couldn't help myself. You make me feel so good that when I want to feel you, I just got to feel you no matter where you are."

My private line rang, so I patted Scorpio on her ass and made her get up. It was Stephon.

"Man, why haven't you been answering your phone? I called you at work and Angela's crazy ass told me to hit you on your private line."

"I was too tired to go in today, bro. Just wanted to lay my head down for an extra day, you know how that is."

"So, I guess Scorpio wore that ass out last night, huh?"

Scorpio stood and listened to my conversation, so I put Stephon on hold.

"Say, baby, do you mind? I need to take this call. Why don't you go to the kitchen and find us something to eat. I'm hungry, aren't you?"

"Alright. I'll try and find something," she said, walking out.

"And baby," I yelled. "Don't cook nothing. Put together a salad or something." She walked back in for a second and rolled her eyes at me. Then she gave me a stick it up my ass sign with her finger. "Now, I'll stick something up your ass if you want me to," I said, laughing.

"Well, we might have to try that later."

She laughed and walked out.

"Damn," I said, shaking my head and putting the phone back on my ear. "Yeah man, I'm back."

"What the hell's going on over there? What's all this nasty shit I hear you talking, my brotha?"

"This woman is bad. She's been over here since y'all left wearing my ass out. I ain't never—and I mean never...Did I say never?"

"Yeah, you did, man."

"Never, had a sista put it on me like that. She done set that shit out."

"Damn, I knew she would be good. She had the look about her. Pussy screamed your name as soon as she walked in the door."

"Yeah, and its been calling me ever since."

"My question is what you gone do with it? You know Nokea and Felicia ain't having it this time. They start acting funny every time you bring somebody new to the circle. And if I can recall, the last time you tried that shit, they were both about ready to kill your ass."

"Nigga, how many times I gotta tell you I got this under control over here. Nokea and Felicia ain't going nowhere. I've been with Nokea for nine years and Felicia for four. If they ain't stepped by now, they here to stay, my brotha."

"You gone on with your bad self. But, uh, I...I thought today you were going to be passing Scorpio to me."

"Now, I know what I said last night but this a different day. Let me enjoy the moment while it lasts and if I get tired by next week, next month, or next year, I'll send her your way then."

"So, I guess you gonna buy that car sooner than you thought?" Stephon asked. I laughed and thought about it for a minute.

"Yeah, I guess she would look pretty damn good in a Navigator or an Escalade, but, uh, she gotta do a little more work on me before I consider that."

"Well, she done stepped up since last night. She wasn't getting a damn thing then."

"And she still might not but...mannn, the way she be popping that thang, whew, it's enough to make a nigga go crazy."

"You got my shit over here on the rise just thinking about it. Let me call one of my ladies so they can shake a brotha down tonight."

"You do that and I'll call you later."

When I hung up, I called Nokea to see what she wanted. She answered on the first ring.

"Jaylin, where have you been? I was coming over to talk to you in about an hour."

"Talk to me about what?"

"About what we talked about last night, silly. You said we could continue our conversation today." Damn, I had completely forgotten about Nokea coming over here today.

"Nokea, baby, I'm sorry. I forgot you wanted to talk. Look, my decision still stands. I don't want you to give yourself to me right now. So, really, there's nothing to talk about."

"I don't care what you say. We have a lot to discuss and I'll be over there in an hour. Tired or not, you're going to hear me out." She hung up.

I didn't call back because I heard something in the kitchen fall. I ran to see what it was, and when I did, I saw that Scorpio had dropped a glass bowl on the floor.

"What are you doing?" I asked, irritated.

"It just fell Jaylin. When I turned around my elbow knocked into it and it just fell."

Since she was in the kitchen with no clothes on, I helped her bend down and pick up the glass and eventually forgave her. We sat on the stools and ate the salad she made. It was cool for a salad. I'd had better, but since I didn't have any meat to put in it, the lettuce and veggies just had to do.

I knew Nokea said she was on her way, but I wasn't going to make Scorpio leave just because Nokea insisted she wanted to talk. If anything, she knew better than pressuring me into doing something I didn't feel like doing. Out of respect though, I explained the situation to Scorpio and asked her to chill out in my room until Nokea and I finished talking. With no questions asked, Scorpio agreed.

Nokea wasn't bullshitting; she was right on time. I opened the door and she looked extremely upset with me.

"Baby, what's up?" I said, knowing that I didn't want to be bothered.

"What's up is whose darn car is that in your driveway?" she yelled.

"Nokea, come in, have a seat and calm down. You know I don't like you yelling at me like that. Besides, it ain't your style."

She walked in and went over to the couch. My baby looked and smelled good as usual. Had her hair all slicked down on the side and spiked in the front. Her sexy little blue dress showed every curve she had on her body. Especially her hips that swayed from side to side as she sauntered into the living room.

"I'm not sitting down Jaylin." She folded her arms. "I want to know whose car that is!"

"Nokea for the last time, don't be yelling in my house like that. My neighbors might hear you and you know these folks in Chesterfield don't play. So, sit down so we can talk." She finally sat her ass down and I sat next to her. I took her by her hand.

"The car outside belongs to a nice young lady that I met not too long ago. She's upstairs in my room watching TV and she's leaving tonight." Nokea snatched her hand away from mine.

"Was she here last night when I called you?" Wasn't no sense in me lying again so I came out with the truth.

"Yes, she was but..."

Nokea took her hand and smacked my face. I closed my eyes and turned my head to prevent myself from fucking her up. But when I realized I deserved it for lying to her, I couldn't do anything but shake it off. She took her hands, covered her face, and started to cry. I felt worse than I had ever felt before because I had never seen her cry like that. I leaned over and wrapped my arms around her.

"Look, I'm sorry. The last thing I want to do is hurt you but it ain't like you don't know my situation. I don't know what you want from me. You tell me you don't want to have sex with me and how do you think that makes me feel? If you say you love me like you do, then there shouldn't be no problem with you wanting to give yourself to me." Nokea continued to cry on my shoulder as I talked to her. "Baby, do you hear what I'm saying to you? What do you want?" She lifted her head and wiped her tears.

"Jaylin, I love you. I've always loved you but you have been so blind to see that all along you've had everything you've always needed. Did it even occur to you if maybe you gave our relationship a chance I would eventually come around and give myself to you? Not once did you give up your women for me. I've always been in this with somebody else. I can't take it anymore. All my girlfriends are getting married, making commitments and I have nothing. I'll be thirty-years-old in a couple of weeks and don't even have a stable-ass simple relationship." She continued to cry.

As she laid her head back and rested it on the couch, I couldn't say anything. I knew what I had put her through but I thought she understood what a man like me needed. I got up and went to pour myself a shot of Martel. When the doorbell rang, I poured a double shot because I felt something heavy about to go down.

When I opened the door, Felicia walked in, Scorpio stepped out of my bedroom and Nokea stood up next to the couch. Damn, I thought. What in the hell am I going to do now? Since Scorpio was my new lover, all eyes were on her. She had on my black silk robe and it was tied so low you could see part of her left breast.

"So, who the fuck is this?" Felicia said, letting herself in.

I tried to play it cool; after all—I had nothing to hide. "Hey, Scorpio, why don't you come downstairs. I want to introduce you to a couple of friends," I said.

As Scorpio walked down the steps, her pretty legs and her private parts peeked through my robe. I know damn well Felicia and Nokea got a peek because they looked like they're insides burned with fire. Scorpio walked into the living room with Felicia and Nokea, who were already moments away from killing each other.

"Ladies, first let me tell you all that I don't want no shit up in here tonight. We're going to settle this like adults and everybody's gonna go home happy, alright."

"Jaylin, I really don't want to be a part of this," Scorpio said. "I can just go. You've already made it clear to me where things stand with you and I, so there's no need for me to stay and battle it out with these two women."

Now that was my kind of woman. "Thanks, Scorpio. I appreciate you not stressing a brotha and all. Just leave my robe on my bed when you change."

"Of course," she said, walking back up the steps.

"Well, Jaylin, it's not that easy for me." Felicia put her hands on her hips. "I need to know what's up right now with you and I. I'm not going to play second to neither one of these bitches. I've done it long enough. When I saw Miss Homebody over there today she said you were leaving me and getting with her. Now, I came here to hear it straight from the horse's mouth."

I looked at Nokea. She didn't say a word, but a look of disgust was written all over her face. But tonight, I was standing my ground. And if someone didn't like it, then step.

"Felicia, I'm gonna say this to you and Nokea—if she's listening. I am not going to limit myself to just one woman. Not now, not never. I enjoy being with the both of you and refuse to choose one over the other. If you can't roll with that, then roll out. If you don't appreciate a brotha's honesty, then I don't know what to tell you. I ain't got time to be going through this bullshit over and over again. So, I'll let you both decide. Either you're gonna be with me or you're not. I'm not going to lose any sleep either way it goes."

There was silence. Scorpio walked downstairs with her white jumpsuit on, and looked just as spectacular as she did when she came in last night. Nokea and Felicia looked at her with jealousy in their eyes as she walked over and kissed me on the lips.

"I'll call you tomorrow," she whispered and walked out of the door.

Damn, I really hated to see her go. "So, ladies, what's it going to be?" I rubbed my hands together, waiting for an answer. Nokea didn't say anything so Felicia was the first to open her big mouth as usual.

"All I wanted to know is if you were ending it tonight to be with Nokea. Since you've made it perfectly clear you're not," she said, looking at Nokea, "I'm cool. The only other problem I have is this Scorpio chick. You've been making love to me and only me for quite some time and I don't know if I can get with you screwing around with her. How long is this supposed to last?"

"Felicia, I don't know. I like the gal but who knows how long she's going to be around. Actually, I'd like to kick it with her like I do y'all but it seems to be a problem all of a sudden."

"You damn right it is! It's a problem because I don't want no damn diseases from this bitch. She looks nasty if you ask me, so I'm calling the shots on this one. When you done with that bitch, you call me. Maybe I'll be there or maybe I won't, who knows? But I don't want to hear from you as long as you're still with her. This one here," she said pointing at Nokea, "I can deal with. But that tramp who just left, I can't."

"Whatever, baby. Don't let the door hit you on the way out." Felicia walked to the door. "Hey, Felicia, don't have a change of heart tomorrow because you know Jaylin don't play that."

She slammed the door.

Nokea sat on the couch like she was in deep thought. "So, Miss Lady, are you a goner too?" I wasn't in no mood for any more bullshit.

"Nope. I'm not going anywhere Jaylin. I've put up with your mess for all these years, I might as well continue. Besides, I'm not going to lose you to women like them. I have enough confidence in myself that I know one day you will come around. I just hope I'm still there." Her eyes filled with water again.

I sat beside her. "Nokea, you understand me better than any woman I've been with. And deep down you know how I feel. So, trust me this time, it'll all work out for the best." She laid her head on my chest and closed her eyes.

"I hope so, Jaylin. I truly hope it does."

8 NOKEA

Today would change my life forever. It was my birthday and Jaylin made plans to take me to Cardwell's At the Plaza for dinner. Afterwards, we arranged to get a room at the Sheraton Clayton Plaza Hotel so I could finally show him how much I really love him. It was time. And just maybe, things between us would be different now. When I talked to him last night, he said he hadn't talked to Scorpio or Felicia. So, it was time to get my man since they both were out of the picture. He apologized for the other night and told me that he'd lost sleep thinking about the things he said to me. I didn't know whether to believe him or not, but there was no reason for him to lie to me anymore. I respected him for being honest about everything but the choice was still mine. I couldn't get mad at him for sleeping with other women if I allowed him to do it. If I could just hang on for a while, this drama would soon be over.

Besides, Daddy loved Jaylin, and so did Mama. They'd always wanted us to be together. When I called Mama the other night and told her about what happened, she told me Jaylin was just going through a phase every man goes through. She said Daddy had done the same thing to her before he decided to settle down. But she also told me she was ready for some grandbabies.

After work, I went to Famous Barr at Northwest Plaza and bought a beautiful powder-blue negligee that accented my light brown skin. The front was lace and had a v-dip all the way down to the tip of my coochie hairs. The back was a thong and showed my butt that Jaylin admired so much. I bought some strawberries & cream bath and body lotion to make sure I smelled extra fresh for him tonight. Then I called him at work to make sure we were still on for tonight, and to thank him for the roses he had delivered to my office today. Angela answered with her usual attitude, and then she asked me to hold.

"Jaylin Rogers," he said, sounding like he was busy.

"Would you like for me to call you back?" I asked, knowing that I would be disappointed if he did.

"Naw, I got a minute. What's up?"

"Nothing, I just wanted to tell you thanks for the roses, and I wanted to find out what time you're picking me up tonight."

"You're welcome—nothing but the best for my lady. And I'll see you around...sevenish?"

"Jaylin, are you sure you want to do this tonight? I mean, I'm ready, but I know you had your doubts before."

"I'm as ready as I'm ever going to be. I want to make sure you're ready. If not, baby, then now is the time to tell me. I've been thinking about your sexy little self all damn day."

"I'll see you tonight." I blew him a kiss before I hung up. It was good to know his thoughts were about me. I just hoped I didn't disappoint him. I'd dreamed of our moment together and everything felt so right.

When I got home, I called the Sheraton to make sure everything was set for tonight. Jaylin had already taken care of everything but I didn't want anything to go wrong. So, I called reservations just to confirm.

In front of the mirror I pranced around in my sexy little number and made sure it looked good enough for Jaylin. I even called my best friend, Patricia, over to get her opinion.

"Girl, you know I ain't trying to see your ass hanging all out in that thing. Personally, I think he don't deserve your ass but anyway..."

"I didn't ask for your negative opinion. I just wanted to know how you think it looks. Would you wear something like this for Chad to turn him on?"

"I guess I would. But honestly, he doesn't give a shit what I put on. As long as I'm naked, he's good to go. And if I know Jaylin, he's the same way. He only cares about what's underneath and that's it."

"I know but I want to kind of tease him a little bit...you know? He's been with all these women and has so much experience, I just hope I can please him."

"Nokea, I ain't trying to be hard on you but you sound like a fool. If you're having doubts about it, then why do it? I've been so proud of you all these years for not giving in to him. I wish there were more sistas like you who would wait until they get married. Really, it's not that hard to do. At the rate these brothas are going, nobody should be fucking."

"Well, you got that right, but I need to do this for me. If I really love Jaylin and know deep in my heart we're going to be together, then why not?"

"I just want you to be sure, that's all. He's hurt you so many times before and I don't know if giving yourself to him is going to change anything about him. He's got some personal issues he needs to work on and it ain't got a damn thing to do with you."

I silently disagreed. After tonight, things will be different between Jaylin and I. After all, seems like he'd almost waited a lifetime for this.

9 JAYLIN

It was good to be off work. I rushed home and changed so I wouldn't be late for dinner tonight with Nokea. She was so sweet. I had put all my bullshit aside for the week just to make her happy. Felicia called and left me several messages but I didn't call her back. I guess she finally realized that when I say something, I mean it. She walked out on me, and for now, she was staying out until I was ready.

My mind though, been kind of fucked up. The thought of fucking Scorpio again stuck with me twenty-four-seven. I thought about her ass at work, at home, and even looked for her at the gym. She called and said she would be out of town for a few days and would call when she got back. And even though I wanted to hear from her, I tried desperately to forget I ever met her.

I dropped the keys on the kitchen table and hurried to my room to change. I put on my gray suit Nokea picked out for me at Saks Fifth Avenue and put on a crisp white shirt underneath. I left a few buttons undone so she could see my chest that she admired so much.

After I put on my Rolex, the doorbell rang. I'd told Nokea I would pick her up tonight, but knowing her, she was anxious to see me and couldn't wait. I jogged down the steps with one black sock in my hand and the other on my foot.

Looking through the glass doors, I could clearly see it was Scorpio. I was pressed for time but I opened the door anyway.

"So, what brings you by?" I closed the door behind her.

"I just got back in town. Kind of missed you and wanted to see you," she said, looking me up and down. "Are you about to go somewhere?"

"Yeah, I was. I have a dinner engagement tonight that I'm running a little late for."

"Do you mind if I stay here until you come home? I promise I'll have something sweet for you when you do get back." She walked up to me and buttoned my shirt.

"Look, why don't I just call you tomorrow. I'd hate to keep you waiting all night long."

"So, your dinner engagement is going to take all night?" She pressed herself up against me and my dick throbbed for her.

41

"No…it shouldn't. I'll try to get back here as soon as I can."

Scorpio turned and walked up the stairs. She wore black shiny leather pants and a black halter-top with a string that crossed in the back and wrapped around to the front. Her black heels had her damn near as tall as me.

She opened my bedroom door and sat on the edge of my bed. I sat on the other side and slid my other sock on. Rushing, I went to the closet and stepped into my shoes. Then I looked for my black belt that was hidden away in the back of my closet. When I came out, Scorpio was already naked underneath the covers and watched my flat-screen TV on the wall. I wanted to stay there but I knew it would be wrong to play Nokea on her birthday.

I took my wallet off my nightstand and headed towards the door.

"Oh, Jaylin," Scorpio said, slightly opening her legs so I could get a peek. "Try not to be too long. I'm kind of anxious to feel you." I walked over and kissed her soft lips. She pulled me down and I eased my body on top of hers. She felt good. Body was so warm as I rubbed her with my hands. My dick got hard, so I quickly hopped up.

"I'll be back as soon as I can," I said, leaving out of the door.

Nokea opened the door and looked amazing. I had stopped thinking about Scorpio at home in my bed so I could give Nokea the attention I thought she truly deserved. She had on a fitted black and white dress that hung off her shoulders, and her eyes shone as she saw me walk through the door.

"Hello," she said, wrapping her arms around my waist. "You look handsome."

"You look beautiful too. Turn around so I can get a good look at you." She turned around and all I could think about was taking her dress off tonight.

"So, are you still taking me to Cardwells?"

"Yes, but first, I want a kiss before we go." Nokea smiled and gave me a few short pecks on the lips. After that, we left.

While driving down Interstate 70, my mind wandered back to Scorpio. Nokea held my hand and made me laugh at her cute little jokes, but no matter how hard I tried, I couldn't focus. I drove to The Lake Front, and after realizing I was an hour away from St. Louis, I knew there was no way in hell I would make it back to Scorpio before the night was over. I parked my car down by the dock and we got out.

"Jaylin, what is this?" she said, looking at the double deck party boat that was surrounded with lights and had a sign on it that said Happy Birthday.

"Come on." I took her hand. "Let me show you."

Nokea and I stepped on the boat. The top deck had a table set with fine China, wineglasses, and a vase of flowers was in the middle. I had even gone to the extreme of hiring some fellows at Freddy's Jazz Club in town to play some soothing music while we ate dinner. As I escorted Nokea to the bottom deck, she was shocked. The room was lit with scented candles, giving it the smell of a flower garden; the bed had rose petals spread all over it; and the sheets were gold satin. There was a Teddy bear on the bed with a T-shirt that read "Happy Birthday! Yours forever, Jaylin." She picked the bear up and held it close to her.

"Jaylin, I don't know what to say. I thought you made reservations at the Sheraton."

"I did. But at the last minute, I changed my mind. I wanted to do something special for you. I told you before how much I appreciate you being there for me, didn't I?"

"Yes, but I didn't expect this. This is too much."

"Not for you though, baby. You're worth more than money can buy. Now, put that Teddy bear down so we can eat. I'm starving."

After we got our grub on, we slow-danced the night away. I held her sexy little body in my arms and tried to forget about everything I'd done to her. I promised her things would only get better.

Soon, I dismissed the jazz players and the waiters because it was time to get down to business. I hadn't had no loving in a little over a week and was ready to release this tension I had built up inside me. I gave Nokea that look and she definitely knew what time it was. She actually took my hand and led the way. One thing I like is an aggressive woman. One who takes charge and knows how to get what she wants from a man.

When we got to the lower level, Nokea didn't waste any time. She laid me back on the bed and kissed me. Then she unbuttoned my shirt and removed my belt.

"I'll be back," she said, walking to the bathroom in the far corner of the room. I stood up and took my clothes off before she came out. I

43

hopped under the gold silky sheets and waited for her. My dick climbed slowly but surely, and when Scorpio crossed my mind again, it was on full rise. I fantasized for a minute about being between those soft pretty legs—but when Nokea stepped out of the bathroom with her sexy blue negligee on, my thoughts quickly changed to her. I smiled as she walked my way. I could see how hard her nipples were through the lace, and the smoothness in her coochie hairs blended in well.

"Do you like?" she said, easing her pretty little self on top of me. "I bought this just for you. I hope you enjoy taking it off me." I smiled and laid her backwards so I could get on top and take control. I'd been with many virgins before so I knew how to handle things in order to keep the rhythm flowing. I eased down her negligee and drew her breasts into my mouth. She could barely keep still as I sucked those, so I knew when it came time for me to lick her insides, she would have a fit. And that she did. Legs squeezed my head so tight that I could barely hear. I held her down to keep her still. My purpose was to wet her just a little so it would be easier for me. But as I gently went in, she backed up.

"Jaylin, I'm sorry. I can't it...it doesn't feel right," she said, painfully staring at me.

"Baby, just relax. Alright," I whispered. "I can't go any easier than I'm already going." She relaxed a bit and I took another shot at it. I back up a bit and slowly eased my way in. Dick felt like it was about to suffocate, but the warmth made me think of Scorpio again. I closed my eyes and tried to get back to business but Nokea messed up my mood again.

"Jaylin, you're hurting me." She pushed me back. "Please stop. I just can't." By this time I was upset. I couldn't get my shit off like I wanted to, or for that matter, how I had planned to.

"Nokea, if you just calm down baby everything will be okay." I couldn't make it any easier for her. I tried but every time I'd move, she'd tightly grab my hips to stop me. If she would take the pain, then after a few more strokes everything would be cool.

Unable to take the pain, she backed up and eased me out of her. Then she apologized and walked off to the bathroom. Damn, I thought. If I had gotten my shit off with Scorpio before I came, I would have been all right. This was bullshit and Nokea knew I was pissed, but fuck it. Ain't shit I could do but try again later.

Nokea came out of the bathroom with a disturbing look on her face. I didn't want her to feel bad about not being able to hang with me, but little did she know, there weren't too many women who could.

"Come here baby. Come lay down with me. At least let me hold you." I held my arms out.

"Jaylin, I'm so sorry. I had no idea it would be so painful. I know you're disappointed but I..."

"Shhh...no need to apologize. At least we tried. I really didn't expect to get that far. But at least I got to taste you."

"Yeah, that was wild. Kind of felt good too."

"Shit, the way you squirmed around, it was better than good."

She laughed and leaned in for a kiss. I put my arms around her and she placed her head on my shoulder. There was silence.

"I love you Jaylin."

Unable to say those words, I responded, "And you know how I feel."

Nokea had crashed out. I couldn't sleep because my thang wouldn't go down, as I thought deeply about Scorpio. It was two in the morning and I knew she was still at my place waiting for me. I quietly went into the bathroom, took a shower, and tried not to wake Nokea. When I came out, I tripped over her shoes that were on the floor and awakened her.

"Jaylin, are you okay? Why are you dressed?"

"Baby, Stephon called and said he had car trouble. He's several miles down the highway on Interstate 70 and Lindbergh so...I'm gonna go help him out. I'll be right back."

"Do you need me to go with you?"

"No, no. Go ahead and go back to sleep. I'll be back before you know it."

"Alright, Jaylin, but be careful."

"I will."

I flew down Highway K and took the quickest route to Chesterfield. I unlocked the door and ran upstairs to my bedroom. When I opened the door, Scorpio was still there. She lay on her stomach in a deep sleep. I slid the covers off her so I could look at her naked body, and then took my clothes off to join her. I slowly eased myself inside her and felt relieved. She flinched a bit and woke up.

"It's about time," she said, getting into position. "I thought you forgot about me."

"Not a chance in hell," I whispered in her ear. "Not a chance in hell."

10 FELICIA

I tossed and turned all night. It was damn near six o'clock in the morning and I was up thinking about that son of a bitch Jaylin. I was furious he hadn't returned my phone calls. I tried to forget about his little fucked-up ways but when I invited this brotha over from the past, I realized how much Jaylin really meant to me. Sex was horrible. Only lasted for about three minutes and wasn't even worth my time. I had even given this brotha at work my phone number. Our conversation was cool, but when he told me he was married, I cut him short.

I missed the hell out of Jaylin. Friday nights were supposed to be our night and when I didn't hear from him, I was really disappointed. I remembered it was Nokea's birthday so I figured he was probably with her. When I drove by his house last night that bitch Scorpio's raggedy ass car was in his driveway. The funny thing was, his car wasn't there. I thought maybe it was in the garage, but when I got out and peeped in there, the only thing I saw was his motorcycle and his red Porsche Boxster. I called his house several times throughout the night but he didn't answer. Even though it was Nokea's birthday, I at least expected to hear from him last night.

After I called his house again and got no answer, I decided to call him on his cell phone. It rang a few times then a female answered.

"Hello," she said, in a sleepy voice.

"Is Jaylin there?"

"Who is this?"

"Just put Jaylin on the phone."

"Is this Felicia?" Nokea asked.

"Yes, it is. But bitch I didn't call to talk to you. Put Jaylin on the phone. I have to ask him something."

"Felicia, Jaylin doesn't want to talk to you. Besides, he isn't here. What are you doing calling him anyway? I thought you didn't want to have anything else to do with him."

"Don't worry about why I'm calling him. That ain't your business. I know you thought he was all yours but that ain't happening. Not if I can help it. You'll never have him to yourself."

Nokea laughed. "Felicia, you are so wrong. I don't know when you're going to wake up and smell the coffee. Jaylin and I spent a

47

wonderful night together. We've done nothing but show each other love since you walked out the other night. As a matter of fact, we spent the entire night on a boat to celebrate my birthday. And just a few more weeks of this, I'll soon be Mrs. Rogers. So my dear, it's really time to move on. Why don't you just go find somebody else to lay you? Jaylin now has me for that so your services are no longer needed." Nokea had me upset but I wasn't going to let her know she had definitely touched a nerve.

"Nokea, all I can tell you is enjoy it while it lasts. I'll be back. You can bet your life on that. And when I do see Jaylin again, I'll be sure to call you and share the details. In the meantime, you need to be worried about that other bitch that's got his ass all wrapped up. If you claim he was with you last night, then what the fuck was her car doing at his house? Don't flatter your fucking self thinking he doesn't have anyone in his life but you. I find it quite sickening you're the one who he keeps stepping on like a piece of trash. Not me, and damn sure not that new bitch." Nokea was silent for a minute. "Miss Homebody, where's Jaylin? I've argued with you long enough. Give him the phone, would you?"

Nokea hung up. I called back to check her ass for hanging up on me but she wouldn't answer. Couldn't believe I was up this early in the morning tripping with her. He was probably laying right there and had her doing his dirty work for him.

I also couldn't believe she had given herself to him. She was probably so desperate to keep him that she thought of it as a last resort. Even though I hated the bitch, I kind of felt sorry for her. She had no clue what she'd gotten herself into with Jaylin. As a matter of fact, I didn't either.

11 NOKEA

I was worried because Jaylin hadn't made it back yet and what Felicia said weighed heavy on my mind. I got up to get my purse, and rummaged through it until I came across my phone book. I looked under the J's for Jackson and found Stephon's number. I knew he had gotten it changed a few times and only hoped I had the right one. When a chick answered I was about to hang up, as I thought I had the wrong number. Instead, I asked for him.

"Who's calling?" she asked with a slight attitude.

"This is Nokea. I'm Jaylin's girlfriend."

"Aw...okay. Hold on a second, Nokea, let me wake him up."

"Yeah," Stephon whispered, sounding sleepy.

"Stephon, I'm sorry to bother you but have you seen Jaylin? He left last night and said he was on his way to get you because you had car trouble."

"Yeah, I saw him. He left though."

"What time did he leave?"

"Shit, uh, I...I can't remember. Not too long ago, I guess."

"What's not too long ago? An hour ago, two hours ago? When did he leave?"

"He left about an hour ago."

"So, where did he meet you at?" I said, pressing some more.

"Nokea, look, I'm tired. You calling here with all these questions and I just got in the bed. He didn't meet me anywhere. We worked on my car in my driveway, okay?"

"Okay, Stephon. Sorry to bother you and thanks for your help."

"You're welcome. And I didn't mean to get upset with you. I'm just tired."

"I understand. Thanks." I hung up.

I knew the moment Stephon opened his mouth that he covered up for Jaylin. He tripped when he said they worked on his car at home. Jaylin told me his car stopped on him right down the highway.

I got out of bed and put my clothes on. I didn't have a car but I did have money for a taxi. I called one and the dispatcher said they'd send one right over. I sat on the bed and racked my brain...what if Jaylin lied to me? There was no way he would disrespect me like that

49

just to be with someone else. It didn't make sense that he would go through all this trouble to get me in bed, then go home and be with somebody else. Just didn't seem like something he would do. I called his house a couple of times before the taxi came. There was no answer.

When the horn blew, I grabbed my purse and my Teddy bear and left. The ride was long; the taxi driver drove extra slow down Highway 40 and the meter added up. I laid my head back on the seat and closed my eyes. I thought about Jaylin trying to make love to me last night. His touch was so gentle and so smooth. I couldn't believe I wasn't able to keep up with him. The way he sucked my breasts and licked my insides made me want him even more. We'd just have to take our time though. He said he'd be willing to give it another try as long as I was.

The taxi was on Chesterfield Parkway, right around the corner from Jaylin's house. My stomach felt queasy, as I had a feeling something wasn't right. As the driver pulled in front of his house, and I saw Scorpio's car in the driveway along with his Mercedes parked next to it, I damn near died. I paid the driver and got out of the car.

As I went to open the door, I turned the handle and it was already unlocked. I quietly closed the door behind me, walked in, and stood in the foyer. I looked around and didn't see any sign of him downstairs—so that only meant he had to be upstairs. Most likely, in his bedroom. I walked up the steps and could hear laughter. I could also hear water.

My heart raced as I walked into the bedroom. His bed was empty. Then I looked into his bathroom and couldn't believe my eyes. Jaylin and Scorpio were in the shower. He had her pinned up against the marble tile and took deep strokes inside of her. They were so into it that they didn't even notice me standing in the doorway. She had her legs wrapped around him and ran her fingers through his curly black hair, as water sprinkled down on both of their naked bodies. I couldn't see his face but by the sounds he made, and the dirty talk between them, I could tell he enjoyed himself.

She was all smiles, and after she kissed him like she was out of her mind, she leaned her head back and closed her eyes. She moaned and shared with him how good her insides felt and he agreed that his dick felt the same. When her eyes opened, they connected with mines. Shocked to see me, she opened them wider and pushed Jaylin back.

"What's the matter baby?" I heard him ask as she continued to look in my direction. He turned his head and looked shocked as well.

50

He then lowered her legs, wiped the water off his face and turned the shower off. I turned my back and took a deep breath as I felt myself about to lose it. Scorpio walked out of the bathroom first, naked. She walked right past me as if I wasn't even there.

Jaylin came out with a towel wrapped around his waist and tossed Scorpio a towel to cover up.

"Say, uh, Scorpio. Would you mind going downstairs so I can talk to Nokea for a minute?" She wrapped the towel around her body and walked out of the door. He stood in front of me and started to explain. "Nokea, I know what you're thinking but it ain't even like that. I came…" I immediately stopped him. My chest ached badly and I felt like I wanted to throw up.

"Jaylin, it's over. This is most definitely the last straw. How could you do this to me, is what I want to know? I did nothing—I mean nothing—to deserve this," I said, holding back my tears.

"I never said you did. I've always said this was my problem, not yours. But it was always good to have you there for me. Don't go. Please don't be mad. I just need time, baby, that's all." He stood in front of me and looked pitiful.

"Jaylin, time isn't what you need. You have a serious problem and you need to search deep within yourself to find out what it is. In the meantime, I will no longer be there for you." I swiftly pushed by him and walked out of his bedroom. On my way out, I could see Scorpio in the bonus room with her legs folded up on the couch like it was her darn house or something. Jaylin came out of his bedroom and called my name, but I continued to walk.

"Alright then Nokea, have it your way baby. Remember though, if you walk out on me, ain't no coming back until I say so."

I slammed the door on my way out. I walked to the Shell gas station on Olive Street Road and called Pat to come pick me up. When I cried, she said she was on her way. I sat on the curb in front of the gas station and lost it. Cried so hard a man stopped and asked if I needed a doctor. I was hurt, and bad. By the time Pat came, she had to get out of the car to help me get in. My body was numb and I shook all over.

"Nokea, what happened? Calm down and tell me what happened," she said driving off.

"You were right," I sobbed. "Everybody was right about Jaylin but I just didn't want to listen."

"I know I was right, but calm down and tell me what happened."

"He left me last night." I wiped my tears. "He left me in the middle of the night to come home and screw this new chick he's been seeing. I had just given myself to him and everything."

"Nokea, you bullshitting, right. Are you telling me he slept with you and then went home to sleep with her?"

"Yes. He wasn't able to perform like he wanted to with me, so he made up a lie about going to help Stephon with his car. In reality, he went home to be with her."

"Now, that's a dirty son of a bitch! You don't even need him in your life if he's going to treat you like that. I can't believe Jaylin. I could just take my ass around to his house and give him a piece of my mind." Pat turned the car around.

"Pat, please. Don't go over there. I don't want him to see me like this. I just want to let it go and move on with my life. I don't have anyone to blame but me. I made him believe that for many years it was okay for him to dump on me like this. For God's sake, that's all he knew how to do. How can I get mad if I was the one in control of my own happiness?"

Pat shook her head. "Yeah, you're right sweetie but you deserve so much better. And if I can help in any way by hooking you up with some of Chad's friends, let me know. They talk about you every time they see you."

I smiled.

12 JAYLIN

Scorpio and I sat in my bed, ate popcorn, and watched the *Lifetime* channel. Snacking in my room and watching a channel that was made for women was definitely out, but since I tried to impress her, what the hell? I laid my head on her lap and she ran her smooth soft hands through my hair.

"Jaylin, I think I'm falling in love with you already. I can't go a day without thinking about you, and when I'm with you, I forget about the outside world."

"Whoa, baby. One day at a time. I mean, I got some deep feelings for you too but let's not go talking this love stuff yet. Besides, as you can see, I already got a full plate right now."

"I know…but you can't tell me that you don't think about me more than any other woman you've been with. We have a connection. It's not only the sex either. Just like now, I feel like I've been here with you forever."

I sat up a bit and looked at her. "I'm not saying I don't feel different about you, but this love talk got to stop. Can we just enjoy the moment? Hell, I don't know nothing about you. I don't know where you live, don't know what you do for a living, and don't even know how old you are. But I do know I enjoy having sex with you. And honestly, that's it. Give me a reason to love you, that's all I'm saying."

"Oh, I can give you several reasons to love me. First, I live in Olivette, I'm a Playwright who's starving to write some new material, and I'm twenty-eight years old. When you do get to know me better, you'll eventually love me because I'm sweet, I'm kind and I definitely know how to please my man."

"Alright, Miss Playwright, come over here and tell me a story," I said, sitting her up on top of me.

She sat with her beautifully curved plump titties staring me right in the face.

"Well," she said, smiling. "There was this sexy fine-ass brotha who just couldn't get enough of this woman who had come into his life and changed his whole world around. She made love to him, over and over and over again, until one day, she got tired. He was afraid to love her back, and eventually she left him."

"Cut," I said, putting my hands on her waist. "It's not that I don't want to love you, Scorpio, it's just that I don't know how. If or when love presents itself, you'll know it. And if it's love I have for someone else, they'll know too. The problem is no woman has given me a reason to love her. If you give me a reason then maybe I'll figure out how. Make sense?" Scorpio didn't respond. She leaned forward and gave me a peck on the lips. I knew she probably wanted more, but for now, it was strictly a fuck thing for me.

Scorpio left late Saturday night. I went up in her about three more times that day before I let her go. Sunday was my day. I wanted to be alone. I was tired—exhausted from all the female bullshit so I took time for myself. I drove to C&K Barbecue on Jennings Station Road and gobbled down a tripe sandwich that I'd craved for. Then I drove by North Oaks Bowling Lanes on the corner of Natural Bridge and Lucas & Hunt to see if Stephon and my boys from the barbershop were hanging out. I'd missed hanging with the fellows since I moved to Chesterfield, so every opportunity I got, I made my way back to the hood.

Since Stephon was nowhere to be found, I went back home and cleaned my house until it was spotless. Scorpio had left a towel here and there, and had me a little upset. I cleaned my desk off in my office and vacuumed the carpet throughout the house. My kitchen took up the most time. I mopped the floor and wiped down the stainless steel appliances. There were a few dishes in the sink, so I knocked those out too.

By early evening, I went into my bonus room and played a game of pool with myself. The thought of calling Nokea to apologize crossed my mind but I didn't feel like hearing her cry again. This was the first time I hadn't heard from her all day. Felicia bugged the fuck out of me, but I wasn't ready to call her back yet. And Scorpio, she left a message that said she was thinking about me. As hard as I tried not to, I thought about her too. Thought about the way she be putting it on me. Even thought about what she said about me. She said she would tear down my walls and make me love her. The only person who I thought might be a little deserving of my love was Nokea. But since she didn't want to hang around and find out, what the hell?

As I was in deep thought, my private line rang in my office. It was Stephon. "Say man, you busy?" he asked.

"Nope. Just sitting around chilling, that's all."

"You don't sound to good my brotha. What's ailing you?"

"Shit...nothing man. Just beat. Ready to get back to business tomorrow. Stock Market got me kind of worried."

"I know how that is because I'm losing money in that motherfucker too. But the purpose for my call is to tell you I had a visitor today."

"Who?" I asked.

"Nokea. She stopped by and apologized for going off on me yesterday morning."

"Going off on you for what?"

"She called looking for you, and I didn't know what to tell her. She said you told her you were coming to help me fix my car and I hadn't a clue what she was talking about. I covered for you but I really didn't know what to say."

"Man, I'm sorry. I forgot to call and tell you what to say just in case she did call. My mind was so fucked up, I didn't know whether I was coming or going."

"Well, all I wanna know is, did you really play her like that? She was in tears over here telling me about what happened. I kind of felt sorry for her."

"Nigga, please. I didn't play nobody. Nokea knew what time it was. She fucked around that night, so I left. Came home and got some from a for-real woman. Now, she's running over there telling you about it. Man, I tell you, women be doing some fucked up shit."

"Yeah, they do, but I ain't never seen you diss her to that level. This Scorpio chick must be a bad motherfucker."

I laughed. "As a matter of fact, she is. I kind of like her ass too."

"You like that pu-tain she be whipping on you. I had a chick set me out like that before, and at times, I still think about her. But, it was over before it started. She got all demanding and shit. Wanted me to fuck her all the time and I couldn't. You remember that chick named Claire, don't you?"

"Yeah, I remember, but I thought the reason you stopped seeing her was because she got married."

"Yeah, that's right. And I got my fucking feelings hurt too. All I'm saying is take it easy with this chick. I have one other question for you too."

"What's that?"

"Is she worth losing Nokea over? That gal's been in your corner for a long time."

"Stephon, you know better than I do Nokea will be back. She's playing that role right now but she'll have a change of heart in a couple of days."

"I hope so for your sake because today when we talked, she seemed pretty confident to me it was over."

"Confident, huh? Did she tell you I tried to make love to her on her birthday?"

"Naw, man, you lying. She finally let your ass get into those panties?"

"Yep, that's how I know she ain't going nowhere."

"How was it dog? Was it everything you expected it to be?"

"It was alright, man. You know how it is when you dealing with a virgin. I'm too old for that 'let me train you how to fuck me' shit, but I was willing to do it for her. So, it was cool."

"Nigga, I don't know what you're going to do but I got your back if you need me."

"Thanks, cuz, I'll call you later."

I sat in my office for a while longer and messed around with my computer. Soon, I picked up the phone to call Nokea. I wanted to see why she went over Stephon's house to dump on me. Who was I fooling? I was actually calling because I hadn't heard her squeaky little voice in a while. When I dialed her number the operator answered.

"We're sorry, the number you have dialed has been changed, at the customer's request, the new number is not listed." I hung up and tried again. I thought I dialed the wrong number.

Again, *"We're sorry, the number..."* Damn, she'd gotten her number changed already? Was she that upset with me that she didn't even want to talk? Ain't no trip. I took my phone off the hook and took my ass to bed.

13 FELICIA

Now, Jaylin was really pissing me off. The phone calls weren't working, so I decided to make my way to his office today. Clowning or not, I needed some answers from him. I knew what I said the other night but I missed the hell out of him. Missed his touch, his kiss, and of course, his loving. I put my braids into a bun, threw on my gray DKNY jogging suit, and my white DKNY tennis shoes. I left my jacket open so he could see my bare flat stomach and my orange sports bra underneath. I wanted to pretend like I'd been to the gym working out because Jaylin loves a woman who keeps herself fit and trim.

I got off the elevator on the 9th floor of the Berkshire's Building, and went to the water fountain to splash water on me like I'd been working hard. I walked through the lobby and found myself standing in front of that bitch Angela.

"May I help you?" she said, knowing damn well who I was.

"Don't play with me bitch! You know who I'm here to see."

"Do you have an appointment?" She tried to be professional but she wasn't nothing but a two-dollar ho that cheated on her white husband with Jaylin.

"Angela, I'm going to say this as nicely as I can...Bitch! Call Jaylin and tell him I'm out here to see him." She rolled her eyes and called Jaylin on the phone.

"He said have a seat, he'll be out in a minute."

"Thank you," I said, sharply and walked over to one of the leather chairs that sat in the lobby.

Jaylin came out with one of his clients, smiling as he shook his hand goodbye. He looked scrumptious. Had on a dark blue Brooks Brother's suit with a cream shirt underneath and some navy blue and cream shoes to match. His hair looked like it had just been trimmed down on the sides. He had his beard cut off and wore a goatee that fit his chin well. I stood up, as he looked at me with his cattish gray eyes, and he motioned for me to come back to his office. He stopped and told Angela to hold his calls. She shook her head and gave me a nasty look.

Jaylin closed the office door behind us and walked around his desk to sit in his chair. The first thing I did was look around to see if he still had the picture of me on his Credenza. When I noticed that gone, I also noticed Nokea's picture missing as well.

"So, what's up Felicia? Why you bugging baby? You said you were finished with my black ass."

"Where's my picture at Jaylin?"

"Cut with the bullshit, Felicia! You didn't come all the way over here to talk about no damn picture. What do you want?"

"Jaylin, just calm down. I know you ain't trying to act a fool up in here, are you?"

"You got one minute to state your business. After that, I'm calling security. So, go," he said, looking at his Rolex.

"Alright, look. I'm sorry about the other night. I was wrong for trying to give you an ultimatum like that but I was upset. I don't care who you mess with, and as a matter of fact, I don't want to know who you're messing with. All I'm saying is I miss you. I miss what we shared on Friday nights and I want to know if you wouldn't mind having me back in your little fucked-up world." Jaylin was silent for a minute; he rubbed his fingers across his lips and thought about what I implied.

"Felicia, you don't miss me. You don't miss a damn thing about me. That's, of course, with the exception of my big dick. Because that's what you miss. Go ahead, tell me, and be honest. That's what it is. You miss my motherfucking dick."

"No, Jaylin, that's not it. I really miss what we had. We shared something special, just in case you can't remember."

"Something special? Yeah, I've been hearing that shit a lot lately. We ain't got nothing special Felicia. All we've ever had was a fuck thang, baby. I like to take good care of my fuck thangs so that's why every once in a while we go do something special. You see, there's those famous words again: Something Special. It really ain't a damn thing special about it."

"So, what are you saying? Do you want to do this or not?"

"You wanna do this, Felicia?" He got out of his chair. "You really want to do this! Come on baby. Let me fuck you. That's what you came here for so let's just get it over with." He removed his belt and unzipped his pants.

"Jaylin no, stop!" I pulled myself away from him as he tried to pull my sweatpants down. He grabbed my face and kissed me. I smacked his face and he stared deeply into my eyes. Knowing that my smack didn't mean a thing, he reached over and turned the lights off. Then he lifted me on his desk.

"Felicia, don't you ever leave me again. If you do, you will never, and I mean never, be able to come back in my life again," he said, forcing himself inside me.

The feel of him was too good to turn away, "I won't, baby. I promise you I won't."

I felt like a million dollars leaving Jaylin's office. When I walked past Angela, she looked at me and rolled her eyes again.

"See you later bitch," I said, as I exited the lobby doors with my leather Coach purse clutched to my side. She knew what we were doing because when she knocked on the door Jaylin didn't answer. I went home, took a shower, and drove to the office to get something else accomplished for the day.

14 NOKEA

I was miserable not talking to Jaylin. But I knew there was no way I would go back to him. My girl Pat would kill me and so would Mama. I told Mama about what happened and she was furious. What I didn't tell her is I gave myself to Jaylin that night. Had she known, she would have died. She basically advised me to get on with my life and encouraged me to meet somebody new. And that's what I intended to do. I had changed my number so Jaylin wouldn't be able to get through if he tried to call with another one of his lies. In fact, I even thought about moving but I knew that would be taking things to the extreme. Since I had just gotten a promotion, I dedicated all my time to my new career.

I was the new sales director for Atlas Computer Company and had to show my colleagues they had chosen the right person. During my first presentation, Jaylin kept coming to my mind. I was so glad when it was finished so I could go somewhere and get a grip of myself. No matter how hard I tried to stop the tears, they just kept on coming. Late at night. Early in the morning. Even while at lunch with a few of my co-workers today I cried. They asked me what was wrong and I told them my grandfather past away in Mississippi. Since he'd died years ago, I felt like I hadn't burned any bread on him by not telling the truth.

After breaking down again in the bathroom stall at work, I asked my boss if it would be okay if I took the rest of the week off. According to me, I was on my way to Mississippi to attend my grandfather's funeral.

On my way home, I stopped to pick up some groceries at the Clock Tower Dierberg's on West Florissant Avenue. Whenever I'm stressed, I always pig out. Before I knew it, my cart was full of junk: potato chips, cookies, ice cream, and pizza rolls. You name it, it was there. I stood in the long line and picked up an *Ebony* magazine to keep myself occupied.

"Shorty?" I heard a voice say from behind. It was Stephon.

"Hey, Stephon," I said, giving him a hug. "How are you?"

"Naw, the question is how are you? I hope you're feeling better since the other day. You had me kind of worried."

"Worried for what? I know you didn't think I would kill myself or anything like that, did you?"

"Nothing like that. I was just worried. You've been with my cousin for a long time and you kind of like family."

"Yeah, well, even family can snake you sometimes." I reached in my cart and laid my groceries on the conveyor belt.

Stephon reached in and helped me—until he came across a bag of maxi pads. He dropped them back in the cart like they were going to kill him or something.

"Now, if you're going to help, those need to be put up there too," I said, smiling. He laughed.

"I'll let you handle those and get the rest of your things."

As the cashier rang up my groceries and gave me my total, I looked at her like she was crazy. I didn't think I'd put that many things into my cart, but I guess I did. I reached into my purse to pay her.

"I got it." Stephon gave the cashier his credit card.

"Stephon thanks but I think I can handle my grocery bill."

"No problem. Besides, I owe you one anyway."

"For what? What do you mean by you owe me one?" Stephon didn't say anything. He just put my bags into the cart and pushed it out of the door. When we got to my car, he loaded everything into my trunk.

"There you go, Shorty. Don't say I ain't never did nothing for you."

"I never did, but why do you owe me one? That's what I want to know."

"Because, I really felt bad about the lie I told you the other day. I love my cuz and everything but I seriously think y'all need to work it out. When I talked to him Sunday, he sounded pretty down. He told me he hadn't heard from you. So, why don't you call him?"

"Stephon, please stay out of this. You of all people know Jaylin has done nothing but manipulate me over the years. Why would you even want me to continue to be with him?"

"Because, you're miserable. He's miserable. Don't make sense for two people who love each other to be miserable."

"You know better than I do Jaylin isn't miserable. He got that...that *thing* over there with him and he's enjoying every minute of the day being with her. You didn't see the way he was all into her, I did.

61

Just standing here thinking about it hurts so badly..." I got teary eyed again.

"Nokea, I didn't mean to upset you. But you know Jaylin. After he gets what he wants from her, he'll be knocking at your door."

"Well, he can knock all he wants to, I will no longer be there for him."

I got in my car and waved goodbye. I hated conversing with him about Jaylin; all he was going to do is go back and tell him.

When I got home, I put my groceries up and slipped into my nightgown. I lay in bed and watched Mandy Murphey on Fox 2 News while eating chocolates. This was the life. I wish I could sit here and do this forever, I thought. After the news depressed me with all the Black folks killing each other, I turned the TV off and grabbed a book to read. I quickly got bored with that and picked up the phone next to me. I dialed Jaylin's number but when I got to the sixth number, I hung up. I knew he probably wasn't home from work yet but the thought of leaving him a message crossed my mind. I could just say I forgot something or I needed him to come pick up something he left at my place. But I realized that wasn't in my best interests, so I dropped the thought, turned the radio on Majic 104.9 and listened to Deneen Busby give the news and local updates. After she gave me the scoop, I dozed off as I listened to some music.

I was awakened by a knock at the door. My house was pitch black so I knew it had to be pretty late. I glanced out the peek hole to see who it was. It was Jaylin, standing on my porch with his hands in his pockets and his head down. I quickly backed away from the door because he looked so good, and I didn't want my hormones answering the door for me. After I didn't answer, he banged harder.

"Nokea, I know you're in there. I saw the light come on, so baby, open the door." Wasn't any sense in me trying to pretend I wasn't home, so I cracked the door enough to tell him I didn't want to talk. "What do you mean you don't want to talk? You've always been able to talk to me, so open the door."

"This time is different Jaylin. I don't want to talk. That's why I got my number changed. So please, just go away."

"No, Nokea. I'm not leaving, so you might as well open the door." I hesitated, and then took the chain off and opened it. "Thanks," he said. He walked in and took his cap off like he intended to stay a while.

"Jaylin, look, we've already talked about this so lets just move on, please."

"Are you crazy? Move on my ass. You know damn well we were meant to be together, so why you tripping?" He moved closer to me. I pushed him back.

"Would you please just go," I said.

"I told you once I'm not leaving until you forgive me. Just a couple of weeks ago you made me a promise. You said that when things got rough between us, you wouldn't leave. As long as I've known you, you've always been a woman of your word. What's the sudden change?"

"The sudden change is I thought I could handle you being with other women. But I can't. Especially after I saw you making love to Scorpio in the shower. That just did something to me. And no matter how hard I try to erase that day from my memory, I can't. The thought of it sticks with me twenty-four-seven..." Jaylin walked up and put his arms around me. He rubbed my back and kissed my forehead.

"Baby, I don't know what to say. I was wrong. If that's what you need to hear me say, then yes, I was wrong. But please don't hold it against me for the rest of our lives. It's awful for us not being together."

The pressure was on and I couldn't even respond to him. He kissed me with his soft thick lips and I couldn't resist.

"Let me make love to you," he whispered in my ear. "I want to hold you tonight and if you still feel the same way tomorrow, then I promise I will never come here again."

He took my hand and led me to my bedroom. He removed my nightgown and rubbed his hands gently over my body. I trembled, as the thought of him making love to Scorpio was still fresh in my mind. He opened my legs and did what he knew best, as I squirmed like a slithering snake.

After I gave him a taste of me, he inserted himself. Tears rolled down my face in the dark. I loved this man so much it was almost frightening. I was vulnerable and weak and he definitely knew what to do to get me where he wanted me. I had made a promise to myself to never let this happen again. But there I was enjoying every gentle stroke he gave me and more.

After Jaylin finished, he rolled over and let out a big sigh with his arms stretched out. The guilt I had for letting myself down immediately kicked in.

"Jaylin, if you don't mind, I'd like to be alone."

"Come on baby. I thought you wanted me to stay the night." He rubbed his hand on my hip as we lay face to face.

"No. I really need to be alone right now. What we shared was beautiful but I need time to get my head straight."

"Alright...if you insist. I told you, if you're not feeling this relationship anymore then I'm not going to pressure you." He got out of bed.

"Oh, I am definitely feeling us, but I can't be with you under these conditions."

"Hey, whatever you say. I hope you find a place in your heart to forgive me so we can get on with our relationship."

"I will." I turned over, and pulled the cover over me. Jaylin bent down and gave me a little peck on my nose.

"Get some rest, and call me tomorrow," he said before leaving.

This was going to be a lot tougher than I thought it would be. How could I get him out of my system? All I had to do was not open the door, but when I saw him, I got weak. There had to be somewhere I could go to get help. I was losing respect for myself, slowly but surely. But, my word as my bond, I promised myself that going forward to take it one day at a time.

15 JAYLIN

"Didn't I tell you I'm the man," I said, talking to Stephon at work with my feet propped up on the desk.

"Man, I just can't believe she gave in like that. She seemed so confident it was over when I saw her at the grocery store."

"Yeah, she was confident alright. Confident that she wanted some of this good loving I be dishing out."

"Jay, you know you crazy. That woman just loves your Black ass, that's all. If she could get past that, she'd be okay. As for Felicia— damn, she just trying to get laid."

"And so am I. That's why when she came here yesterday, I waxed that ass all on my desk and had her begging for more."

"You wild dog. Straight up fucking wild. How much pussy can a nigga get? After one time a day my ass wore out. If I had to go two or three times, that would kill my Black ass. And then with different women, shit...I hope you're strapped up good."

"Well, you know how it is. Sometimes I do, sometimes I don't. Depending on who it is. With Felicia I most definitely break one out because ain't no telling who been up in that. But Nokea, that's all good. I'm the only brotha who will ever have a mark on her stuff. As for Scorpio, it depends. Her shit be so good, I just like to get the real deal. You know what I mean?"

"Yeah, sure in the hell do. Been there and done that, so I ain't knocking you at all, my brotha. Hey, listen, while I have you on the phone, Ray-Ray proposed to that skinny dark chick he's been dating for six months. They haven't set a date yet, but he told me to tell you to hook a brotha up with some nice females at his bachelor party. He's looking for something a little extravagant—none of that Pink Slip action, please."

"Oh, yeah? Tell a brotha I said congrats and I'll see what I can do." Angela walked in and told me one of my clients was there to see me. "Say man, I'll call you later." Stephon hung up and Angela let Higgins in my office.

"Jaylin, what's up bro?" he said, shaking my hand.

"Hey, how you doing Mr. Higgins. Have a seat, sir." He sat down and lit up one of his cigars. The smell of it drove me crazy but since he was one of my major clients, what the hell?

"Jaylin, I never received confirmation on those additional shares I talked to you about. I checked the market today and this company is moving. How are we looking?"

Damn. I had forgotten to take care of that for Higgins. With all the bullshit that had been going on, it totally slipped my mind.

"Let me see…" I said, turning around to my computer. Looks like everything is going okay. It is moving but not that much to brag about."

"Any extra money I can make, Jaylin, is enough to brag about. What I would like for you to do is call up some of my buddies who are clients of yours and let them know what it would cost to buy into this stock immediately. That way, we'll all be rich." He looked for an ashtray to dump his ashes.

"Here you go," I handed him a Kleenex. "I don't have ashtrays in here because I'm allergic to smoke. And I'll be happy to call everyone to let them know about Mason Technologies."

"Thanks, Jaylin. I'm not going to take up much more of your time. Just keep in touch; you've been a hard man to catch up with lately. I guess that lady who was screwing your brains out the other day got you tied up, huh?"

"Nah, nothing like that. Anyway, sorry for the interruption. She just couldn't get enough of me that day," I said, laughing. He laughed back and reached into his pocket to give me an envelope.

"Here's a little something extra my wife and I put together for all your hard work and dedication to making us very wealthy people. I trust you with my life and hope you'll continue to make good decisions so we can have everything we'd always dreamed of."

"Thanks, Mr. Higgins." I reached for the envelope. "And as always, you can count on me."

I could hear Higgins outside my office as he flirted with Angela. If I didn't know any better, I'd think they had slept together before. Angela was a gold digger, and looked for anybody who had money. She tried to work that thang on me but I wasn't having it. After I found out she was married to my boss's son, I ended it. He treats her like a queen but for her, that's still not enough. He even told her she doesn't have to

66

work but she insists on being out of the house. That's what I have a beef with the white man about: always wanting their women to stay at home and shit. Two salaries are always better than one, I don't care what anybody says.

Shortly after I heard Higgins leave, I opened the envelope he'd given me. Enclosed was a check for $25,000 and two tickets for a cruise to the Bahamas. Seven days and six nights. Already paid for. I'd been to the Bahamas before with Felicia, but we argued so much it was ridiculous. So, taking her again was definitely out of the question. Nokea was still mad at me and hadn't called all day, so it was obvious she needed more time to get herself together. I'd take Scorpio. She would be perfect to kick it with in the Bahamas. Besides, with her I knew I'd be getting my fuck on every single day.

Before I called her, I called Higgins and left him a thank you message for him and his wife. I then sat back and tried to fix the problem I had with not buying his shares when he asked me to. When I figured out how much of my own money I had to put up in order to correct the problem, I was pissed. I had no one to blame but myself.

I called Angela in to see if she would stay late and help me make some calls, so I could get Higgins' buddies invested as well. All of them had been nothing but good to me, so the more money I made them, the better off I would be.

Angela and I were in the office until nine o'clock trying to cut deals over the phone for Higgins' buddies. Since they made up at least sixty percent of my salary, I didn't care how long it took. Exhausted, I took my jacket off and sat back on the small hunter-green sofa in my office. Angela came in with a glass of wine for each of us; she knew how well it relaxed me. She sat on the floor directly in front of me with her legs folded. I could see right up her short skirt and I'm sure her intention was to let me see.

"Jaylin, let's give a toast." She kneeled down in front of me.

"Toast to what? To how tired I am?"

"Well, if that's what you want to toast to, then go right ahead. But I was thinking more like a toast to mo money, mo money, and mo money."

"Now, I'll drink to that." We both laughed and clinked our glasses together. She smashed my glass so hard the wine splashed on my slacks. "Damn, Angela, what are you doing?" I said, jumping up so the wine wouldn't seep through my expensive pants.

"Sorry, I didn't mean for that much to spill on you."

"What do you mean, you didn't mean for 'that much' to spill on me? Did you do that shit purposely?" She looked at me and smiled.

"You know I did. I hope you'd take them off and send a sista home with a smile on her face like you did Felicia the other day." I walked over to my desk and wiped my pants off with my handkerchief.

"Angela, I ain't trying to go there with you. Old man Schmidt would kill me if he knew what you and I used to be doing up in here. Sorry, baby, I can't take the risk anymore. Besides, ain't that white man you married to satisfying your needs?"

"No, he's really not. I mean, he's satisfying my financial needs but my physical needs can only be satisfied by you."

"Um...sorry to hear that. I can't help you though. Once again, there's too much risk involved."

Angela came over and kneeled down in front of me as I sat in my chair and wiped my pants off.

"So, let me at least have these pants cleaned for you." She started to unbuckle my belt. I grabbed her hand and couldn't believe I tried to turn down some ass.

"Look. This ain't right and you know it. I can't go out like that Angela, I'm sorry."

"All I want to do is taste it Jaylin. You don't have a problem with me doing that, do you?"

I didn't say anything. My thang was on the rise so wasn't no sense in trying to fight it anymore. Besides, a little blowjob never hurt anyone.

I closed my eyes and allowed her to go to work. She must have really been practicing on her husband because she had my ass on cloud nine. She wasn't good at it before but I guess practice makes perfect. As I was in a trance leaned back in my chair, I heard two people talking and so did Angela. She hopped up and I quickly buttoned my pants. No sooner had I zipped them, Mr. Schmidt stuck his head in my office. He introduced Angela to one of his friends.

"How do you do, sir, it's nice to finally meet you," she said, nervously shaking his hand.

"Doug wasn't kidding. He does have a beautiful wife. It's finally good to meet you too."

"And this here is my top investment broker Jaylin, Jaylin Rogers. And Jaylin, this is Roy Johnson. He's going to be our new sales and marketing manager." I stood up and shook Roy's hand only to notice my belt was still on the floor. I pretended I didn't see it, but Roy had to open his big mouth.

"Say, Jaylin, your belt is on the floor. You might want to pick it up before you slip on it."

"Ah, okay. I'll get it. You know working late can really make you exhausted. And after eating such a heavy dinner, I felt like I was about to bust." I picked up the belt and Angela looked at me and smiled.

"Jaylin, Angela, we'll let you two get back to work. Angela, Doug said he's been calling, trying to reach you. Give him a call to let him know when you're going to be leaving."

"I sure will Pops. I'll call him right now." She gave him a kiss on the cheek.

Now he had the fragrance of my thang on his face. Never—and I mean never—again. I closed my door and picked up the phone to call Scorpio. Since my thang was still hard, might as well finish off the night with a good one. The sound of her sexy voice made me smile.

"Say baby, it's Jaylin."

"I know who this is. Not only that, I know what you want."

"Oh, yeah? And what might that be?"

"You want me to meet you at your place and make love to you all night long."

"You're partially correct. First, I want to invite you to go on a cruise with me to the Bahamas in a couple of weeks, then I want you to meet me at my place tonight so we can exchange some juices."

"Well, what if I tell you I'm busy or I can't find a sitter? Will you call someone else to exchange some juices with tonight?"

"Good question, baby, but nobody can juice me up the way you do. So, what time should I expect you?"

"Give me an hour and I'll be there. Don't have me waiting because I don't like to wait when I'm anxious."

"You, wait on me? Shit, never. I'm leaving the office now."

"And Jaylin, I like swimming pools too. Why don't I meet you in the pool area? Let's say the Jacuzzi?"

69

"I'll go home and get it warm for you."

I hung up and got my ass out of the office as quickly as I could. Angela and I took the elevator down to the parking garage and when I rushed her to her car, she started in with the questions.

"Jaylin, who were you talking to? I heard you tell somebody you were on your way," she said with one leg hanging out of the car.

"Angela, don't go questioning me. We don't have that type of relationship so please don't start. And as for what happened in my office today, it will never happen again. We could have lost our jobs if those two had been just a minute earlier."

"Now, you know that ain't going to happen. Pops trust me and so does Doug. They have no idea what went on with you and I in the past, and they damn sure don't know what's up with us now."

"Well, good, because there's nothing going on with us now and I'd like to keep it that way. So, goodnight and be careful." I closed her door. She rolled her big bubble eyes and started her car. I didn't care how mad she was, I just couldn't continue to do shit like that. My career meant more to me than anything.

Somehow, I managed to get stuck in traffic on Manchester Road since I tried to take a short-cut home. But by the time I got home, Scorpio's car wasn't there so I figured I had time to warm up the Jacuzzi and put on some soothing music. I got out of my work clothes, showered, and went into the kitchen to get some chocolate-covered strawberries I had in the refrigerator just in case I wanted to set the mood.

I went to the pool area and turned the Jacuzzi on so it would be nice and warm before Scorpio came. Then I put on some soft music and stepped my naked body into the Jacuzzi and waited for her to come. I poured myself a glass of wine and sat her glass next to the tray of strawberries. I left the front door slightly cracked so she wouldn't have to knock when she came.

As the water bubbled and steamed, I closed my eyes and dozed off. Shortly after, I was awakened by the touch of her soft wet lips. But when I opened my eyes, Felicia stood over me.

"So, are you expecting someone Jaylin? I know you ain't sitting out here butt naked in the Jacuzzi by your damn self."

"Yes, I am Felicia. Why don't you go home and I'll give you a call tomorrow."

"Nope, can't do that. I've been leaving you messages all day long and you haven't returned any of them. I thought we had an understanding."

"Look, I've been busy! That's why I haven't returned your phone calls. I planned on doing so but I just hadn't got around to it."

"But you've gotten around to calling some other bitch over here. Who is it? I hope it ain't who I think it is."

"Felicia, it ain't none of your business. I told you before, don't be coming over here unannounced or unless I ask you to. It used to be cool, but since you tripped like you did the other day, the rules have changed."

"So, you got rules now, huh? I'm scared of you. Look, I'll let you have your little shin-dig over here tonight, but when I call you, you need to return my phone calls."

"And you need to go before my company gets here."

Felicia put her hand in the water and tried to grab my goods. I grabbed her hand and asked her again to leave.

As soon as Felicia stood up, Scorpio walked out and closed the sliding glass doors behind her. She looked delicious. Had on a red fishnet bikini that revealed everything. She dropped her flowered wrap at the door and strutted over to me like Felicia didn't exist. Her long black shiny hair was slicked back and her curls dangled on the left side of her shoulder. Felicia couldn't help but notice how stunning she looked.

When Scorpio picked up her wineglass and sat in the Jacuzzi beside me, it was time for me to escort Felicia out. I stepped out of the water bare-bodied and all, and told Felicia it was time to go.

"I'm leaving, Jaylin, but would you at least have the decency to walk me to the door?"

I bent down and gave Scorpio a kiss and she touched my face with her hand. "I'll be right back. Don't you go nowhere," I said.

"Hurry now. I can't wait much longer," she said, starting to remove her bikini top.

Felicia rolled her eyes and shook her head. I pulled the sliding door over and motioned for Felicia to follow. When we got to the living room, she stopped.

"This is just ridiculous and you know it. This bitch ain't nothing but a freak. And the both of you walking around here with no damn

71

clothes on like it's a fucking freak fest or something." She gazed at my stuff, and knew damn well she wished it was her in that Jacuzzi instead of Scorpio.

"Look, Felicia, this is what's going to happen when you come over here unexpected. I'm not doing this to hurt you, but when you go searching for shit, you're definitely going to find it. So stop searching. I'll call you tomorrow. Just maybe, I'll see you on Friday."

"This is bullshit and you know it. One day, you're going to regret every fucking thing you're doing to me."

"If you say so, Felicia. Only if you say so."

She slammed the door and Mama's picture on the mantel fell. I walked over and picked it up. I stood there for a moment and thought about Mama. I wondered if she was proud of me. Wondered if she knew what I'd been through after she left. And wondered if she was pissed at me for not being with Nokea. I placed my lips on her picture and put it back on the mantel.

When I went back outside, Scorpio was in the Jacuzzi and had taken several bites of the chocolate strawberries. I got back in and wrapped my arms around her. She put a strawberry in my mouth then poured wine on her breasts for me to suck them. Her nipples were at full attention when she interrupted me.

"Jaylin?"

"Yeah baby."

"I don't ever want to see her over here again. She's becoming a pain and I don't like to be hurt."

"I'll take care of it. Don't you worry your pretty little self about her, she won't be coming back any time soon." I put Scorpio into position on my lap.

16 FELICIA

Friday came before I knew it, and Jaylin hadn't returned any of my damn phone calls. I was pissed and didn't know how to handle it. This Scorpio bitch took up too much of his time. Even time away from Nokea. I had no clue when he saw her because seemed like she was put on the back burner like I was. If that was true, then maybe it was time for us to pull together and try to get Jaylin to come back to reality. He was somewhere in fucking la-la land thinking that all he needed to satisfy him was Scorpio. She was nasty looking to me. I didn't care what he said. I mean, she had a nice body but did she have to flaunt that motherfucker in front of females? I wasn't interested in looking at the ho, but any time a woman got a red rose tattooed on the back of her ass, you can't help but notice. She might as well had showed up naked. Tiny-ass red bikini wasn't hiding a damn thing. Jaylin didn't think I noticed, but he was full of lust as he watched her. I was afraid he'd fuck her right there in front of me. He never looked at me like that, and I can't even recall if I've seen him look at Nokea like that either. He'd definitely fallen for this bitch, and the only one who could come between them, other than me, was Nokea.

When I got home from work, I called Nokea's house. Her number had been changed and when I tried her cell phone that had been changed too. What was up? Something wasn't right and I was anxious to find out what it was. I called up my ex-boyfriend, Damion, and told him to meet me at my house at ten o'clock. I refused to be alone on another Friday night, and since Jaylin was full of games, Damion would just have to do. I changed clothes and decided to pay Miss Homebody a visit at her house in Barrington Downs. I knew she would be stupid enough to let me in, especially if I pretended I was looking out for what was in Jaylin's best interests.

Her black Acura Legend was parked in front of her house. I could see a light on in her bedroom and that was it. The rest of the house was dark. I rang the doorbell repeatedly and didn't care if she was asleep or not. I could see her through the glass beveled-edge door.

"Who is it?" she asked, as if she really couldn't tell it was me.

"Nokea, it's me Felicia. I just want to talk to you for a minute, if you don't mind."

73

"About what Felicia? You and I have nothing to talk about."

"Yes we do, so please open the door."

I couldn't believe I begged the bitch to talk but I was desperate. She opened the door and looked terrible. Of all the years I'd known Nokea, I'd never seen her look so bad. She had bags under her eyes like she hadn't slept in days; her hair was in rollers, and her pink bathrobe was a wrinkled mess.

"Come in, but make it quick. I'm tired and need to get some rest." She put her hands in her pockets and stood by the door.

"Do you mind if I at least have a seat? It won't take long but I really need to talk to you about something."

We walked over to her sofa in the living room. She had really done up the place since I'd last seen it. I'd come over about three years ago when I found out she dated Jaylin and confronted her. Her place wasn't that spectacular then, but she had it fixed up like an African exhibit or something. All kinds of black art covered the walls and she had black statues in each corner that damn near reached the twelve-foot ceiling in her living room. She had a plush loveseat and sofa covered in Nefertiti cloth and a border that surrounded the room in the same print. An old black baby grand piano jazzed up the room, and a huge honey-mustard, green, and burgundy rug with swirls covered the shiny hardwood floors. She had candles burning that gave the room a nice subtle fragrance.

"So, Felicia, what trouble are you here to cause today?"

"I'm not here to cause any trouble. I just want to find out where things stand with you and Jaylin. I know he's been spending a lot of time with Scorpio and wondered if you've seen him lately."

"What do you mean by he's been spending a lot of time with Scorpio? How do you know how much time he spends with her?"

"I know because every time I call him she's over there. I stopped by his place the other night and they were in his Jacuzzi together having sex," I said, spicing things up like I had seen it for myself.

"So, you had the pleasure of seeing them in action too, huh? I walked in on them in the shower, and after that, I ended it...well, I tried to end it."

"What? You saw them together in his shower? What did he say?"

"He didn't say much. You know, the usual. He came over Monday night and apologized. And, stupid me, I was so vulnerable that I forgave him."

"Monday night, huh? I had just seen him Monday afternoon. I went to his office and he couldn't keep his hands off me. Tried to have sex with me right then and there. I went ahead and gave in, but I told him if he wanted to make love to me again, it would have to be in a better place."

Nokea was quiet. She turned her head and I could see her throat move in and out as she took a hard swallow.

"Felicia, Jaylin came over here Monday night and made love to me after work. I felt something wasn't right but I let him do it anyway. How could I be so stupid?" She yelled, and then walked over to the piano bench and took a seat.

"Shit, how could we both be so stupid? I'm just as guilty so don't feel bad. The question is what are we going to do about it? If you want things to change then we got to figure out what we can do to change them."

"I'm not doing anything. I don't want Jaylin anymore. I haven't talked to him since Monday, and for me, that's only the first step. If you want to fight for him, you go right ahead. But you won't be battling with me."

"Nokea, you know you've said that a million times before. What makes you think this time it's a for sure thing?"

"Because, I know. I feel it in my heart and in my soul. The only thing I need to do is figure out a way to get my energy back. I feel beat. I'm exhausted from all this crying and it's wearing me down."

"I don't mean any harm, Nokea, but I can tell. I ain't never seen you look like this. The difference between you and I is Jaylin will never bring me down no matter how hard he may try. I always keep my head up and make sure I got somebody on the side just in case he get to tripping."

"No, Felicia. The difference between you and I is I love him and you don't. That's why it's harder for me than it is for you. I'm not saying you don't care for him, but that's all it is. You will be able to walk away whenever you eventually get tired. Me, it's going to take time. More time than I anticipate. But for now, as long as I don't see him, I'm doing okay." Even though I hated to admit it, Nokea was right.

I didn't love Jaylin as much as she did, but the thought of him not being a part of my life was killing me.

I left Nokea's house on a good note. I didn't tell her what I intended to do but she made it perfectly clear that she was out of it. I couldn't blame her; she had to be the one who suffered the most pain from Jaylin. I had only stepped into this mess four years ago and was already exhausted from the bullshit.

When I got back home, I called Jaylin and left him a nasty message for not calling me again on Friday night. I changed clothes and waited for Damion to come over so I could get some type of satisfaction for the night.

17 NOKEA

It had been three whole weeks since I last talked to or seen Jaylin. I went to Infiniti Styles on the corner of Chambers and West Florissant Avenue to get my hair done, and then I shopped at Jamestown Mall to find some outfits for the fall. As far as I was concerned, I was back in action. I didn't only look good again, but I felt good as well. That was until late Sunday night. I'd eaten some greasy fried chicken at Pat's place and it had my stomach upset. I went to the bathroom and threw up. I thought it would make me feel better but afterwards, it didn't; I felt nauseous and faint.

I went home, lay down in my bed with a cold rag across my forehead, and tried to figure out what was wrong with me. And by morning, I threw up again. I called my doctor to make an appointment and then called my boss and told him I would be late. The thought of food poisoning crossed my mind because for some reason the chicken didn't taste right to me.

I arrived at Dr. Beckwith's office in the Central West End about nine thirty. The nurse called my name immediately so I didn't have to wait long. When he came in, he asked me all kinds of questions about my period, what I had eaten, and if I had any other symptoms. When I told him what my symptoms were, he said it didn't sound like I had food poisoning and told me he wanted to give me a pregnancy test. Since I hadn't missed my period I knew it wasn't possible. Besides, Jaylin and I only had sex one and a half times. Since I knew one time is all it took, I anxiously waited for the results.

Dr. Beckwith came back into the room and pulled a chair next to me. He had a smile on his face and he looked me in the eyes.

"Nokea, I have good news and more good news. Which one would you like to hear first?" I'd been with Dr. Beckwith since I was a little girl, and he always joked around with me when something was wrong with me.

"Well, Dr. Beckwith, if it's double good news then let's hear it," I said, grinning back at him.

"First, you don't have food poisoning, and second, you're going to have a baby." The grin on my face vanished.

"What—what did you say?"

Brenda M. Hampton

"Yes, Nokea, you're pregnant. And we're going to do everything possible to make sure you have a healthy baby."

I couldn't say a word. When Dr. Beckwith left the room, I dropped my head and burst into tears. I never thought I would have a baby out of wedlock. Mama and Daddy were going to kill me. If not me, they were going to kill Jaylin. For the last few months, I had really been a disappointment to myself. Why did I have to make so many messed-up decisions? Decisions that cost me big time.

Dr. Beckwith's nurse came in and congratulated me. She gave me a hug and noticed immediately that I'd been crying.

"Are those tears of joy?" she asked, helping me off the examination table.

"No...I don't know. I'm confused right now. Really, I don't know how I feel."

"Well, I know it comes as a shock today but once you get home and think about how much happiness this baby is going to bring to your life, you'll feel a whole lot better. It's normal for you to feel the way you are. Just don't go making any decisions until you've had time to think about it."

"Thank you," I said, giving her a hug.

I called work to ask my boss if I could work temporarily from home, and he didn't seem to have a problem with it. Occasionally, I had to work from home just to get out of the office environment where so much he said, she said bullshit went on.

In the car, I thought about how Jaylin would feel about this. I knew how much he loved his daughter, who was taken away from him years ago, so I knew he wouldn't have a problem loving the baby I carried. Would this baby finally change our lives? I thought. Was this a sign from God we needed to be together as a family? The big question was, when would I break the news to him—or would I do it at all?

I needed advice so I went to Barnes Jewish Hospital on Kingshighway where Pat worked to see if she would take an early lunch with me. After she told her boss it was urgent that she left, she grabbed her purse and we headed to the Pasta House on Euclid Avenue.

"So, why are you dragging my ass out of the office like this couldn't wait until I got home?" Pat said, sitting down. The waiter poured our water so I looked at her like, wait until he leaves. He walked away only to quickly return with our menus.

78

"If you don't mind," I said. "Give us about ten minutes and we'll be ready to order." The waiter smiled and walked away.

"Okay, Nokea, out with it. He's gone so what's on your mind?" I reached my hands across the table and held hers.

"Pat, I'm having a baby. The doctor confirmed it this morning and I'm confused about what I need to do." She squeezed my hands tighter and smiled.

"Girl, I'm so happy for you! But please don't tell me it's Jaylin's baby. I know he's the only one you slept with but just make up somebody, please."

We laughed.

"Girl, you know I can't lie like that. You know its Jaylin's. The question is what am I going to do? I haven't called him in weeks and I've been working hard trying to get him out of my system. And just when I thought things were going well, bam—I'm pregnant."

"I know I'm your best friend but when it comes to Jaylin, I'm not one to give you good advice."

"Yes you are Pat. You've always given me good advice. I just never do what you tell me to do because I think what I'm doing is always in my best interests."

"Well, I'm going to tell you how I see it. If you decide to listen to me, then fine. If you don't, I won't be mad."

"Okay, that's fair enough. I just need to hear your input. Then you can tell me what you think I should do about telling Mama and Daddy."

"Shit...I forgot about them. They're going to kill you Nokea. But then again, as much as they like Jaylin, they might be forgiving."

"You mean as much as they *used to* like Jaylin. I told Mama about what happened and she told me to move on with my life. Daddy came by to see me the other day and when I cried on his shoulder about our ups and downs, he wasn't too happy. Actually, he said he was going by Jaylin's place to have a few words with him about how he's been treating me lately."

"Well, I'll start with your parents first because they love you and they'll definitely understand. You're a grown woman and I don't think they're going to be disappointed in their thirty-year-old daughter for having a baby out of wedlock. You have a damn good job and you'll definitely be able to provide for this baby. As for you and Jaylin, don't tell him."

"What? Now, why wouldn't I tell him?"

"I mean, don't tell him right now. Wait a while. And if he starts showing you some love without knowing you're pregnant, then work things out with him. If he doesn't call or come around, then raise this baby by yourself and do the best you can. The worst thing you can do is have him think you had this baby just to trap him. If he thinks that, you're going to hear about it for the rest of your life."

"But, Pat, you know I didn't get pregnant on purpose. Jaylin is going to be excited when he finds out, and I know that for a fact."

"I'm not saying he wouldn't be. All I'm saying is he's going to hold it against you for the rest of your life. You know how men are. Always thinking somebody's trying to trap their ass when they're right there making that baby with you."

"Well, I don't care what Jaylin or anybody else thinks. I didn't get pregnant on purpose to trap him."

"Okay, Nokea, do what you want to. If you want to tell him, by all means, do. If it's meant to be, then shit will work itself out." That was the best thing Pat said to me all day. Her advice wasn't what I wanted to hear but I always appreciated her input.

After lunch, I decided to stop by the barbershop to see Stephon. Since he knew Jaylin better than anybody, I thought he might be able to offer me better advice than Pat did.

When I walked in, he was on the phone while working on somebody's hair. He looked at me and smiled, then shortly after, ended his conversation.

"What's up Shorty? I know you didn't come in here to get your hair cut."

"No, I didn't. I wondered if you had a minute to talk."

"Yeah, let me finish this young man's hair and I'll step outside with you to chat. In the meantime, get a soda out of the machine," he said, handing me a dollar bill. "And get me one while you're at it."

I went to the machine, got us some sodas, then walked over to his workstation and put his soda on the counter. Then I looked at his pictures he had lined up on his mirror. Him and Jaylin, that's about all there was. He had a few pictures of some females but you'd have thought Jaylin was his girlfriend. I looked at one where Jaylin had a

80

black gangster hat on with a toothpick in his mouth. He looked ghetto, and was kneeled down with a peace sign held up. It was a good picture, but trying to put on the ghetto look wasn't working for him.

After the fellows in the shop rambled on about women, I found myself a chair and took a seat. They didn't care if women were around or not; they dissed women so badly that I was almost forced to say something. Just when I was about to intervene, Stephon had finished his customer's hair.

"Come on Shorty. Let's go to my car," he said, opening the door for me. He opened the door to his BMW and I hopped in.

"So, what's so important that you came to see little ole me on the job."

"First, I want to know if you've talked to Jaylin."

"Yes, that was him I talked to when you walked through the door. He's in the Ba—"

"Don't stop now. Where is he?"

"Nokea, why you always making me tell you shit about Jaylin? You know how tight we are. I don't want to be caught in the middle of this chaos between the both of you."

"I don't want you caught in the middle either but I have a serious problem I'm trying to work through right now. So, the more I know what's going on with him, the easier my decision is going to be."

"What kind of serious problem do you have?"

"Where is he and I'll be happy to tell you about my problem."

"He's in the Bahamas. He'll be back on Monday night. So, what's your problem?"

"Who is he with? I know it isn't Felicia because she came to see me the other day and said things were on the down low with them. And I also know he isn't there alone."

"Well, then I guess you answered your own question."

"Tell me, what is it with him and Scorpio? Is he in love with her?"

"Nope, don't think so. I just think she got a hold on him right now. If you know Jaylin, this phase will be over soon."

"I don't know, Stephon. I see more to it than just that. He's different. He's had this I-don't-give-a-fuck attitude about everything lately, and that's a side of him I have never seen before."

"Yeah, he has changed a little bit, but men always get excited about something new in their lives."

"Well, I hope he gets excited about his baby I'm carrying."

"What? Nokea are you pregnant?"

"Yes…And I don't quite know how I'm feeling about it. I just found out this morning, and since then I've laughed and I've cried—don't know if I'm happy or sad."

"Well, I'm happy for you and Jaylin," he said, reaching over and giving me a hug. "And if you came to ask me if Jaylin is going to be excited about the news, yes. He's going to be ecstatic. He misses the hell out of his daughter and you know how bad he's wanted another child since then."

"Yeah, but since things haven't worked out between us, he might feel differently."

"Nokea, that's not so. Things are going to work out for you two. There's no way you can let another woman stand in your way. When he gets back on Monday, you go right over there and tell him."

"I want to have a nice dinner for him and then tell him, but I don't know…I'll think about it for a while and then decide how and when I'm going to tell him."

Stephon kissed my forehead and said he had to get back to work. Now, that's the kind of advice I needed to hear. He lifted my spirits up so high that I stopped by Babies R Us and bought two outfits for my son. I also threw in a bib that said I love my daddy and some pacifiers. I had a deep feeling it was going to be a boy but a girl would be all right with me too.

18 JAYLIN

Scorpio and I had the time of our lives in the Bahamas. She was good relaxing company for me and was exactly what I needed to get my head on straight. The moment we arrived on the ship, it was on. Men checked her out like she was some kind of beauty queen or something. I had the women all checking me out too, but not like the men rode Scorpio. And seemed like the harder they looked, the closer she clung to me. She didn't leave my side. She didn't complain about anything, and she definitely had enough sense not to bring up Nokea or Felicia on our vacation.

Before we'd left St. Louis, I'd gone to Saks Fifth Avenue and bought her two beautiful evening gowns to wear for dinner. One of them was black with pearls that gathered around the neckline. The back was open and the bottom had a tail-like flare. The other was short and red with a sheer throw scarf that draped on her side as she walked. The edges were trimmed with rhinestones and matched the red sexy shoes I bought perfectly. The dresses and shoes cost a fortune but when I saw her in them, she looked ravishing. She was definitely fit to be in Jaylin Rogers' world.

At our first dinner, we got so many compliments as a couple that we lied to people and told them we were on our honeymoon. For me, that took shit a bit far, but when Scorpio said it, I just went with the flow of things.

She really knew how to keep a brotha happy. Rubbed my feet at night, massaged my body with body oil, and washed me up in the shower. Of course, I returned the favor and rubbed her body too but she did it to the extreme. And the sex— whew—it was on. Every time we stepped foot in our room, we were at it. Could barely get the door open before we ripped each other's clothes off. Shit, I had even got some of that ass at three o'clock in the morning on the upper deck of the ship while mostly everybody else was sleep. She was creative. I enjoyed being with this woman, and frankly, I hadn't thought about kicking her to the curb anytime soon.

Our second to last night in the Bahamas, I took her to a jewelry store and bought her a diamond Rolex she seemed to be infatuated with when we browsed earlier. She didn't know I'd purchased it until we got back to the room. After I showed it to her, her eyes filled with tears and she cried. She made love to me that night like sex was going out of style. Fucked me so good, I damn near cried myself.

But after tonight, it was time to get back to reality. I had to decide where I was headed from here. I was tired of the bullshit with Felicia and Nokea and was ready to put it all to rest.

Scorpio and I put on our swimming gear and went for a late night swim on the upper deck with some of the other couples. She laid her pretty self between my legs as we looked up at the sky and tried to count the stars.

"I counted 670 of them, Jaylin, how many did you count?" she asked.

"I only counted ten. Ten over here, ten over there. I don't know...why don't you help me count?" I picked up her hand and we reached for the sky. We counted together and when we got to twenty, I took her hand and kissed it.

"Jaylin, what's on your mind baby? You've been awfully quiet today."

"Nothing much. Just thinking about how much I've enjoyed these past several days being here with you. Thinking about how good it's been to get away from all that bullshit at home. That's all."

"Well, I'm glad you asked me to come along. I never imagined the Bahamas being so beautiful. And Paradise Island, it's to die for. Just amazing." She leaned back and I put my arms around her waist.

"I'm glad you had a good time too. Next time, though, I'm going to take you somewhere even better."

"Jaylin, please, it doesn't get any better than this. I don't care where I am as long as I'm with you."

"Aw, trust me, it gets a whole lot better than this. There are places we can go that are more beautiful than you'd ever imagined."

"And I'll still say as long as I'm with you. It's just so funny how well I've taken to you. I thought I was in love with you before, but now I definitely know I am." Damn, there go those words again, I thought. Every time they come up, some bad shit always follows. "Jaylin, I know you didn't want to hear that, but what else am I supposed to say? If I feel a certain way in my heart, why should I have to hide it because those words frighten you?"

"Scorpio, I didn't say that I didn't want to hear it. All I'm saying, as I said before, is love complicates things. I'm just not ready for that kind of relationship, baby."

"You also said you haven't had a woman in your life that has made you love her. If I'm not making you love me then you tell me what else I need to do. I'm trying but eventually, my energy is going to run out." For the first time with me, she touched a nerve. She was already talking that running out bullshit and since everybody else was, I guess it wouldn't even matter any more.

"Baby, please. We are having a good time. Don't spoil it talking this nonsense. Can I please just enjoy my last day here with you?"

"Sure. But since you don't want to talk about that, can we talk about what happens when we get back to St. Louis? I really would like to know where things stand between you and I."

"What do you mean, where things stand? I thought things were cool just the way they are."

"They are…but I want to be in your life at all times. In fact, I'd like to move in with you. Be with you around the clock to take care of your manly needs."

"I don't know if I'm ready for that. When we get back we'll talk about it then…okay?"

Scorpio laid her head back on me and closed her eyes.

When we got back to the room, I guess she was a bit upset because she went right to sleep without upping no booty. I couldn't sleep so I slid on my sandals and some shorts and went for a walk around the ship so I could clear my head. The wind blew a settle breeze and the blue water splashed waves against the boat, making it rock.

I rested my arms on the rail, and thought about what I planned to do about my situation. I loved being with Scorpio better than anybody, but I wasn't sure if I was ready to give up my relationships with Nokea and Felicia. They had always been there for a brotha when I needed them—up until lately. Nokea talked about all this time she needed to get herself together, and as far as I was concerned, time wasn't on her side. I was the one who called the shots, so by now, if she hadn't figured out what she wanted to do, then fuck her. And Felicia? I just wanted to make sure I had some back-up booty if things weren't going cool with Scorpio and me. But since they were, I really didn't need her like I thought I did.

85

As I stood and watched the water rock the boat, Scorpio came up from behind, wrapped her arms around me, and rubbed my chest in a circular motion.

"I guess I know what you're thinking about," she said. I turned around and held her in my arms.

"I'm sure you do know. First, I want to apologize for snapping at you earlier. You didn't deserve that and I know exactly where you're coming from." I kissed her on the nose. "Second, when we get back to St. Louis, I want you to move in with me. I know I still have some unfinished business to take care of, but I'll work that out when I get back."

"Jaylin, are you sure? I mean, I do have a daughter too you know? She'd have to move in with us as well."

"Yeah, I know. I thought about that too but it's okay. I can hire a nanny to come in and take care of her during the week. She can have the room I fixed up for my little girl before she moved away with her mother."

"Are you sure you want to do this? It's going to be a big change for you, and I don't want you to do this unless you're ready to."

"Scorpio, it's time. It's time for me to chill out. I can't make you any promises about being faithful, but I at least will try."

"I'm not tripping off you being faithful or not. I'm going to make you so happy, you're not going to have enough time to think about another woman."

I picked her up and laid her on one of the recliners behind us on the deck. I covered my ass with a towel and fucked her well, not even caring if other people were around. There were only a few other couples on the deck, but they seemed to have the same idea we did at four o'clock in the morning.

I hoped I hadn't made a bad decision by letting her move in with me. The worst thing that could happen was I'd fall in love with her—but there was no way a brotha like me would slip.

19 FELICIA

After not hearing from Jaylin for a couple of weeks, I tried to move on. I left him a few messages just in case he decided to return my phone call, but fuck it. I'd become banging buddies with Damion and was making the best of it. He wasn't that bad after all. As a matter of fact, as long as I pretended he was Jaylin, everything was cool.

I'd gotten so lonely that I made a connection with this white dude name Paul from work. He was a fine-ass man that had all the qualifications that I required in a Black man. I invited him over to my place on Saturday night and he was good company. Our conversation was tight and flowed like we'd known each other for years. He was such a gentleman and treated me like his African princess. He talked about how he'd had his eyes on me for a long time but he wasn't sure if I was interested in dating white men. Told me all of the white men wanted to get to know me better. I laughed because I never thought none of them would be interested in a sista like me.

After dinner, I thought he'd try to get some booty but he didn't. He walked himself to the door, gave me a kiss and said he'd call me tomorrow.

And that he did. I admired a man who kept his promises. He even had five dozen yellow, pink, and red roses delivered to my house the next day and thanked me for such a wonderful time last night. I was flabbergasted. The only thing I worried about was rushing things with him. I'd heard all the nightmares about white men not being as competent as Black men were in the bedroom and was a little afraid of taking our relationship to the next level.

One thing about me: a man must be able to lay my ass out. If not, he'd eventually be history. That's what I liked so much about Jaylin. There was no way a woman would leave his bedroom unsatisfied. He went above and beyond the call of duty. Did what ever he had to do to make sure a woman's needs were met. And if you did go home feeling unfulfilled, and he knew it, he'd be sure to make it up to you the next day.

I just couldn't understand why things had to change between us. Our sex life was off the chain until that bitch Scorpio came into the picture. If he hadn't met her, we'd probably be sexing each other up right now. Just the thought of him being with her upset me, but I knew for the time being I had to keep myself occupied elsewhere.

For lunch, Paul and I went to Café Calimino not too far from work. We tried to keep things on the down low so no one would find out about us. People always seemed to make a big fucking deal about mixed relationships and I wasn't prepared to answer any questions. Seemed like everybody and their Mama from work came in the café and spoke to either Paul or me. They didn't question us but we could see and hear all the whispers going on. After we got many stares, I asked Paul if we could leave and invited him over to my place for dinner tonight. He didn't seem the least bit bothered by all the attention we got and asked me to stay. When I refused, he paid for lunch and we left.

I left work early so I could go home to prepare a nice dinner for us tonight. I stopped by the Ladue Market on Clayton Road and picked up some fresh veggies to steam and a couple of porterhouse steaks to put on the grill. Everything was perfect. I set the table and put on some soft music to set the mood. I changed into a silk red nightgown and left my panties off just in case Paul decided he wanted to get down tonight.

As I lit the candles on the table, the phone rang. I knew it was probably Paul calling to tell me he was on his way but when I answered, it was Jaylin.

"Surprise, surprise," I said, filled with excitement just to hear his voice.

"Hey, Felicia, I need to see you tonight. Do you mind if I come over?" He sounded like it was important.

"Uh…sure, why not? What time should I expect you?"

"Give me about an hour and I'll be there."

"Okay, I'll see you in an hour."

I hung up and rushed to call Paul to cancel our dinner. Before I could, he rang the doorbell. I had to get rid of him. I missed Jaylin too much to turn him away. I'd make it up to Paul some other time, but tonight, my ass belonged to Jaylin.

"Pauuul," I said, smiling. He had a red rose in his hand and gave it to me as he entered.

"Hello, Felicia." He kissed me on the cheek. "You look wonderful."

"Thanks. You look nice too," I said, trying to think up a lie to tell him so he could leave.

"Dinner smells delicious. What are we having?" He took his jacket off and put it on the coat hanger.

"I grilled some steaks and steamed some veggies but I...I just got a call from one of my girlfriends. She had an argument with her husband and asked if I could come by and talk to her. She's one of those emotional type women and I'm afraid if I don't go, she might try to do something to herself."

"By all means, Felicia, go. Would you like me to wait for you until you come back?"

"No—I'm not sure how long I'm going to be and I'd hate to have you here waiting for me all night. Can we make plans another time?"

"Sure. No problem. I hope everything works out for your friend, and she's very lucky to have a friend as caring as you are."

"Yes she is. I tell her that every day," I said, handing him his jacket so he could hurry up and leave.

"I'll see you tomorrow at work."

"Okay, Paul. Thanks for being so understanding."

I waved goodbye, shut the door, and ran upstairs to change into something more sleezy for Jaylin. What I had on hid all my good body parts and if I wanted to compete with Scorpio, I had to reveal something. I put on my purple see-through nightie with a purple silk bra and thong underneath. I sprayed myself with a dash of Beautiful, and put the food on the table so Jaylin and I could talk over a nice dinner. When the doorbell rang, I grabbed the phone and pretended as if I were in deep conversation with somebody important. He walked in and looked out of sight. Had a deep tan that made his gray eyes glitter even more. I could tell he hadn't been home yet to change clothes after work because he still wore his navy blue tailored suit and multi-colored tie. As he waited in the hallway for me to end my call, I saw him check out the five dozen roses Paul bought me that were all over the living room. I turned and walked back towards the kitchen so he could get a glimpse of my ass that he could see so well through my nightie. When I turned to face him, I could see the come-fuck-me look in his eyes. I gave a few more laughs on the phone and told no one on the other end that I'd have to call them back because I had company.

"Jaylin, don't just stand there. Come have a seat. I fixed you a little dinner because I figured you'd probably be hungry by the time you got here." He walked into the dining room and sat down.

"Felicia, how did you cook dinner that fast? It only took me an hour to get here."

"Please. It don't take me long to cook. When you called, my steak was already finished. All I had to do was throw you one on the grill."

"Okay, if you insist. But look, I really didn't come over here to eat dinner—"

"I know you didn't. It was supposed to be a surprise. I've missed hearing from you. Not only that, I miss being with you. Do you ever think things will be the way they were before between us? I really didn't think it would bother me this much by not being with you but it's killing me."

"Felicia, that's what I came over here to talk to you about. I just got back from the Bahamas and when I got home, I got all twenty-nine of your messages. Baby, this gotta stop. If a brotha don't return your phone call, that means he doesn't want to talk."

"Ya see, I had no other choice. You kept telling me you were going to call but you didn't. I guess it was because you've been in the Bahamas. And I guess I don't have to ask you with who, do I?"

"And I guess I don't have to feel any shame when I tell you I was with Scorpio."

"So, what is it with you and her? Don't I mean anything to you anymore?"

"Felicia, I'm here to tell you it's over. I can't continue to see you because it just ain't enough of me to go around. Besides, I'm tired of all the bullshit and I need to start making some sense out of my life."

"So, just like that it's over? Do you really think you can go without being with me, Jaylin? Every time you meet somebody different, I get set aside like a day-old piece of bread. Do you think I'm going to let you continue to do this to me?"

"This time is different. I've never came to you before and asked you to end this either. So, if we end this tonight, then no, I won't continue to do this to you."

"I don't believe your sorry ass! This bitch got your mind all fucked up and you got the nerve to come over here and tell me it's over? Just tell me one thing. Are you in love with her?"

"I ain't in love with anyone. I'm just trying to live decent for one time in my life, that's all. Scorpio gives me something you or Nokea have never given me, and that's a peace of mind. She don't nag, she don't bitch, and anything I ask her to do for me, she does it. Most of all, her patience and tolerance level is remarkable. And right now, she's all I need in my life. Will that change, I don't know. But if it does, I won't be coming back your way any time soon."

I was lost for words. Here I had spent four years of my fucking life putting up with this son of a bitch and his bullshit, and he had the nerve to step up in here and brag about another bitch? I felt like getting a gun and killing his ass right then. As I felt my emotions about to explode, I held back.

"So, I guess you'll be having this same conversation with Nokea? That's provided you already haven't."

"Yes, I will. I haven't seen or heard from her in a while, but I'll be sure to let her know as soon as possible where things stand between us." Knowing that Jaylin didn't seem to be bullshitting this time—I got desperate and tried to somehow keep him in my life. I stood up, took off my nightie, and walked over to his side of the table.

"Jaylin, if you want this to end, make love to me. Just this last time, please. If you do, I promise you I won't interfere with your relationship with Scorpio. And whenever she fucks up, because she will, I'll be there waiting." I placed my ass on his lap and kissed him. He rubbed his hands on my ass, but then he pulled away.

"Felicia, I'm not playing. It's over," he said, trying to push me away from him.

"Please don't do this, baby! Don't leave me like this." I begged as I tried to kiss him again.

He resisted again, and the tears trickled down my face. All the years I'd been with him, I never cried in front of him. But this time, I couldn't hold back because no matter how bad things got between us, he never turned down making love to me.

"Felicia stop!" He pushed me away. "Stop making a damn fool of yourself. It ain't like our relationship was all that anyway. You know you played second best to Nokea for a long time, so cut the act and let me go." I ignored him and continued to try and pull his jacket off. By the time he made it to the door, I managed to pull it off and ripped his shirt. "Damn, Felicia! What did I tell you?" He took the shirt off and threw it on the floor. "Come on! Let me fuck you! Even though things aren't going to be different tomorrow, just let me give you what you want so you can get the fuck out of my hair!" he yelled, pushing me up against the wall.

He pulled my braids back and gave me a hard wet kiss like he just didn't want to be there. He pulled the string on my thong so tight that it ripped and he threw it on the floor. Then he unzipped his pants and as they fell to his ankles, he lifted me and forced himself inside of me. I held his neck tight as he pounded my back up against the wall.

"Are you happy now Felicia! Is this what you wanted! Is this all the fuck you wanted!" he said, pounding me harder against the wall.

"I want you baby! That's all I want is you." I continued to cry as the feel of him sliding against my walls excited me. After I felt the warmth inside of me, he slowed down his pace. Then he rested his sweaty head on my shoulder while he held my legs in his arms up against the wall.

He gave me a quick peck on the cheek.

"Felicia, I know how bad you want me. But, you can't have me." He dropped me on the floor and he slid back into his pants.

I sat on the floor in tears as he stood proudly with a smirk on his face and had no sympathy for me.

"Get out Jaylin!" I yelled as I helped myself off the floor. "Get the fuck out!"

He looked at me and continued to get his clothes together while looking in the mirror. I went to the dining room, picked up the plates on the table, and threw them at him. If anything, I tried to cut his motherfucking face up.

"I hate you!" I yelled as I continued to throw damn near every piece of china that was on my table at him. My aim wasn't worth a damn but he ducked a few times as he tried to unlock the front door.

By the time he slammed it, food was everywhere. I'd made a complete mess, but it was certainly a good way to let go of my frustrations. I sat in a chair with my knees pressed against my chest, and cried like I'd just lost my best friend. Deep down, I really did. I knew Jaylin wasn't coming back my way anytime soon.

20 NOKEA

I probably jumped the gun, but I'd been to Babies R Us about five more times looking at clothes and furniture for the baby. Jaylin was back from the Bahamas, according to Stephon, so I wanted to wait until the weekend to surprise him with the news. He was probably exhausted after leaving the Bahamas then going straight to work on Monday. Besides, the more rest he had, the better my news would be for him. I still contemplated on when I would break the news to Mama and Daddy, but Jaylin had to be the first to know. If I didn't get it out of my system now, I'd probably listen to Pat and never tell him.

Either way, when Saturday morning rolled around, I didn't hesitate. I got up, showered, and cooked a fulfilling breakfast so I wouldn't feel lightheaded when I talked to him. Then I hugged the Teddy bear he'd given me and put it in the room that would soon have our new baby in it. I drove slowly down Wild Horse Creek Road to his house and thought about what he would do. We'd probably sit around all day thinking about what to name the baby or discuss who it would look like. There was no doubt in my mind that Jaylin would be happy, but when I turned the corner and saw Scorpio's car in his driveway, my heart raced. It was nine o'clock in the morning so she must have spent the night with him.

I started to call him on my cell phone, but I was there to tell him about his baby and that's what I intended to do. I rang the doorbell because I didn't want to use my key and walk into what I did the last time. It took a minute for someone to come to the door, and it was Scorpio. She had Jaylin's burgundy silk robe on and looked at me like, what the hell was I doing there?

"Hi, Scorpio, is Jaylin here?" I tried to show her a little respect since I was uninvited. She didn't say anything; she just opened the door and let me walk in. I went into the living room and sat down. I immediately noticed toys all over the floor. Soon, Jaylin walked out of the kitchen with what looked to be a four or five-year-old beautiful little girl on his shoulders. I was shocked.

"She's here to see you," Scorpio said, as she walked back into the kitchen. Jaylin put the little girl down, and after she kissed him, she ran back into the kitchen after Scorpio.

"So, what's up Miss Lady?" he said, picking up the toys on the floor.

"No. You tell me. Seems like you got yourself a new family over here."

"Something like that. So what brings you by?" I wasn't about to tell him about the baby until I found out what was up with him and Scorpio.

"Is that her daughter?" I asked.

"Yes. Her name is Mackenzie."

"So, what is she doing over here? And why are all these toys here?"

"Because, Nokea, she lives with me. Both of them moved in with me after we came back from the Bahamas. Is there anything else you'd like to know?"

"Yes...yes there is. What's going on with the two of you? I mean...is this some kind of commitment you're making to her?"

"Nope. It's a commitment I'm making to myself. See, when you were busy trying to decide if you were going to be with me or not, I decided for you. I'm moving on Nokea. Moving on to bigger and better things. Leaving all bullshit behind me, baby."

"In other words, you're ending our nine-year relationship to be with this woman and her daughter?"

"Pretty much. You didn't make my decision any harder. You were the one playing games like you didn't want this, so like I said, it's time to move on. Now, if you don't mind, I was in the middle of eating breakfast. Do I need to show you the way out or can you find it yourself?"

I couldn't believe Jaylin's attitude. He'd never talked to me like that and had an attitude like he just didn't give a damn. There was no way I would tell him about the baby. He'd definitely think it was a trap thing right about now and I didn't want my baby being raised with a father who had such an attitude. I got off the couch and walked towards the door.

"Hey, Nokea?" he said as I slowly walked to the door. "Do you still have the key to my house?"

"Yes, I do." I turned around and took a hard swallow.

"Leave it on the table on your way out." He walked back into the kitchen.

My eyes filled with tears as I dug in my purse and removed his key from my key ring. I laid it on the table and shut the door behind me. I barely made it to my car before I gagged and threw up all over myself. I started my car, jetted down the street and thought about my only other option: abortion. There was no way I would raise this baby alone. How could I have been so foolish to think he'd be happy about me having his baby? He already had his homemade family and seemed to be just fine with it.

I was so miserable and needed someone to talk to. I didn't feel like talking to Pat; all she was going to say was I told you so, and I wasn't in the mood to hear that. I decided to stop by the barbershop and give Stephon a piece of my mind, since he was the one who told me to tell Jaylin.

I went home first and cleaned myself up, then headed to the shop to see him. By the time I got there, my eyes were so puffy from crying that he stopped cutting this guy's hair to come outside and talk to me.

As soon as he walked out, I grabbed him by his shirt.

"Why did you tell me to go see him Stephon? You knew how he would react, didn't you!" I said, hysterically.

"Hold on, Shorty." He grabbed my arms. "What are you talking about? Calm down and tell me what happened!"

"He doesn't want me anymore! He doesn't want this baby! He asked me to leave and told me to give him his key back!"

"I said, calm down! Did you tell him about the baby? I know he wouldn't have told you to leave if you told him."

"After he told me he was moving on, I couldn't tell him about the baby." I wiped the tears from my face. "If I had, he still would have asked me to leave. He basically said he was with who he wanted to be with so there was no sense in me hanging around."

"You should have told him about the baby Nokea. I knew Scorpio had moved in with him but I thought once you told him the news, things would be different. If you don't tell him, I'm going inside right now and call him."

"No, Stephon! Please don't call him. Please!" I begged.

"Well, then when are you going to tell him? He needs to know that he's got a baby on the way. And I can't make you any promises that I won't tell him." I looked at Stephon with serious hurt in my eyes.

"Stephon, please. Let me decide how to handle this. I don't even know if I'm going to keep this baby."

"Now, that ain't even an option. You're definitely going to keep it. If I'm going to keep my mouth shut, you gotta promise me you won't have an abortion. If Jaylin finds out you did, he's really going to be upset. Not only at you for doing it, but at me for not telling him. So, go home and think about being a good mother to this baby you're carrying. I'm kind of looking forward to having a little Jaylin around."

I smiled and Stephon wrapped his arms around me. He always seemed to be there for me when I had problems with Jaylin. Not only that, he was the only one who could turn a bad situation into a good one.

I thanked him and headed for home with a better attitude. An abortion was out of the question. If Jaylin didn't want anything to do with me then maybe it was time to move on. I had a bigger thing in my life to worry about now than trying to get him to be with me. This baby was going to need all the love and support a mother could give. If I continued to stress myself with his mess, I'd probably have a miscarriage or something. From what I heard those ain't no picnic.

I felt so confident that I stopped by my parents' house to tell them about the baby. I stood on the porch, as they'd just come home from a prayer meeting at church. Seemed like they lived in church. I didn't mind going but my Saturday's always kept me occupied.

Mama got out of the car and put her arms around me; she'd said no matter what, she could always tell when something was wrong with me.

"Nokea, are you all right?" she asked as daddy opened the door.

"Yeah, Mama, I'm fine. I just came over to see how you and Daddy were doing."

"Well, you could have called to see how we were doing," Daddy said.

Daddy and I sat at the kitchen table while Mama poured us a glass of orange juice. I took a few sips.

"So, how was church? Did Reverend James preach today?"

"Church was good, Nokea. And Reverend James always preaches a good sermon. Even on Saturday. Now, you know that. Everybody's been asking about you. Asking when you're going to come back to church. You haven't been there in a while. Why don't you make plans to go with us tomorrow morning?" Mama said.

"I don't know, Mama. I've been going to Pat's church with her. Kind of like hers a little better, that's all."

"Okay, well when you're ready to come visit, let us know."

"I will. I promise you I will." I finished up the orange juice and got up to pour another glass. Mama and Daddy looked at each other.

"Nokea, what's on your mind girl? You've always been able to talk to us about things, so come on, out with it," Mama said, seeming to get tired of all my fidgeting. I stood in front of the sink and took another sip of orange juice. I put the glass on the counter and looked directly at Mama first, then Daddy.

"Mama, Daddy," I said, swallowing. "You're going to be grandparents." Mama smiled immediately. She then stood up and embraced me in her arms. Daddy didn't say a word.

"Oh, Nokea, I'm so happy for you," Mama said. "I thought you'd never say those words to me. How far along are you? Do you know what you're having yet?" She leaned back and looked at my stomach. She didn't notice Daddy's demeanor like I did.

"Daddy is everything okay?" I asked.

"Where's Jaylin?" he asked in a deep strong voice.

"He's at home, I guess."

"Are the two of you planning on getting married?"

"No. As a matter of fact, we're not. Sorry to tell you this Daddy but Jaylin and I never got back together. I happened to get pregnant my first time having sex with him, and I'm not going to force him to be with me because of the baby."

"No, Nokea, that's nonsense. You're not going to raise this baby alone. If Jaylin helped you make it then it's his responsibility to take care of it too," Daddy said, raising his voice.

"I'm gonna have to agree with your father on this one Nokea. You and Jaylin need to try and work things out so you two can raise this child together," Mama said.

"Mama, you and Daddy both know women raise children by themselves all the time. I've already talked to Jaylin and he doesn't want to have anything to do with me. He's with somebody else so I can't make him be a father if he doesn't want to."

"Well, whether he likes it or not, I'm going over there to talk to him tomorrow—"

"Daddy, don't. Please stop treating me like a little girl, and let me handle my own business. I'm a grown woman and I'm quite capable of making the right decision."

"Nokea, I thought you and Jaylin always talked about waiting until you were married to have sex. He promised me not too long ago that he would wait until you all were married. What happened? Was it all just a bunch of lies?"

"Daddy, believe me when I say we tried to wait. Hell, we waited a little over nine years. I don't regret giving myself to him because I'm going to have a beautiful baby. And the two of you are going to be wonderful grandparents. Just please be happy for me, okay?" I gave him a hug.

Daddy smiled and when Mama saw he wasn't tripping, she smiled at me too. By the time I left, they were planning for everything. Even for the baby's education. I just threw my hands up in the air, thanked them, and told them goodbye.

21 JAYLIN

The nanny didn't show up today, and since Scorpio was still asleep after coming in late last night, I worked from my office at home. I couldn't get much done because Mackenzie drove her Barbie around in a toy car on my desk. My papers dropped on the floor and when I talked to one of my clients on the phone, she disconnected it.

"Mackenzie! What are you doing sweetie?" I tried to calm down, as I looked at her cute little face that looked exactly like her mother's. I sat her on my lap as she reached out her arms for me.

"Nothing, Uncle Jaylin. I just want somebody to help me play with my dolls."

"Well, as soon I get off the phone, I'll play with you, okay?"

"You said that the last time but you didn't. Do you promise this time you'll play with me?"

I felt so bad about lying to her that I decided to play with her dolls in the middle of my office floor. I felt like such a damn fool as I put on different outfits for these dolls to look like they had some real money.

When the doorbell rang, it saved me. Mackenzie asked me to drive her Barbies to the mall to buy some more clothes.

"I'll be right back Mackenzie. When I get back I'll take them."

"Okay," she said. "I'll get their purses so we can go."

I smiled at her and went to the door. When I looked out, it was Stephon. I hadn't seen him since I got back from the Bahamas.

"What's up, my nigga?" he said, as I opened the door.

"You got the best go. What brings you by?" I said.

"I had a few things on my mind I want to holla at you about. You got a minute?"

"For you, always, my brotha." I walked back into my office where Mackenzie was still on the floor playing with her dolls. I sat in the chair behind my desk and Stephon sat on the sofa. Mackenzie looked at Stephon and climbed on my lap. She put her arm around my neck.

"Uncle Jaylin...who is that? Is he your brother?"

"Naw, sweetie. That's my cousin. We like brothers, but he's my favorite cousin." She looked at Stephon and looked at me again.

"He looks like your brother. But you're a lot cuter than he is."

Brenda M. Hampton

Stephon and I laughed. "Nigga, what you laughing at? The girl got good sense. She know a fine brotha when she see one," I said.

Stephon chuckled. "Only in the eye of the beholder. You know damn well you ain't got nothing on me." I threw one of Mackenzie's Barbie dolls at Stephon and he ducked. Mackenzie even tried to help, but she aimed at my expensive lamps and damn near broke one.

"Thanks, Mackenzie. Why don't you go upstairs and try to wake up mommy," I said, taking her off my lap.

"Okay, but will you still play with my dolls when your cousin leaves?" I looked at Stephon and I could tell he was cracking up inside.

"Sure, Mackenzie. I'll play with your dolls." She ran out of the door excited about my offer.

"Man, I thought I would never see the day when you played with dolls. I knew you had a thing for them when you were little, but ain't you a tad too old for that shit?"

"Yeah, right. Don't be over here talking that bullshit. You know damn well I don't like playing with dolls. I'm just trying to make a little girl happy."

"Well, you seem to be doing a pretty good job at that. She's crazy about you already. But, what's up with this Uncle Jaylin stuff?"

"Look, I asked her not to call me that. I told her to call me Jaylin. I don't want her thinking I'm her father so I always remind her to call me Jaylin. She's the one who insists on adding the uncle. It bothers me a bit, but eventually she'll learn to call me by my name only."

"You know, you've really changed. I haven't figured out if it's for the good or the bad. I dig what you're doing for that little girl, but I think you're rushing things a bit."

"I know you do. And sometimes I think I am too, but so far, I have no regrets. My house ain't been nothing but peaceful. The things Mackenzie says and does remind me of my little girl. Remind me how much I could kick Simone's ass for taking her away from me. So, if she can fill that void for right now, I'm okay with it."

"What if things don't work out with you and Scorpio? She's going to take Mackenzie and you'll be right back where you started. Personally, I think it's a bad idea that you're getting so attached to her."

"Who says Scorpio and I aren't going to work out? Man, believe it or not, that's a good woman up there. I mean, she might not have all the glamorous material shit like the other women I've messed with, but her personality counts for everything."

"So, honestly—and I mean honestly, Jay—are you falling in love with this woman?"

I didn't respond for a minute. I got up and shut the door. Then I sat on the edge of my desk and looked Stephon directly in the eyes.

"Honestly, my brotha, I can't say I am. I mean, I dig the shit out of her but I...I don't understand why I can't love a woman like I should. You of all people know I had some type of love for Nokea, but lately, I'm not sure what it was."

"So, what about Nokea? Are you ever going to try and work things out with her?"

"Nope, not right now. I'm going to play this out for a while and see where it leads me. If things don't work out, I won't sweat it. Maybe I'll see if she's available then. I think we needed a break anyway. I need this time away to figure out who or what I really need in my life. And in the meantime, I'm going wherever my heart and my dick lead me. Right now, that's with Scorpio."

"Well, I can definitely tell you it sounds all good, my brotha. And whatever you decide to do, you know I support your black ass all the way."

"Thanks. You know I appreciate it. It's good to know I at least got some kind of family who supports me in what I do."

Scorpio woke up and cooked Stephon and me some hamburgers and fries. She had my kitchen in a mess, but she learned slowly but surely how to be a better housekeeper. Her and Stephon got along well. She laughed when he told her about a few good times that we had growing up. Everything from the ass-whippings he gave me to the girls we tried to sneak in the basement. I was embarrassed. And since Stephon exaggerated some shit, he made the stories sound even more dramatic than what they really were.

When Stephon was ready to go, he pulled me aside in the bonus room where we had just finished up a game of pool. Scorpio was in the kitchen with Mackenzie washing the dishes.

"Man, you know what I said to you earlier about how I didn't know if this was a good thing or a bad thing?" he said.

"Yeah, I remember. Why?"

"Let me just say that I like this change in you. She's a lot better than I thought she was, and if that little girl can bring joy to you like she has, then it's got to be all good. There is one thing I want you to do for me, though."

"What's that?"

"Go see Nokea. Just tell her how happy you are and why. I think she deserves to know a little more than you told her the other day—and let her know just maybe, there's still a chance for you and her."

"I'm sorry, my brotha, I can't do that. I already told Nokea what was up and I'm afraid if I go see her, I'm going to wound up sleeping with her like I did Felicia when I tried to end it. Right now, I'm leaving well enough alone."

"Not even for me?"

"Not this time, not even for you. You know better than anybody when I stand my ground, it's hard to make me change my mind."

"Alright," he said, giving me a hard handshake. "I'm going to let you get back to your beautiful woman and her daughter. I've taken up enough of y'all time today already."

I walked Stephon to the door then went in the kitchen to check on my sweet ladies. Mackenzie had water all on the floor and tried to mop it up. Scorpio wiped down the counter with a rag and didn't hear me come into the kitchen. I picked up a jug of cold water that was on the table and looked at Mackenzie to tell her to be quiet. She smiled because she knew I was getting ready to pour the water on Scorpio.

"Mommy!" she yelled. "Watch out!" Scorpio turned around so fast that she knocked the jug out of my hand and the water splashed on me.

"See, that's what you get for playing so much," she said, as her and Mackenzie laughed. "Now go upstairs and take those wet clothes off." I held her waist and kissed her.

"Only if you come and help me out of them. After all, you're the one who wet me up." Scorpio looked down at Mackenzie still trying to mop up the water on the floor.

"Now, you know she's not going to let us be alone," she whispered. "I'll make it up to you later since I was so tired last night."

"You, tired? When did you start getting tired?"

"Ever since you've been making love to me two and three times a day. You know a sista got to have some down time Jaylin."

"I guess I'll let it slide this time, but only this time, beautiful. As a matter of fact, why don't you slide on you and Mackenzie some clean clothes so we can go shopping? I saw this cute little pink toy car for her to drive in the paper today and I want to go get it."

"Really? Her mother needs a cute little car too, you know?" she said, rubbing her fingers through my hair.

"I know. So, like I said, why don't you go change clothes and maybe I can help you out in that department too." I hit Scorpio on the ass and her and Mackenzie left the kitchen. Afterwards, I cleaned up a little better than they did and went upstairs to get out of my wet clothes.

By ten o'clock that night, Mackenzie had her pink 4X4 Jeep wagon and Scorpio's old car was hauled away by J's Towing Service to make room for her new red convertible Corvette. She was in tears most of the night. And Mackenzie was right in bed with us as we watched TV and talked.

"Jaylin, I don't know what I would do without you. Why are you so good to me?"

"Scorpio, I ain't no stingy brotha. I take care of those who take care of me. You and Mackenzie do a damn good job of that, so like I said, when you take care of Jaylin, Jaylin takes care of you. It's as simple as that."

"But this is too much. First the cruise, then the dresses, and then the watch. The watch must have cost you a fortune. Now, a car? And not just any old car—an expensive car. I don't know how I'm ever going to be able to repay you."

"Woman, please. You don't have to repay me anything. All you have to do is keep making Jaylin happy, that's all. Now, it doesn't get any easier than that."

"Jaylin, I can't compete. The only time I make decent money is when I get a call like I did last night from Jackson. He looks over my scripts and if he likes them, he pays me. If he doesn't, then I don't get a dime. I love to write but it's not getting me the money I need to buy nice things for you like I want to. I don't want this relationship to be all on you. Maybe, I need to give up writing and go back to school to study business. I've been thinking about it for a long time, and since you've hired a nanny to take care of Mackenzie, this might be the perfect opportunity for me."

"Sounds like a plan to me, Scorpio. An education never hurt anybody. I'll even front you the money if you're sure that's what you want to do."

"I'm sure, but you don't have to pay for it. I will. I'll do whatever it takes to pay for my education without your help. Not that I don't appreciate the offer but I want to do this on my own."

"Alright, Miss Lady. I'm not going to argue with you about that but if there's anything I can do, let me know."

Mackenzie had fallen asleep in my bed. I picked her up and carried her into her bedroom. Just when I got ready to close the door, she stopped me.

"Uncle Jaylin, are you and Mommy going to get married?" I smiled and walked back into the room.

"It's Jaylin, Mackenzie, not Uncle Jaylin. And no, right now we're not. If we do, you'll be the first one to know. Okay?" I tucked her into bed.

"Would you read me a bedtime story?" She looked around the room for a book. I opened the closet and pulled out *Cinderella*. I sat on the bed next to her and started to read. I tried to hurry so I could go back and make love to Scorpio, but Mackenzie held me up asking questions as I tried to finish the book. After reading it four times, she was sound asleep.

Scorpio was already in the tub waiting patiently for me. I slid in behind her but the water was slightly cold.

"I'll warm you up, so don't worry about how cold it is," she said, pecking me on the lips.

"Then stop talking and start warming."

"Jaylin, I love you," she whispered in my ear, as I rubbed her silky smooth body with my hands.

"And you know how I feel."

22 FELICIA

Paul was all I needed to get my mind off Jaylin. But when he tried to make love to me the other night, I didn't feel a thing inside of me. I was so disappointed but couldn't find it in my heart to dismiss him after all he'd done for me. He was constantly all over a sista at work and at home, but after I told him we had to cut the chatting at work, he backed off a little. I didn't mind him coming over to my house to see me, but when he showed up without calling, I had to bring it to his attention. Damion was still coming over from time to time and I didn't want the two of them meeting up at once. It was okay for a brotha to get caught in his game, but a sista—we had to play it cool. Pretend like we were only with one brotha at a time knowing damn well some of us be knocking two or three behind closed doors. I had learned a lot from Jaylin. Like him, I had specific days I asked Paul to come over and specific days I asked Damion to come over. Everything was right on schedule. I had Damion over when I needed some good loving and Paul over when I needed a good friend to chill with.

The only problem was, Paul was falling in love with me. During dinner last night at the Macaroni Grill, it was his second time telling me since I met him. I know I put it on him the other night, but this love shit was too soon for me.

Hell, I still hadn't gotten over Jaylin. I knew it would be a matter of time before he came back to me, but the question was when? I called his house a few times but when his bitch answered, I hung up on her. She had to be living with him because every time I called she answered. When I called him at work, that bitch Angela made up excuses for him. Saying he had just gone to lunch or he was in a meeting or something. I wanted to pay him another visit on his job, but I decided to just sit back and let this shit play itself out. Anyway, wasn't like I didn't have two other men in my life occupying my time.

I even thought about Nokea. I saw her the other day at the Quik Trip, on New Halls Ferry Road, pumping some gas and she looked a mess. Looked like she had put on a few pounds and her clothes didn't even match. I really felt bad for her. If she would have just had another man on the side, she might not be in the situation she's in now. I know she didn't expect Jaylin to settle down and marry her. Then again, shit...I thought some day he would marry me. Well, I'm not writing him off just yet. Whenever he's able to be alone with me and not make love to me, then I'll write him completely off. Until then, the door is always open.

Paul picked me up at seven so we could go to the movies. His dark brown hair was slicked back and he had on some loose fitting Levi's with a black button down shirt. His dark tan almost had him looking like a brotha. And his black shades covered his pretty green eyes.

He opened the door to his SLK 230 Mercedes Benz and I hopped in feeling like a million dollars as I rode with him. At every stop, people checked us out. I didn't know if they glared at us because we looked good together or because he was white and I was Black. And when we got to the movie theatre, the stares continued. Paul always liked to hold hands and kiss in public, but I was uncomfortable with everybody checking us out. I loosened my fingers from his hand and pretended I had to sneeze. When nothing came out, I dropped my hand by my side.

As we stood in line waiting to get some popcorn, Paul looked at me.

"Felicia, why are you so uncomfortable with me?"

"I'm not uncomfortable with you; I'm just uncomfortable with all these people looking at us like they ain't never seen a mixed couple before."

"All you have to do is pretend they're not there. Just focus on me. If you do, you won't even know they exist."

"So, really, why don't all the stares bother you? One thing about Black folks, we can't stand to be stared down. It's harder for me to ignore them than it is for you."

"No, it's not. I refuse to give them the attention they want. Besides, I'm here with a beautiful woman, and if I'm happy, who cares what other people think?"

I smiled because I knew Paul was right. I even reached over and gave him a kiss. Some girls behind us in line looked at each other and rolled their eyes. Paul saw it, and then he embarrassed the hell out of me. "Excuse me everyone," he said, with an English accent. "As you can see, I'm white and my stunning date here is Black. We've been noticing all the frightful stares we've been getting and would like to say thank you. You've made us feel like celebrities. So, my name is Paul and this is Felicia. We just got married yesterday, so would you all be so kind as to give the gorgeous bride a big round of applause."

Paul clapped and so did everybody else. When he kissed me, the applause got louder. I couldn't believe how he embarrassed us but it was quite funny. As we walked through the theatre to our seat, some people smiled and told us congrats. And even though it was a stupid thing to do, it worked. I felt more at ease with him and the stares had turned to smiles.

I gripped Paul's muscles through his shirt every time a scary part came on the screen. He laughed but held me tightly in his arms. "Felicia, are you really that scared? If so, we can go watch something else."

"No, Paul, this cool," I said, chewing on some gummy bears. "I just like snuggling up with you if you don't mind."

"Of course not. Whatever you want, my dear." He held me tighter.

After the movie, we headed back to my place. The first thing I did was check my messages to see if Jaylin had called. When he hadn't, I went into the living room and entertained Paul. If he was a bit more aggressive when it came to sex, maybe I would like him better. I always had to be the one to initiate it. It was like he was nervous or scared to touch me. But when I changed into my black teddy, and straddled his lap, he couldn't keep his hands off me. He laid me back on the couch and laid my coochie out with his to tongue. Now, this was one thing white men sure knew how to do better than Black men. For the first time, Jaylin had nothing on him. I could barely keep still. Damn near broke his neck as I squeezed it tightly with my thighs. But then when he slid himself inside me, the excitement went away. Damn, I thought. Why couldn't he just keep licking? I moaned and groaned like it was the best thing ever, and when he left, I called Damion over to finish the job. In the meantime, I'd have to work on Paul until he got better. Eventually I think he would, but only time would tell.

23 NOKEA

I ate everything in the house from the rooter to the tooter. Pigging out and wasn't even hungry. The stress from not talking to Jaylin added to my bad eating habits. I was only a few months pregnant and had picked up seven pounds already. Dr. Beckwith said if I didn't slow down, I was headed for a difficult pregnancy.

When I left his office, I stopped by Burger King on West Florissant Avenue to get my last taste of a double Whopper with extra cheese and some French fries. Then, had the nerve to stop at Krispy Kreme and get three glazed donuts. By the time I got to the office, I felt like a pig. I had to struggle just to make it up the stairs. I went to the bathroom and looked at myself in the mirror. I could still see my curves but if I kept at it, I knew they would soon disappear. I decided to take my doctor's advice and cut back on the fattening foods. From now on, it would be just a salad and some Jell-O. If I splurged, it would only be on the weekend, or if I felt like going out to dinner with Pat and her husband.

She was a charm. Since she was the closest friend I had, I confided in her a lot. She even started to pick up weight with me and forever brought me ice cream and a bunch of other fattening foods. Every Saturday she took time away from Chad to come by my place and keep me company. She knew I missed Jaylin and tried to do everything in her power to make me forget him. But no matter how hard she and I both tried, he could never leave my memory. We had too much history together, and since we had a baby on the way, it would be even more difficult to get him out of my system.

Pat was right on time Saturday with some salads she made and movies she brought from Hollywood Video. She rented *Two Can Play That,* and *Training Day.* She knew that Morris Chestnut and Denzel Washington was definitely a way to snap me out of my misery. We sat in the den mesmerized by the fineness in both of them and munched on our salads.

"Girl, I'm so hungry that I'm going to imagine this is the hamburger and fries I ate earlier this week," I said, picking all the meat out of the salad first.

"Nokea! I thought you said you weren't going to eat any more fast food."

"That was after I stopped at Burger King. Since then, I've been doing pretty good. And since it's Saturday, and I can splurge on the weekend, can we please order a pizza with everything on it?"

"No, Nokea. You know you need to eat a little healthier. If not for you, then for the baby."

"I didn't think it would be this hard for me to watch my weight, but this salad stuff is driving me crazy."

"Look, if you want to order a pizza, you go right ahead," Pat said, chewing on the salad like she really wanted me to order a pizza.

I reached over to the coffee table, picked up the phone, and ordered a supreme pizza with extra mushrooms and olives from Pizza Hut. "Okay, don't blame me when your ass get all fat. Then I'm going to have to listen to you bitch about that. In the meantime, what I don't understand is…why didn't you tell them to put extra cheese on the damn thing? Girl, call them back and tell them to add more cheese," she said.

We laughed, as I picked up the phone and called Pizza Hut back. The man gave me a new total and I hung up.

"I'm sorry but that salad was just not cutting it. And I made it. Shame on me for bringing that bullshit over here," Pat said.

"Well, at least you tried. And as hard as I tried to make it taste like a hamburger, it wouldn't."

"But at least we got a good laugh out of it. I haven't seen you laugh like that in a long time. So, seriously, how have you been? And don't tell me what I want to hear, tell me the truth," Pat said, putting *Training Day* on pause.

"It's been tough, Pat. Really tough. Sometimes I want to pick up the phone and curse Jaylin out for doing this to me. And other times, I thank God he's out of my life. Then there's a part of me that thinks this is some day going to work itself out. How? I don't know, but I really wish that it would. I cry myself to sleep almost every night, torturing myself over seeing him with Scorpio. Wondering why it couldn't be me living there with him? With our son? He seemed so excited about her little girl that I don't even know if he's going to be excited about his baby when he finds out—"

"What do you mean when he finds out? Are you planning on telling him?"

"No, but what if he does find out? I can't keep this from him forever. It would be impossible."

"Look, Nokea, nothing's impossible. You tried to tell him and he didn't want to hear it. So, fuck him. Raise this child by yourself. You never know, somebody decent might come along and be a good father to him. He doesn't need a father like Jaylin setting bad examples for him. Especially when it comes to how to treat women."

"You're talking like you know it's a boy. I hope it's one. And I hope he looks just like Jaylin. If I can't love the big one like I want to, then the little one will just have to do," I said, rubbing my belly.

"You are out of your mind. All I can say is go with your heart. It'll take you places no one else can."

"But my heart is with Jaylin, Pat."

"For now it might be, but you'll find somewhere else to place it. Just give it time." She took the movie off pause. "Who knows, maybe somebody like Denzel Washington will come your way. And if he does, will you be so kind to a friend and share him with me?"

We laughed. "Now, I'll share Jaylin, but Denzel or any man like him I will not. Denzel is the kind of man you want to keep all to yourself."

"Okay, fine, keep Denzel. But when I show up at your door next week with Morris Chestnut, don't be mad at me."

"Only in your dreams, Pat. Only in your dreams."

The delivery driver came and we ate the pizza so fast that we ordered another one. When he came back, he laughed because I had pizza sauce all over my white T-shirt from the first one. Pat only had two slices of the second one and I damn near ate five slices all by myself. I hate the thick edges, so when I pulled them off, it actually only accounted for four slices. No matter how many it actually was, I paid for it and so did Pat. We lay on the floor in the den with cold rags on our bellies to cool them down.

"You are a mess. Look at you, Nokea. I told you this was a bad idea." Pat rolled over on her side.

"No, you didn't Pat. You told me to call them back and add more cheese. And if you forgot, you were the one who suggested a second pizza."

"Damn, I was, wasn't I? And I have to drive home and face Chad looking like a big fat pig. You know, he's noticed this sudden weight gain I've had since you've gotten pregnant and told me if I gained one more pound, he would leave me."

"Girl, please. That man loves you. I don't care how fat you get he isn't going anywhere."

"I know, but girl we got to slow down. We got six more months to go and if we're eating like this now, shit…we both gonna be some fat bitches by the time you deliver."

"Okay, starting Monday. No more of this pigging out after Monday. I promise."

After *Two Can Play That* was over, Pat helped me clean up the den and headed home. She called Chad to tell him she was on her way and gave me a sista hug before she left. I didn't know what I would do without her in my life. Mama and Daddy tried to be there for me, but I couldn't sit down and talk to them about everything like I could Pat. And even though I wanted her to be accepting of Jaylin, there was no way she would be. Especially after all he'd put me through.

I went to the kitchen and poured a soothing cup of the hot Chinese tea Mama had given me to relax. It didn't have any caffeine so I had no problem taking my butt to sleep.

The phone awakened me at one in the morning. When I heard Stephon's voice on the other end, it scared me.

"Stephon, is everything okay?" I asked.

"No. Not really. I just wanted to call and let you know that my mother passed away last night. You know she's been battling this drug addiction for years, and last night…she, uh…she decided to take her life."

I could hear the pain in his voice.

"Stephon, I'm so sorry. If there is anything I can do, please let me know. I know how you felt about your mother doing drugs but at least you had the courage to make peace with her years ago. God will bless you for that and you will be able to go on knowing you did all you could for her."

Stephon was quiet. "Yeah, but I guess it wasn't good enough. She called me last week and asked for some money, but I wouldn't give it to her. I knew what she wanted with it but…but now I feel bad because I didn't give it to her."

"How could you feel bad about not contributing to her habit? Look at all the good things you did for her. Out of all her children, you were the one who stood by her. Please don't go dumping on yourself because you did the best you could."

"Well, I'll call you in a couple of days and let you know about the arrangements. Sorry to call you so late. So, go back to sleep Shorty and get some rest."

"Stephon, before you go…how's Jaylin taking the news? I mean, I know he's probably thinking about his mother at a time like this."

"He's doing okay. I think he's more hurt because I am. He never really cared too much for Mama anyway, but I think it bothers him knowing he wasn't there for her either."

"Alright, Stephon. Thanks for calling and call me as soon as you find out the arrangements."

I couldn't sleep a lick as I thought about Stephon's mother. The memory of her leaving them at home, night after night, when they were kids kept coming to mind. My mother even stepped in a few times and fed them when she was out on one of her drug binges. And Jaylin, she treated him like crap. One of her boyfriends beat him with an extension cord so bad one time that he came to school with whip marks all over him. I couldn't blame him for not being hurt about her death, but I knew he would always be there when it came to Stephon. And so was I.

24 JAYLIN

The funeral was torture. Stephon, his two other brothers, who I didn't get along with, and me sat in the front row of the church with our black suits and dark black shades on. I guess the glasses were to hide the tears, because I found myself thinking about Mama when she left me years ago to live in heaven. Stephon took it the hardest. And when he fell to his knees in front of her casket, I damn near lost it myself. I walked up and put my arms around him. He grabbed my leg and asked the Lord why? Why did He have to take her?

My other cousins sat there with a few tears here and there, but that was it. I wanted to take my foot and kick all of them straight in the ass. One of the assholes was a crack-head his damn self and had the nerve to sit there like his shit didn't stink. And the other two were broke as hell, didn't have shit going on but thug-ass women and a street corner. Basically, didn't have a pot to piss in or a window to throw it out of. Stephon was the only decent one. They couldn't stand either one of us because we didn't turn out like they did.

Stephon's girlfriend and I helped him back to his seat. And when I got back to mine, Scorpio was right there waiting to comfort me. She held my hand and rubbed my back. I held back the tears because I definitely didn't want my woman to see me cry. I didn't care how bad things got.

When the funeral was over, the lower level of the church held a dinner in remembrance of Aunt Betty. Stephon sat in a chair in the corner all by himself like he didn't want to be bothered. When I looked up, Nokea stood close by and talked to him. She looked beautiful. Had on a long dark blue fitted dress and some high-heeled dark blue shoes. Her eyebrows were perfectly arched and her short hair had been freshly cut. She even looked as if she'd thickened up a bit and wore the extra weight well. Especially in the breasts area.

Before my mind went into the gutter, I had to think about where I was. I couldn't be in church thinking about sexing up women, could I? But with all the fine women running around, it was hard not to. And since Scorpio watched my every move, I backed off. Especially on this nice little tender who mugged me from far across the room. She stared me down like she wanted to break a brotha down right then and there, however, now wasn't the time nor the place.

After we chowed down, I walked to the water fountain and got a drink. When I lifted my head, Nokea stood close by and waited for me. Since I saw Scorpio looking at me, I kept on walking like I didn't even see Nokea.

She grabbed my arm.

"Listen, I'm not trying to come between you and your woman, but I wanted to tell you how sorry I am about your aunt. I know this has probably been a difficult time for you, and I wanted to tell you if you need anything, call me." She handed me her new telephone number.

"Thanks." I leaned forward to give her a hug just so I could feel her in my arms again. "I appreciate it. And…and take care."

I went back over to the table where Scorpio was and sat next to her. She smiled and encouraged me to go talk to Stephon because he seemed like he was out of it. I tried to give him some space because men don't like all that attention when they're feeling down. We like to get our thoughts together and deal with it whenever. But since Scorpio pressed the issue, I went over and pulled up a chair next to him.

"Man, are you going to be okay? I know it hurts because you know I've been there before. But, it gets easier, my brotha. In due time, it gets easier," I said, knowing exactly how Stephon felt.

"I know, man, but why did she have to kill herself? If she was going to do that, she should have done it years ago. Just don't make sense. And then to make us suffer because she didn't want to any more…"

"Those suffering days were over a long time ago. For us anyway. Now, Aunt Betty had a choice. She could have cleaned her act up and you gave her the opportunity to do so. I know when you asked me for that fifteen grand you gave it to her. I know every time that you borrowed from me you put it right into her hand. All I'm saying is you can't feel responsible for something she done to herself. And if you do, then that's too bad. But she knew out of everybody, you were the one who took care of her." There was silence. Stephon closed his eyes and took a hard swallow.

"Jay, I don't know what I'd do without you. After the way Mama abused you when you were growing up, you knew the money was for her all along, didn't you?"

"Yeah, but I also knew if I didn't give it to you, I'd lose the only family I had. I wasn't prepared to lose you just yet."

"Naw, you knew if you didn't give it to me, I would kick your ass like I did when we were little," he said, laughing.

"Whatever, nigga. I held back because I didn't want your brothers jumping in it trying to help you kick my ass. But now, I wish I would have fucked all y'all up." We both laughed again. Just to get one smile out of him made me feel good.

I looked over at Scorpio and blew her a kiss—only to see Nokea reach out her hand and catch it. I smiled and went back to conversing with Stephon.

"Say, man. Did you see Nokea? She's looking good, my brotha. Looking damn good," Stephon said, like he wanted to hit that.

"She looks au-ight. I mean, she look like she's picked up some weight if you ask me," I said. There was no doubt in my mind that Nokea looked spectacular.

"Weight is good, bro. Especially if you're wearing it like she is."

"So, what are you trying to say? You trying to get a piece of that action?"

"Naw...Naw... I'm just telling you like I see it. The woman got it going on. Right about now, she'd give Scorpio a run for her money."

"Nigga, please. You know damn well Nokea don't even compare to Scorpio when it comes to looks. They both fine but Scorpio gets a ten-plus in my book. Nokea only gets a nine. With the exception of today; today I'll give her a ten."

"Well, I have that reversed. You're only thinking about the putain but I'm strictly talking about appearance. And appearance-wise, Nokea got Scorpio beat."

"You are out of your mind. Look at them. Take a look at both of them now and tell me Nokea look better than Scorpio." I looked back and forth at them and so did Stephon.

He hesitated for a moment.

"Alright. You got me convinced but...but Nokea is the bomb."

"Like I said, she's workable, but she ain't got my baby beat. Besides, why you riding Nokea so tough? Are you finding yourself a bit attracted to her?"

Stephon hesitated again and gave me a serious look.

"And if I was, would you be mad?" I dropped my head and thought about it for a minute. Then I gave him the most serious look he'd probably ever seen on my face.

"Man, we like brothers but that's one woman we'll never share."

"So, are you saying she's hands-off when it comes to me? Or to anybody?"

"All I'm saying, is that's one woman we'll never share." My palms started to sweat as I could tell where this conversation was headed.

"But, that's what you're saying. And I'm saying she deserves to have a good man in her life, don't she?"

"And, I'm saying that man won't be you, so let's drop it." Stephon hopped up and grabbed my hand. I grabbed his hand back and we gave each other a pat on the back.

For the rest of the evening, I felt a tension between us. Tension I had never felt before. And when Nokea said goodbye to everyone, Stephon got up and offered to walk her to her car. Deep down I was pissed but I managed to keep myself under control.

Scorpio said she was ready to go, so I told her to wait in front of the church while I went to get the car. As I walked to it, I noticed Stephon in the car talking to Nokea. Looked like they were in a deep conversation, but once again I kept my cool. When they saw me, Stephon got out and waved goodbye to her, then walked towards me.

"Man, what you looking all uptight for? I was just thanking her for coming," he said.

"Hey, that's cool. I ain't tripping. If you want my leftovers, that's all on you," I said, getting into Scorpio's Corvette.

I drove off, and then saw that sweet little tender that had her eyes on me all day. She flagged me down and I stopped the car.

"Hey, sexy. Can a sista get your phone number to call you sometime?" she asked. I looked at her shiny thick thighs that begged me to open them.

"Let me get yours and I'll call you when I get time." She wrote down her number as I watched for Scorpio. I quickly took her number and put it in my pocket, then drove around the corner to pick up Scorpio.

25 JAYLIN

The stock market was a serious blood bath. Everybody was calling like crazy trying to sell out. I'd even sold a few of my own stocks since they'd done so badly. If anything, losing money wasn't the name of my game.

A little after noon, Mr. Schmidt stepped in my office to talk. I thought it was about how badly the market was doing, but when he talked about my performance, he quickly got my attention.

"Jaylin, you're still my number-one producer, but lately you haven't been as dedicated to this company as you were before. And since you haven't, I've been losing money. If we could bring in some more business, it will make up for some of the losses when the market drops like it has today. So, I'm bringing Roy in to help you. I want you to train him to be like you and then we can go from there."

"What!" I said, getting angry. "Train him to be like me? Mr. Schmidt, there's nobody up in here like me. And there never will be. So, I don't care how well I train him, he's not going to be as productive as I am and you know it." It seriously sounded like this sucker was trying to replace me.

"You're right, Jaylin. That's why I need a second man. When you don't feel like giving one hundred percent of yourself, he can step in and fill the gap. Trust me, it'll all work out for the best. You'll see."

"Look, Mr. Schmidt, you're running the show around here. And whatever you say go, so let's roll with it. But I hope you understand if the situation get sticky, I'm packing up and going elsewhere. Remember, I really don't have to be here." I said, sternly.

"Fine, Jaylin, but at least give it a try. Will you do that for me?"

"It's whatever, Schmidt. Again, let's just roll with it."

For the rest of the day, I was pissed. I asked Angela to hold all my personal calls so I could finally get some shit done. Besides, Roy watched my every move. He listened in on my conversations with my clients and followed me around, trying to learn 'how to be like me,' according to Mr. Schmidt.

I took a break and went downstairs to Barb's Coffee Shop to get a cherry Danish. Something about eating the filling out of the middle excited me. Roy came with me and tried to make conversation, but when I found myself dazing off, thinking about how good Nokea looked at the funeral, I ignored him. I thought about calling to take her up on the offer she made: if I needed anything, call. But, I didn't want to start complicating shit between Scorpio and me.

She took a few classes at a St. Louis Community College and stayed out late nights with her play-writing bullshit. By the time she got home, Mackenzie and I would already be asleep. Sometimes I was so tired I didn't even hear her come in. If I rolled over and tried to get some ass—sometimes she would and sometimes she wouldn't.

Mackenzie kept me busy, though. She had me running around the house like a slave: Jaylin, cook me this, read me this, write me this, comb my doll's hair, and play hide-and-go-seek with me. I did everything for her and wasn't even her daddy. I had no clue where her biological father was, but he was a fool not being a part of her life. She wasn't only a beautiful little girl, but was smart and funny as hell. Best thing about her was she filled a void I had from not being with my own daughter.

As I sat in the coffee shop thinking about her, I took my cell phone out and called to check on her. When Mackenzie answered, I pretended to be somebody else.

"Jaylin, I know it's you. When are you coming home?"

"Mackenzie, I'm going to be late tonight. It's kind of busy today, so I'll see you when I get home."

"Well, what if I fall asleep? Will you wake me up and read a story to me when you come home?"

"Yes, I will. And I have a surprise for you too."

"What! What! Tell me what it is."

"Now, it wouldn't be no surprise if I told you, would it?"

"No, so I'll see you later. Nanny B wants to talk to you." Mackenzie put the nanny on the phone, and I told her I would be late but she could leave if Scorpio came home. She was cool because we paid her a fortune to watch Mackenzie. And I kicked her out extra because she kept the place spotless since it had gotten to be such a mess when Scorpio moved in.

I finished my Danish and my half-ass conversation with Roy. When we got back to my office, a dozen of yellow roses were on my desk.

"These came in for you while you were out," Angela said, standing with an attitude. "So, who are they from?"

"None of your business, Miss Secretary. Roy you have to excuse my secretary; she tries to be my mother sometimes." I had to clear things up because Angela was tripping like we still had something going on. And since Roy was tight with her husband Doug, I'd have to really watch it.

I opened the card and it read: *I know you thought these were from one of your lil' breezys but I just wanted to say I'm sorry for reacting the way I did the other day. Love always, your only true brotha, Stephon.* I smiled and Angela rolled her eyes and walked out of the door. I wanted to call Stephon to thank him, but I didn't want Boy Roy all up in my business so I decided to wait until later.

Roy and I didn't shut down until eleven o'clock. I was exhausted and so was he. Actually, he seemed like a pretty cool dude. Seemed to really know the business and could possibly be what I needed to get things flowing again.

After he left, I called Stephon to thank him for the flowers. I had never gotten roses from anyone, and if I ever did, I was sure they would come from one of my ladies. When Stephon answered the phone he sounded like he was asleep, but when I heard a moan, I knew he was fucking.

"Damn, dog, if you were in it, why did you pick up the phone?" I said, wishing I was doing the same.

"Because, I saw your number on the caller ID, that's why."

"Well, I'll let you get back to business. I just wanted to say thanks for the bitch-ass flowers you sent today. I always knew you had a feminine side to you."

"Yeah, that feminine side of me working it right now. So, your welcome and I'll holla at you tomorrow." He rushed me off the phone.

"Hey man?" I whispered.

"What!"

"That ain't Nokea over there is it?" I said, jokingly.

"I wish. Damn, I straight up wish."

He hung up on me.

I smiled and hung up as well. I also knew Stephon wasn't playing either. We pretty much had the same taste in women so I know if I was thinking about tagging that ass, he was too. As a matter of fact, he was crazy about her when we were little. Since she always had her eyes on me, she never gave him a chance. But who was I to tell her who she could or couldn't date? I was doing my thing with Scorpio and doing it well.

I stopped at a twenty-four hour super store and bought Mackenzie a Barbie that was bigger than her. My purpose was so she could have a friend to play and sleep with when I had to work late nights. I'd even thrown in a small CD player so they could listen to music together and Mackenzie could show her how to dance. And Scorpio, she liked books. I went through the book section and tried to find her one she didn't already have. I picked up "SLICK" and read the back. Definitely interested, I threw it in the cart for myself to read as well.

By the time I put the shit in the car and drove home, it was one a.m. in the morning. I didn't see Scorpio's car in the driveway so I knew she hadn't made it home yet. Nanny B had fallen asleep on the couch, while watching TV in the bonus room. I didn't even wake her. I went to the closet, got a blanket, and covered her with it. I took Mackenzie's doll and put it in my room. And since the house was freezing, I turned up the heat. Then I went to Mackenzie's room to check on her. When I opened the door, she was up in bed crying.

I rushed in. "Mackenzie, are you okay?" I sat on the bed next to her. She continued to cry. I held her in my arms and moved her long pretty hair away from her eyes. "Tell me, what's wrong?" I asked again.

"I didn't think you were going to be this late. I got up three times and went in your room to look for you." She hugged me back as the tears rolled over her cute little cheeks. I took my hands and wiped them.

"I'm sorry. I had to work late. I promise you if I work this late again I'll call and talk to you until I'm on my way home, okay?"

"Okay," she said, wiping her face. "Now where's my surprise?"

"It's in my room. Come on." I took her hand.

We walked into my room and when I opened the door, she had a fit. She saw the big Barbie box lying on the bed and couldn't wait to tear it open. I helped, and when she pulled the Barbie out, the smiles went away.

"What's wrong, Mackenzie? Don't you like her?" She scratched her head and looked at me.

"She's too big, Jaylin. I thought it was a bunch of little ones in the box."

"Oh…but do you think you can give her a chance to be your friend? And if you don't like her, I'll take her back to the store in a couple of days."

"Okay," she said, looking disappointed.

She didn't even play with the damn thing. It sat on the floor for the rest of the night while she lay in the bed next to me, sound asleep. I put my reading glasses on and started "SLICK." I had gotten so into it that I didn't even notice the time. When I heard the front door shut, I looked at my alarm clock on the nightstand and it was four-fifteen in the morning.

When Scorpio walked in, she was surprised to see me up in bed with a book. I tilted my glasses and gave her a hard stare.

"So, you're reading now," she said, taking her coat off and putting it on the chaise.

"Hang it up!" I yelled. "I mean, would you please hang it up instead of laying it there."

"Excuse me." She walked over to the closet to get a hanger.

"What's up with you strolling your ass in here at this time of the morning, Scorpio? You haven't called or anything. How's a brotha suppose to know where his woman at if you don't call?"

"Jaylin, you don't call me when you stay out late. Besides, I thought this was supposed to be an open relationship. You do your thing and I do mine. Right?"

"I can't recall saying all that, but if you're doing your thing with somebody else, why don't you just get your shit and go live with him?"

She looked at me with hostility in her eyes.

"Are you putting me out?"

"No, I'm not putting you out. All I'm saying is show a brotha a little respect. Don't be strolling up in here at four in the morning like you don't owe me an explanation."

"Listen, I'm sorry. It's been a long and trying day. I had tests today in all of my classes, and from there I went straight to Jackson's place."

"Who the hell is Jackson?"

"You know, the one who reviews my scripts for me."

"Aw, that's right. So, what did he say?"

"Honestly, he said he didn't think I had what it took to be a Playwright. He went over my script at least a thousand times and made changes to it. Finally, he gave up. Said he'd call me when he had some new ideas." She sounded disappointed.

"Sorry to hear that. Don't give up though. Why don't you take your shit to somebody else to look at? Sort of like get a second opinion?"

"I don't know Jaylin. I think it's time to give up on writing and focus on my education. I'm spending too much time away from Mackenzie and you. The last thing I want is to come in here every night arguing with you."

"That's the last thing I want too. And since it's our first real disagreement, let's make it our last," I said, getting out of bed. I wrapped my arms around her. "So, uh, are you tired?"

"Oh, I'm tired. But never too tired to make love to my man. Especially since I've been thinking about his sexy ass all day. Let me take Mackenzie in her room, hop in the shower, and then give you this loving you've been waiting on."

"Now, you've been waiting just as much as I have."

"I concur. So, I'll hurry." She kissed Mackenzie and carried her into her room. Then she took her clothes off and stepped into the shower.

My dick was so hard that I couldn't wait to feel her. I slid off my silk pajama pants and opened the glass door to the shower. I grabbed her wet body out and we made our way to the floor. I rubbed her soft wet breasts and massaged them together as I licked her nipples one by one. Then I floated my tongue around her insides, as I rubbed her clitoris with the tip of my finger. When she was wet, and ready, I took my goodness and rubbed it up against her walls until she begged me to give it to her.

"Jaylin!" she said, grabbing my hand. "Stop teasing me, baby. Don't make me wait when I've waited all day to feel you." I ignored her and continued my foreplay. And when I did give it to her, I waited until her body responded then pulled out. She grabbed my ass and tried to force me back in, but I wouldn't let her.

"Why are you teasing me like this tonight?" she asked

I lay over her with my hands holding me up on the floor. Then, I stared deeply into her eyes. "Because, I don't want you to forget how good I am to you. And if you ever think about going somewhere else, you'd better think twice."

I lifted her and carried her to my bed. She turned over on her stomach and I straddled her from behind. I stroked her insides so good, I could hear the juices flowing. The sound of it excited me. As I held on to her ass, and worked her slowly from side to side, she hollered my name.

"Jaylin what baby?" I said, continuing with my strokes. "What do you want from Jaylin? Whatever you want, Jaylin got it right here for you."

"I want you to love me. I want you to fuck me all day and all night. But then I want you to love me too," she said, moving her sexy slim body to keep up with my rhythm. And when I felt her body getting tired, I didn't give a fuck. I turned her over on her back, rested one of her legs on my shoulder, and slid nine plus inches of my loving right between her legs. She couldn't hang as I rubbed, licked and teased many of her hot spots all at once. She screamed as if she'd lost her mind and I could tell she'd never been to that level before.

I didn't finish my business with Scorpio until damn near eight o'clock in the morning. She lightly kissed the ridges of my six-pack and then rolled her pretty self over and went to sleep. I knew she was probably upset with me for sexing her up all night, but when I got to wait two days for some sex, it's a fucking crime and she knows it. I was glad it was Saturday because if I had to go into work, my Black ass wouldn't have made it.

By eleven, I woke Nanny B up and paid her extra for staying so late. She offered to cook us some breakfast, and after she did, she left. I sat on the kitchen stool with a piece of toast and read the *St. Louis American Newspaper*. There was a picture of Felicia shaking the CEO's hand at her architectural firm as he handed her an award. It was probably for fucking him, knowing her, but the article said it was for designing the best creative design. I wanted to call and congratulate her but I didn't want to start the bullshit up with her again since she'd chilled out. She still called every once in a while, but I hadn't returned any of her phone calls. When I say I'm done, I'm done—until I get ready to come back.

Scorpio slept most of the day. Mackenzie and I went back to the store and exchanged her big Barbie doll for fifteen small ones. She had the nerve to throw in outfits and shoes for each one of them to change into. Damn dolls were dressed better than I was. Couldn't believe I spent my money on this bullshit, but seeing the smile on her face made my day. After we left the store, we went to Wehrenberg Theatres on

Manchester and watched a kiddy movie she was dying to see. It was packed. Women were all over me, telling me how cute Mackenzie was and many asked if she was my daughter. When I told them yes, Mackenzie was all smiles. I think she enjoyed being with me more than she enjoyed the movie.

On the way home, she played with two of her Barbies in the back seat. When I turned up the music, she yelled for me to turn it down.

"Jaylin, that's too loud. My dolls are trying to sleep."

"They don't look like they trying to sleep to me. They actually look like they getting ready to go clubbing or something."

"No, they don't go out. They go to work like you and Mommy do."

"Well, that's good. Then I'll turn the radio off so they can get some asleep." Mackenzie laid her dolls on her lap like they were sleep.

"Jaylin?"

"Yes Mackenzie."

"Are you really my daddy? I heard you tell those women you were but you told me you wasn't."

"Mackenzie, I'm really not your biological father. I just told them that because they were being too nosy."

"If I be nosy would you be my daddy then?"

I laughed. "But it's not nice to be nosy, Mackenzie. Being nosy can sometimes get you in trouble."

"Okay, then I won't be nosy. But will you still be my daddy?"

I didn't want to confuse her, but I knew if I told her I wouldn't, it would probably hurt her feelings. I also knew if I tried to avoid the question, she would find another time to ask me. For a little girl, she was smart—and had smoothed me over better than anybody had done before.

"Jaylin, you didn't answer my question," she said, looking up at me with her big light brown eyes. "Are you going to be my daddy or not? If not, I'll find me another one," she said, pouting.

"Stop pouting, Mackenzie. I'll be your daddy only if you stop pouting when you don't get your way." She put on a fake smile and showed her pearly-white teeth.

"So, I can call you Daddy now instead of Jaylin?"

"No, Mackenzie. Continue to call me Jaylin. Daddy's have names too, okay."

I was so glad when we got home. When we pulled in the driveway, Scorpio's car was gone. Mackenzie helped me get the bags from the car and we carried them in the house. There was a note on the kitchen table from Scorpio that said she went to Jackson's house to pick up her script and she would call later. She even left his number for me to call if I needed to reach her. I threw the number in the trash because I wasn't the type of brotha to check up on his woman.

Mackenzie ran to her room and played with her Barbies. When I heard the music from her CD player up loudly, I went to her room to tell her to turn it down. I stood in the doorway and watched her dance like she was damn near twenty years old. Twisting and turning her body like she was putting on a show.

"Mackenzie!" I yelled. "What are you doing? Little girls aren't supposed to dance like that. Who taught you how to dance like that?"

"My Mommy. She dances like this all the time. She makes a lot of money when she dances like this," she said, doing another one of her mother's moves.

I picked up Mackenzie and took her into my room. I sat her on the bed and put one of her Barbie dolls in her lap to keep her busy. Then I ran downstairs and searched the trashcan for Jackson's number. When I called, no one answered; the phone just rang and rang. I tried three more times only to get the same thing. No, this bitch ain't no stripper, I kept thinking. She couldn't be.

I jogged back up the stairs and went straight into my closet. All her shit was lined up on one side and mine was on the other. I went through her clothes piece by piece until I came to a gray garment bag that looked thick and full. It was in the far back of the closet hidden away from all the rest of her clothes. I laid it on the bed next to Mackenzie and unzipped it. The evidence was all there. All kinds of sexy slutty outfits. Leather and lace two-piece sets. Belts and whips. There were even a few pictures of her with a little of nothing on. I guess she gave them out because her signature was on the bottom of them.

I was furious and the only thing I could think about was packing up her shit and kicking her ass out. But when I looked on the bed at Mackenzie, I didn't know what to do. I put Scorpio's belongings back in the garment bag and back into the closet. As I searched for more evidence in the closet, the phone rang. Mackenzie answered and talked, so I knew it was Scorpio. When Mackenzie gave the phone to me, I took a deep breath.

"Hey, baby, you miss me?" she asked, like shit was all good.

"Miss you so much, I need you. Right here and right now," I said, trying to show Mackenzie a little respect by not dissing her mother.

"You know, I've been thinking about that good loving you gave me last night."

"Really," I said, wanting to snatch her ass through the phone and beat the shit out of her. "Well, how soon can you get here so I can give you some more?"

"I was calling to tell you I'm on my way. Jackson made some changes to my script and it looks pretty good. I'll tell you all about it when I get home."

"Sure, can't wait."

I hung up.

Mackenzie gave me a funny look. "Daddy, are you mad at me for dancing like that?"

"No, Mackenzie, I'm not. But do you think you can do me a favor?" I asked sitting her on my lap. She nodded. "Do you think you can take a bath and go in your room and play with your dolls?"

"Sure. I need a nap anyway. Can I borrow your pillow? Yours is more thicker than mine is," she said, taking the pillow off my bed and heading to the door. "Goodnight, Daddy. Thanks for the dolls and the movie today. I almost forgot to thank you."

"You're welcome, Mackenzie. Anytime." She ran back over and gave me a squeezing hug. Then she gave me a long wet kiss on the cheek. She wiped the spit off my cheek with her hand and smiled.

"Daddy?"

"Yes Mackenzie," I said, trying to hurry her off.

"I love you, Daddy."

I was silent. She caught me completely off guard. She looked at me and waited for a response. And for the first time in my life, I felt good about saying, "I love you too."

She strolled out of my room with two of my pillows like her dolls needed one too. My heart ached; if I put Scorpio out she would leave too. I was in a no-win situation and had no idea what I would do.

126

No sooner had I tucked Mackenzie into bed after her bath, Scorpio walked up the steps. I met her at the top of the stairs right after I closed Mackenzie's bedroom door.

"Did I hurry enough for you?" She dropped her purse on the floor, put her arms around me, and gave me a kiss. I moved my head back to avoid her kiss and took her arms from around my waist.

"We need to talk," I said, walking into my bedroom.

"Jaylin, I hope you're not upset with me. I left Jackson's number so you could call me. And this time, I did call to check in." She followed me into the bedroom. I sat on the chaise, and slowly rubbed my hands together. Scorpio stood on the other side of the bed. I knew she could see the fire burning in my fucking eyes.

"You got one chance to tell me the truth. If you fuck up, I'm gonna knock your ass straight to Egypt," I said, sternly.

"Jaylin, you're scaring me. Are you that upset with me—"

"What in the fuck is your occupation?" I yelled.

"What? What do you mean by what's my occupation?"

I hopped up and stood right in front of her. "Please, don't make me do this," I said. "What in the hell do you do for a living?" She took a deep breath and removed her jacket. She laid it on the bed and that's when I lost it. "Hang the motherfucker up!" I grabbed her hair. "Stop leaving shit around the damn house and hang the motherfucker up!"

"Jaylin, what is wrong with you? Let my hair go!" She tried to move my hand from her hair. I grabbed it tighter and slung her ass on the bed. When she fell down, I hopped on top and held both hands down above her head so she couldn't move.

Soon, she started to cry. "Stop, Jaylin! Please stop! I'll tell you if you just please get off of me!" I continued to hold her hands down tightly, and when I was just about ready to release them, the bitch tried to kick me in my motherfucking balls. I grabbed her ankles and pulled her off the bed as hard as I could. She went flying and her head hit the floor. "Jaylin, stop! Would you please stop and just listen for a minute?"

I sat on top of her again and held her hands, as she tried to scratch me. We tussled for a minute, and then I smacked her face. She cried and finally calmed her ass down and covered her face. A red handprint swelled on it, and I got up and went into the bathroom. I could see her in the mirror, as she sat up beside my bed and continued to cry. I took a towel from the closet and wet it.

"Here," I said, giving the towel to her. She looked up and took it out of my hand.

"Are you ready to listen to me now?" she said, looking at me with tears flowing down her face.

"No, I don't want to hear anything you have to say. All I want is for you to get your things and go." I calmly poured myself a drink.

"Jaylin, don't do this. Things have been going so well for us. The reason I didn't tell you about being a stripper is because I slacked up when I met you. I've been trying to better myself by going back to school and trying hard to get my script together."

I took a few sips of my drink and looked at her with disgust. "So, are you saying all these late nights you've been coming in, you haven't been out doing your thing?"

"Twice, Jaylin, that's it. I did two parties just so I could pay for my tuition. I didn't want to ask you for the money so I did what I had to do to get it myself. They were just parties, Jaylin. And after I made my money, I left." I had firsthand experience with these strip parties, so I couldn't do nothing but stand my ground.

"Scorpio, just go. Listen, you don't owe me an explanation. Just get your shit and leave." I walked out of the door because I didn't want to hear anymore of the bullshit. I went downstairs to my office and sat in my chair. She followed.

"Baby, I'm sorry. I never wanted to lie to you, but there would be no way to earn your respect if I told you what I did for a living. You would have thought that sex was all I was good for. I hoped that maybe one day I would be able to look back at this and laugh. Laugh with you when I told you what I had to do to get my education paid for and make a better life for Mackenzie and me."

"Scorpio, cut the fucking act. You flat-out lied to me and that's all to it. One thing I can't stand is a lying bitch. Especially, a lying conniving-ass woman. You are not the type of woman I want to be with. When you get that education you're talking about, or when you become a real Playwright, holla at me. Until then, let me go upstairs and help you pack your shit."

Scorpio stood there and cried, as I moved her ass out of the way and went back upstairs to my room. I pulled her things out of the closet and laid them on my bed. She walked up and stood with her arms folded like she wasn't going anywhere.

When I put her last piece of clothing on my bed, she broke down and pleaded with me again.

"Why do you have to be so stubborn? You know people make mistakes sometimes. All I'm asking for is another chance. I promise I will never take my clothes off for men again. All I care about is being here with you."

"And all I care about is you getting the fuck out of here. Now, if I have to tell you one more time, Scorpio, I'm gonna put you out of here my damn self."

I guess she got the picture because she started to make progress and got her clothes off the bed. Shortly after, she hesitated.

"Jaylin, what about Mackenzie? If you want me to leave, you go wake her and tell her she's got to go with me." I dropped my head and thought about Mackenzie for a minute.

"Come pick her up tomorrow. Better yet, send somebody over here to get her. I don't want to see your face, so your cousin or sister will be just fine. Tell them to come late because I need time to tell her what happened."

"Never mind. I'll wake her and take her with me."

"No you won't. I told you to send somebody over here tomorrow to pick her up, didn't I?"

"Well, I don't care what you said. She's my daughter and I said she's coming with me."

"Scorpio, you know damn well if I wake Mackenzie and ask her if she wants to go with you or stay here with me, you know what she'll say. She's well aware of your trifling-ass ways and doesn't take too well to you as it is."

"What did you say?" She walked over to me. "Trifling? Did you have the nerve to call me trifling?"

"I call it as I see it; now get the fuck out of my face." I pushed her away.

She took her hand and smacked my face. I felt a scratch as my face burned. I put my hand on the scratch, only to see a dab of blood on the tip of my finger. Before I knew it, I grabbed her hair again and slung her ass damn near across the room. I sat on top of her and smacked her around a few times, then tried to push her down the steps to get her the fuck out of my house. I threw bunches of her clothes and shoes over the handrail and they landed in the middle of the foyer. Then, I ran downstairs and shoved her and her fucking clothes out of the front door. I wanted the bitch to take a cab, but since I wanted her out so badly, I didn't even care that she took the damn Corvette.

When I threw the last piece of clothing on the front lawn, I went back into the house and slammed the door. I watched as she walked back and forth loading her car up with her things. I was so mad that I wanted to go outside and kick her ass again. I had never stooped to this level with anybody and if a bitch had made me go that far, I didn't need her.

As I went back upstairs to my room, I heard her car speed off. I picked up my drink and stood at the bar cart thinking about how this bitch had lied to me and then made me kick her ass. Flat out tried to provoke me, when all she had to do was tell the fucking truth. I picked up a wine bottle and threw it at my glass bedroom doors. They shattered and the wine spilled on the walls and all over the carpet.

Seconds later, Mackenzie came down the hallway. "Mackenzie, watch out for the glass!" I yelled as she tried to step over the shards on the carpet. I picked her up to make sure she didn't cut her feet.

"Daddy, what happened?" She rubbed her eyes. "Is Mommy home yet?"

"Mackenzie, Mommy won't be home until tomorrow. Get in my bed and go back to sleep."

I was glad that she didn't ask any more questions because I wasn't prepared to answer her. I went into the bathroom and ran some bath water to relax me. As I closed my eyes and thought about what tomorrow would bring, I dozed off in the tub.

26 NOKEA

I started to show and busted out of everything I had in my closet. When Pat and I went to Jamestown Mall to buy me some maternity clothes, I saw Stephon there with one of his boys waiting for their food in the food court. He told me Ray-Ray was getting married and said they were at the mall to get fitted for their tuxedos. When I asked about Jaylin, he didn't comment. He pretended like he didn't hear me and quickly changed the subject. I knew something was up, so after talking for a while, I invited him to my place for dinner. Pat had already entertained me last night and I was sure Stephon would entertain me by giving me the scoop on Jaylin.

Stephon came in with what looked to be a bottle of wine. When I took it out of his hand, it was a bottle of Welch's sparkling white grape juice. I laughed and carried it to the kitchen where I was in the midst of finishing dinner.

Stephon looked remarkably well. He always kept his head clean-cut and shaven, and his goatee was trimmed and shaped perfectly. He had on a FUBU blue jean outfit and some clean white FUBU tennis shoes. When I asked for his jacket, I could see his thick muscles busting out of his white oversized T-shirt.

"So, Shorty, what you cooking?" he said, standing over me, while looking into the pot on the stove.

"I'm cooking some spaghetti with cheese and some garlic bread. I was going to fry some fish but I forgot to thaw it."

"Naw, this cool. Actually, smells pretty good."

"Here, would you like to taste it?" I put a dab of sauce on the tip of the spoon. "It's hot, though, so be careful." Stephon blew on it and I put it into his mouth. He moved it around in his mouth, and then shook his head.

"This pretty good, Shorty. Jaylin told me you couldn't cook." He laughed.

"Oh, no, he didn't. I can cook when I want to. Besides, we always used to go out. But when I did cook, he loved it."

"Before you go getting all upset, I'm just playing. Actually, he said you were a good cook."

"Alright, then. Don't go talking about a woman's cooking when she's in the midst of cooking for you."

Stephon set the table, then took the garlic bread out of the oven so I wouldn't burn myself. By the time the spaghetti was good and ready, I was tired from being on my feet. He pulled up a chair in front of the one I sat in so I could elevate my feet. Then he served out both our dinners.

I had questions about Jaylin but I didn't want to rush into it. Stephon went on and on about his job—how he was ready to do something different—and the women in his life. He and Jaylin had so much in common, only he seemed to treat his women with a little more respect than Jaylin did.

As I sat listening to him, I observed his muscles tighten every time he lifted his fork. I couldn't resist so I reached over and gave his muscle a squeeze.

"You've been really working out, haven't you?" I said, moving his sleeve up so I could see the Q-Dog symbol on his arm.

"Yeah, Jaylin and me both. We've been meeting at the gym every morning trying to relieve some of this stress we've been under."

"Really? What kind of stress? I didn't know you and Jaylin work out to relieve stress. I thought you all just find a woman to relieve that." Stephon looked at me and stuffed some spaghetti in his mouth. He chewed for a minute.

"Now, you know that ain't so, Nokea. A piece of ass doesn't relieve stress; it only adds to it if you ask me. If you took me in your room right now and fucked my brains out, I'd still be stressed." He sounded like he wanted me to convince him.

"See, if I wasn't pregnant with Jaylin's baby, I'd take you up on that offer. Stress is all in the mind. When sex takes your mind to a different level, you forget about it. Wouldn't you agree?"

"Depends on who you're having sex with. If it's somebody like you, then maybe. But for the most part, I'm stressing no matter what."

"So, what are you trying to say? You sound like you got something on your mind."

Stephon was quiet and stared at me like he was in deep thought. He got up and put his plate in the sink. I checked his bulge out as he walked back towards the table. Looked like he was hard to me. And if he wasn't, sistas know they be in trouble.

He took my hand and walked me into the living room. "Come here, Shorty. Sit. I have something I've been wanting to tell you for a long time."

I was a bit nervous because I didn't know if this was one of Stephon's jokes or not. After I took a seat on the couch, he sat next to me with a serious look. Now, I knew he wasn't joking.

He took my hands and closed them tightly with his. "Shorty, I think you're a beautiful woman and I'm finding myself attracted to you. I've always been crazy about you, but recently, my feelings have been beyond my control. Since you and Jaylin have been apart for a while, I think it's time you move on. You need to find happiness in your life; and not only that, you need a good father figure for this baby." He rubbed his hands on my stomach. "I can give you both of those things and more. I've seen the way you've been checking me out too, and I say if you want to, then let's do this. Time is of essence and I don't want to sit around wasting any more time not being with the woman I've always wanted to be with."

I took a deep breath and pulled my hands away from him. I was shocked. He was right about me checking him out, but what's so wrong with a sista checking out a good looking brotha when she sees one? I thought. Especially, if she's horny.

Before I could even respond, he leaned forward and placed his lips on mine. I put my hand on the back of his head and pulled him closer to me. As we floated our tongues around in each other's mouth, I backed up.

"Stephon, this ain't right. I can't do this with you."

He stood up and removed his shirt. The sight of his dark-brown skin, broad thick shoulders, and six-pack weakened me. He sat back down on the couch, and I lay on my back so he could lay on top of me.

"We can do this, Shorty," he whispered in my ear. "Just between you and I we can do this."

I rubbed his back and closed my eyes as he kissed down my neck. He lifted my shirt and pulled it over my head. Then he put his mouth between my breasts and unhooked my bra with his teeth. I smiled as he dangled it in his mouth like a tiger and growled. He stared at my breasts, and then slowly manipulated them with the tip of his tongue. My insides steamed. I couldn't wait to see what else he had to offer so I unbuttoned his jeans just enough to reach my hands down his pants to rub his ass. Solid as a rock but smooth as a baby's bottom.

When he stood up and took his pants off, I damn near fainted. Body was cut in all the right places and dick hung longer than Jaylin's. I had no idea what I was about to get myself into, but I had some needs that needed to be met. Stephon pulled my jeans off but left my panties on.

He sat up on the couch, and put me on top of him. He massaged my breasts with his strong hands and held them like they were the most precious things he'd ever held in his hands before. I closed my eyes as he sucked them, and rubbed one of his hands on my back. Then he reached his hands inside my panties and rubbed them gently across my hairs. He could tell how excited I was, and took both sides of my panties and tore them. Then, with all of his strength, he lifted me under my arms and placed my goodness right on his face. My legs straddled his face and I held on for dear life.

"Relax, Shorty. I got you." He gently licked my walls, and as I got more excited, it was hard for him to keep me balanced. He kissed my thighs and laid me back down on the couch.

"You taste good, Shorty. I wish you would keep still, though, until I'm finished with you." He licked his lips.

"Stephon, I can't. I'm just not used to all of this," I said, looking into his hazel eyes.

"Well, get used to it. I don't think this is going to be my last time here." He laid my legs on his chest, as he kneeled in front of me. He put his lips on my feet and tickled them with his tongue.

As he pressed himself up against me, I reached down and put him inside me. I closed my eyes as I painfully felt every bit of him. Slowly, he moved from side to side and continued to hold my legs close to his chest. I figured he was trying not to lean on the baby, but when he opened my legs and leaned in forward, I knew the baby felt him because I sure in the hell was. He rubbed my hips with his hands and closed his eyes as he felt my body respond so powerfully to his. He sucked in his bottom lip and he changed to another rhythm—one I kept up with very well.

"You feel good baby. I knew it would feel like this. That's why I couldn't get you out of my mind," he whispered.

"Stephon, what if Jay—"

"Shhh...I don't want to talk about Jaylin right now. We can talk about him once we're finished. Besides, right about now, I ain't stressing. Stress is a thing of the past."

Suddenly, I stopped my motion. "What's wrong, Shorty?" he asked, then gave me a kiss.

"Stephon, we don't ever have to talk about Jaylin again. Feeling as good as I do with you, you'll never hear his name come out of my mouth again."

Stephon smiled and continued making love to me. He was a gentle lover and definitely knew how to excite the hell out of me. By the end of the night, he had taken me to my room and loved me all over again. I felt like a new woman. And by the time he left, which wasn't until Monday morning, I never wanted to see Jaylin again.

27 FELICIA

It had been months since I'd last slept with Jaylin. And I couldn't believe how well everything flowed without him. Paul and I made the best of our mixed relationship and I had even kicked Damion to the curb. His baby's mama called here with some of that, 'When's the last time you seen him?' bullshit. After I told the bitch what he had on, he had the nerve to call and curse me out. I told him, "Don't ever pick up the phone and call me again if you're going to put this out-of-shape, baby-having bitch in front of me." Since then, I haven't talked to him.

Paul, though, he'd been a true gentleman. Had done anything I asked him to do and had gotten a little better in the bedroom. There was no way to keep our relationship a secret at work. Since we spent so much time together, of course, people started asking questions. I wasn't ashamed of Paul's fine ass so I didn't deny shit. And since I was like some kind of prize for the white men, he was definitely the winner.

For the weekend, we planned a fast trip to Chicago. Deep in my heart, I thought he would ask me to marry him because he hinted about having beautiful children together and about us living together. If anything, I didn't know what I would say.

While at home packing up my things, I got a call. It was Jaylin—and it was definitely a setback for me. All he said was for me to be there for him when he needed me. When I asked what was going on, he told me he'd call me later. I tried to call him back but he didn't answer. When I called him at work, Angela said he didn't come in today.

I was confused, so I put on some clothes and drove to his house. When I got there, I rang the doorbell but got no answer. His cars were in the driveway so I knew he had to be there. After banging for a few more minutes, I left.

I didn't know where else to go for answers but to Nokea's house. If anybody knew what the hell was going on, she would. I knew she didn't have the guts to stay away from Jaylin as long as I did, but if he really needed me, there was no way I would turn my back on him.

I rang Nokea's doorbell and she opened the door in her work clothes.

"Felicia, what are you doing here now? Why do you keep coming over to my house like we're the best of friends or something?"

She looked as if her face had swelled. When I looked down at her stomach, I could tell immediately what was going on.

"You're pregnant?" I asked.

"Why? What's it to you?"

"I just want to know. If you are, then maybe that's what's troubling your man." She walked away from the door and I walked in and shut it behind me. "Girl, look, I ain't here to start no trouble. I came over to find out if you've talked to Jaylin. And evidentially you have. Looks like you've done more than talk to him."

"So, now what, Felicia? Yes, I'm pregnant but it's not Jaylin's baby."

"Girl, shut your mouth! Since when did you become a little hoochie mama?"

"Since I learned from your trifling butt, that's when. So, if you don't have anymore questions, would you please go?"

"Ouch. Now, that hurt coming from a bitch who pretended to love Jaylin so much. If you did, you wouldn't be knocked up by another man. And I thought you had a little more class about yourself. I should have known better. Once you lost your virginity, you just couldn't get enough. Could you?"

"Felicia, why don't you take your butt home? If you came over here to find out anything about Jaylin, I don't have an answer for you. I haven't seen or heard from Jaylin in months. And frankly, I don't think I ever will. So, if information is what you're looking for, I suggest you find Scorpio. I'm sure she's got all the answers you want."

I shook my head as I walked towards the door and got ready to leave. "So, who's the lucky man, Nokea? Is it anybody I know?"

"No, Felicia. It's not anybody who you've had the pleasure of giving yourself to."

"I don't know now...you never know. I do get around, bitch, so watch your back," I said, slamming the door behind me.

I jumped in the car and backed out of Nokea's driveway. As I got ready to make a left onto New Halls Ferry Road, I saw Stephon in his white BMW. He looked directly in my face, but when he saw me, he turned his head like he didn't see me. I looked in my rearview mirror and watched as he drove by Nokea's house. I turned the corner like I was on my way out of her subdivision and drove around on the other street for a few minutes. When I drove on a street where I could see the front of Nokea's house, Stephon pulled in her driveway and got out with a box of Kentucky Fried Chicken in his hand. She opened the door and smiled as she let him in. Instantly, he leaned forward and gave her a kiss.

I was in disbelief. Where in the hell had I been? This bitch was pregnant by Stephon. No wonder Jaylin sounded upset; he probably just found out about the bullshit. Damn, I thought. Now would be the perfect time to get back with him. He for damn sure would need me now. And since Paul didn't mind playing second best, I was willing to give it another shot with Jaylin.

I drove back to his house and wasn't leaving until I got some answers from him. I knocked and banged until he finally cracked the door to talk to me.

"Jaylin, would you open the door so we can talk? I know something is wrong; I could tell by the sound of your voice. Please open the door. All I want to do is talk."

"Not right now, Felicia. I'm not in the mood for any company," he said softly.

"Why did you call me then? All you wanted to know is if I'd be there for you when you needed me—and yes, I'm here. So open the door."

He opened the door and let me in. I damn near melted as he gave me a hug. Had his shirt off and some silk paisley-print boxer shorts on. I could tell he had just gotten out of the shower; his hair was wet and so was his body. When he walked up the steps, I followed and wished like hell he'd put it on me tonight. But by the sadness in his eyes, I could tell wasn't nothing going on with us—tonight, anyway.

At his room, I noticed the doors weren't tinted anymore. Looked like he had some new ones put in because they were clear and you could see straight into his room now. He held the door for me as I walked in. There was a cute little girl on the floor in his bedroom watching the *Rug Rats*. She looked up at me and smiled.

"Daddy, who is she? Is this your new girlfriend?"

"No, Mackenzie. This is Felicia. Felicia this is Mackenzie."

I said hello to Mackenzie but I couldn't believe she called him Daddy. I'd definitely been away too long if this was his daughter.

"Mackenzie, would you go in your room and watch TV? I'll come in and read you a story in a minute," Jaylin said. She picked up her dolls and went into the other room. I looked at Jaylin like, what the fuck is going on? "Look, Felicia, I know you got questions, but right now I'm not in the mood for them. I just called you because I hadn't heard from you in a while."

"Jaylin, don't bullshit around with me. Tell me what's going on. And is that really your daughter? I mean, she's cute but she doesn't look like you."

"She's not my daughter. She's Scorpio's daughter, and since we fell out the other night, she's been here with me."

"So, what is she doing here with you? Did Scorpio just run off and leave her with you?"

"No. Her sister came to get Mackenzie but I didn't open the door. I've really gotten attached to her and I'm not ready to give her up yet."

"Jaylin, you have to. That's kidnapping. You can be in a lot of trouble for that."

"Yeah, I know. But she's brought so much joy to my life these past several months. She reminds me of myself when I was little. How curious I used to be about shit. I can't let her go. Besides, she doesn't want to leave me anyway. She told me she wanted me to be her daddy and she wanted to live with me forever."

"But she's just a kid. You need to take her back to her mother before this shit gets out of hand. Where's Scorpio at anyway? I thought she was here with you."

"She's gone but I don't want to talk about her right now. I'm waiting to hear from my lawyer so he can tell me what I need to do. I know he's going to probably tell me nothing, but there's got to be something I can do to keep Mackenzie."

Jaylin sat and looked pitiful. I couldn't believe how much love he had for this little girl. No doubt, I was kind of jealous. Four years with his ass and brotha still didn't have no love for me. I couldn't offer him any advice because what I said to him, he wasn't trying to hear. He was going to do shit his way whether I liked it or not.

And it was obvious he didn't know about Stephon and Nokea. Because if he did, I knew he would have probably said something. But maybe he did…"Hey, have you seen Nokea lately?" I asked.

"Yeah, why?"

"So, you know she's pregnant?"

Jaylin looked at me like he saw a ghost. "She's what?"

"Yes. I saw her today and she's pregnant. I asked her who the baby's father was and she wouldn't tell me. However, she did tell me it wasn't yours."

"Really?" He paused. "How many months is she? Or did she tell you?"

"Naw, she didn't say but I could tell she was pregnant the moment I saw her. You might want to ask Stephon," I said, spicing things up a bit. "He might know since he's been kicking it with her and everything."

"What do you mean, kicking it with her?" His thick black eyebrows raised; he was mad.

"I mean, I just left her place not too long ago and he was over there. Looked like they were a couple or something."

Jaylin jumped up and went into his closet. He put his jeans on and a T-shirt. He grabbed his keys off his dresser and asked me to stay there until he got back. Mackenzie came running out after him but he kissed her and begged her to stay with me. When she cried, he kissed her again and wiped her tears. Motherfucker didn't even give me a kiss and I was the one who gave him the scoop. I picked up Mackenzie and we went back in his room to watch the *Rug Rats*.

28 JAYLIN

I was on a rampage. I was already upset about the shit that went down with Scorpio, and now this. I drove about ninety miles in the Cedes on Interstate 270 and when I hit a bump I almost lost control of the wheel. Felicia had to be bullshitting. I knew damn well Nokea and Stephon weren't kicking it like that. I had just seen him Friday at the gym and he didn't say nothing about Nokea. And pregnant? That just didn't sound right to me. If she was pregnant by Stephon that would mean he'd been screwing her at the same time I was. But she was a virgin so that couldn't be true.

I racked my brain and tried to figure out what the fuck was going on. I thought about Stephon's and my conversations about Nokea over the last few months. I made it perfectly clear that out of all my ladies, I didn't want him to ever screw Nokea. He could have fucked with anyone of them he wanted to, but she was off limits.

I continued to roll the Cedes, and when I flew past a police officer without seeing him, he damn near pulled me over. He pulled his car next to mine and motioned for me to slow down. I nodded and calmly drove the rest of the way to Nokea's house.

As soon as I turned into Barrington Downs subdivision, I could see Stephon's BMW in Nokea's driveway. I swung my car in her driveway and almost hit Stephon's car in the rear. I got out and slammed the door, as I knew I was about to get my clown on. I didn't even knock on the door; I took my foot and tried to damn near kick the motherfucker down.

After I kicked it a few times, Nokea came to the door and opened it.

"Jaylin, what are you doing?" I pushed the door open and helped myself in. I looked down at her stomach and she for damn sure was pregnant.

"So, what's up Nokea? Who's the fucking father of your baby?" I asked. Her eyes watered as she looked at me in fear. Just then, Stephon walked out of the kitchen.

"It's me, man. The father of her baby is me."

Brenda M. Hampton

I looked back at Nokea. "Is this true? Is Stephon the father of your baby?" She cried and Stephon walked over and put his arms around her.

"Jaylin, man, just go. Can't you see she's upset right now? I'll come over to your place after I leave and explain everything to you." I looked at Nokea and Stephon; somebody was about to get fucked up. Wasn't sure which one it would be, but I wanted some answers.

"Nokea, how long have you been fucking my cuz?" I said, as she turned her head on Stephon's shoulder.

"Man, look, it ain't even like that. Why don't you just go home and chill out? I said I'll be over there to explain things to you in a minute."

"Shut the fuck up talking to me! You sorry motherfucker. You always had to have every damn thing I had, didn't you? Couldn't stand to see me with anything I called my own. Your ass just had to have a piece of it, didn't you?" I said, laughing. "Even when we were kids, you had to take everything. Just so I could be miserable. You and your fucking selfish-ass brothers. And your mother, aw...now, we ain't gonna talk about how she raised such a lowlife-asshole when she was one her damn self, are we?"

"Alright, man, that's enough!" Stephon said, grabbing my shirt and pushing me back. "Get the fuck out of here! And if I—" I didn't give Stephon a chance to say another word. I took my fist and stole him straight in his jaw. "Son of a bitch!" he yelled. "You wanna fight! Is that what you want? You want my lady to see you get your ass kicked?" While he talked, I stole his ass again. Without any hesitation, he punched back. Then, it was on. We scrapped so hard that we broke two of Nokea's vases and her glass table. I wasn't letting up and neither was he. She tried to break us a part but I pushed her down and didn't give a fuck about Stephon's baby she carried. When he seen her on the floor, the asshole really tried to get tough. He grabbed my waist and pushed me into the wall with every ounce of strength he had left. My whole body went through the wall and the picture above it came crashing down on top of him. I picked it up and tried to bust his damn head open with it. He dodged it a few times and then tried to grab my legs and knock me on the floor. When he realized he couldn't do that, I pushed him back into Nokea's baby grand piano and flipped his ass over the top. Nokea screamed and ran to the phone. As Stephon lay on the floor holding his back, I ran over and snatched the phone out of her hand. I pulled the cord out because I knew she would call the police on me.

When I stood in front of her, she cried hysterically and shook like a leaf. I balled up my fist and was just about ready to punch her in her damn stomach. She put her hands over her face.

"It's your baby, Jaylin! Please don't do this, it's your baby!" she yelled, and then fell to the floor. I threw the phone down on the floor.

"You lying bitch! You'll do anything to keep me won't you?" I said, wiping the sweat from my face. "I hope you and my cousin have a happy fucked-up life together. You had me fooled though, baby. I thought you had a bit more respect for yourself. But, I guess you ain't no better than all the other fucked-up women in my life. Excuse me, did I say women? Naw, you're not women. You all are undependable, unpredictable, and unreliable bitches. Every last one of y'all. Including my damn mother who left my ass years ago. Shit actually started with her. And then his sorry-ass mother stepped in and tried to pick up the pieces when the only thing she could pick up was a crack pipe." In a rage, thinking about the bullshit, I took my fist and pounded it into the wall. Nokea screamed for me to stop but I couldn't. I looked at her and couldn't let the situation go.

"Let's see who else there is…there's Simone who left town with the only fucking thing I had to love in my life. And let's not count out Scorpio. Boy, she was a charm. Had me paying for her shit. Big dollars. Only to find out the bitch had other motherfuckers paying her too. And now, you. Little innocent-ass virgin-bodied Nokea. Pretending all along that she loves Jaylin so much, she can hardly see straight. And now: 'Guess what Jaylin, I'm pregnant and it's yours, but I'm fucking your cousin too.' Bitch, get real! You were the worst one of them all because you stabbed me in my back purposely. Everybody else, at least they made mistakes—but you, you had it out for me all along. So, you know what bitch?" I walked over to her and lifted her face with my hand. "If it is my baby, you raise it your damn self. I'd be too damn ashamed to tell it that it's got a whore for a mother."

Nokea was on the floor crying, with her hands covering her ears so she couldn't hear me. I wanted to take my damn foot and kick her in her face but I was tired of the drama. I knocked one of her expensive statues on the ground and jetted. As I was leaving, I backed my shit up and went full force into the back of Stephon's BMW. I saw the front end of my shit fold like a piece of aluminum foil and his shit was smashed like a train hit it.

By the time I pulled up in my driveway, the Cedes smoked and the front dangled off. Felicia came rushing out of the house.

"Where's Mackenzie?" I asked because I didn't see her come after Felicia.

"Jaylin, her aunt came over here and got her. I didn't have a choice but to let her go. Mackenzie cried for you but you wasn't here."

"You opened my damn door and let her take Mackenzie! Is that what you're telling me Felicia?" I grabbed her by the neck. "Where in the fuck did she take her?" I yelled, as I knew Felicia couldn't tell me because I had a strong grip on her neck and she couldn't talk. She gagged and tried to pull my hands away from her neck. When I let go, she fell to the ground like a piece of paper. She lay there for a while and coughed. I didn't give a fuck. I shut the door and turned off the light so the bitch couldn't see.

I went into Mackenzie's room in hopes that Felicia lied. But when I got there, there was no sign of her. I sat on the edge of her bed and dropped my head. I was hurt, and bad. Didn't know how I got myself in such a fucked-up situation. I had depended on too many people for my happiness and every last one of them failed me. I was so mad that I could have killed somebody. But wasn't no telling who I would go for first.

I lay back on Mackenzie's bed and placed my hands behind my head. I looked up at Mama first and apologized for disrespecting her. I told her how upset I was with her for making me go to an orphanage only to hear her apologize to me back. She told me I'd not only disrespected her tonight, but also, I'd been disrespecting women for a long time. Said it was only a matter of time when my shit caught up with me. I told her about all the good fortune I'd come into by doing things for myself. She said that she was proud, but acknowledged that I still had a long way to go before she could say I was the man she wanted me to be.

When I tried to touch her, I woke up, while still lying in Mackenzie's bed. It was a dream. It was all a dream. But when I looked around for Mackenzie, she was still gone.

It was damn near light outside so I pulled my shoes off and lay across my own bed. I watched the early morning news and dozed off again. When the phone rang, it woke me and when I looked at the alarm clock, it showed that it was almost noon. I looked at the caller ID and it was Angela.

"Jaylin, Mr. Schmidt is really upset with you. Why haven't you come in or called or something?"

"Because I don't fucking feel like it. Tell your damn father-in-law to kiss my Black ass." I hung up. She called back several more times and I finally picked up.

"Don't you hang up on me," she said. "Now, if you're having some problems, I'll cover for your ass but don't go hanging up on me."

"Sorry, Angela. I'm just not in the mood for doing any work right now. Tell Schmidt I'm taking a leave of absence. In the meantime, ask Roy to handle all my accounts for me. Don't call me unless it's a matter of life or death, please."

"Okay, but you know he's going to want to talk to you."

"Well, fine! Have the motherfucker call back soon so I can tell him to go fuck himself."

"Jaylin, calm down. I don't know what's bugging you, but ain't nothing worth losing your job over. So, when he calls, you'd better change your attitude."

"Yeah, yeah, yeah. Whatever. Just tell him to call me."

Ten minutes later Schmidt called from his office on speakerphone. Roy was in the room with him, and in so many words, Schmidt said if I didn't come in to work, I didn't get paid. That was quite hilarious because I had plenty of money stashed aside from my inheritance. In addition to that, most of my salary came from Higgins and his buddies anyway. I told Schmidt I would be back in action within sixty days and he agreed to let me come back then.

For the rest of the day, I chilled. Took my phones off the hook, and watched *Judge Joe Brown* and *Judge Judy* as they showed no mercy for people in their courtroom. My body was sore from fighting with Stephon; I soaked myself in the tub about five times that day. I had several bruises and couldn't stand the sight of them.

The only phone call I made was to my lawyer to find out if there was anything I could do about Mackenzie. When he said there wasn't, I told him to go fuck himself and fired him. Then I called another one, who said if I could prove Scorpio was an unfit mother, then I possibly stood a chance. I wasn't trying to hate on her but I wanted Mackenzie

145

back in my life and bad. I told him I would think about it for a while and get back with him.

After lying across the bed most of the day drinking shots of Martel, I found myself getting horny. Right about now, Scorpio was probably fucking a brotha and fucking him well. It had been almost five days since I kicked her ass out and my thang felt kind of lonely. I looked in the pocket of the suit I'd had on at Aunt Betty's funeral and found that tender's phone number.

When she answered and realized it was me, she was excited. I talked to her for an hour on the phone and managed to coax her into coming over to see me. I jazzed myself up a bit so I could look good enough to get some.

When she rang the doorbell, I watched the last five minutes of a sitcom and made her stand outside and wait. As she saw me approach the door, she was all smiles. I opened it and checked her out from head to toe, and made sure I wanted to go there with her. She wasn't no dime but her plump juicy ass in her tight red mini-skirt kept her in the running. I noticed her fingernail polish was chipped, and I immediately knew she couldn't be in Jaylin's world if she tried. She looked a bit young too, but when I asked how old she was—she told me she was twenty-seven. Which usually meant she was either twenty-four or twenty-five. As long as she was legal, that's all I cared about.

I escorted her upstairs to my room and didn't waste any time. "Hey, uh, what did you say your name was?" I asked, already forgetting what she told me on the phone.

"Brashaney."

"Can I get you something to drink?" I poured myself another drink.

"No, no thank you. But if you have some water, I'll take a glass of that."

"Nope. I don't have any water. Better yet, I don't serve water to my guests. If you want water, you go home and get it."

She looked at me and sort of rolled her eyes. I smiled, then put my drink on the nightstand and asked her to come stand in front of me.

"Why?" she said, starting to become a pain.

"Because, I want you to take your clothes off. You don't mind if I watch, do you?"

146

"No, but can we listen to some music or something before we get down like that? I mean...I haven't been here five minutes and you already talking about taking my clothes off."

"Brashaney, I don't have time for games baby. I invited you here tonight because a brotha liked what he saw. If you want to sit here all night and listen to some music, fine, go right ahead. But I asked you to come here so I could make love to you. So, what's it gonna be?" I said, already removing my pants. "Are you taking your clothes off too, or do I put on some music?"

Brashaney started to remove her clothes. I could tell she was young because she had young fresh titties. Nipples didn't even look full-grown yet. But when she got on top of me and swallowed my dick like a shark, I wasn't really sure.

I slid on a condom and just laid there as she tried to put it on me. I rubbed her ass a few times and that was it. She took my hand and tried to make me feel her insides, but I couldn't get with it. The thought of Stephon fucking Nokea was fresh in my mind. I remembered how he told me he be airlifting bitches, sucking they pussy and I wondered if he'd done that to Nokea. I also wondered if she liked the feel of him better than me.

Unable to focus, I stopped Brashaney.

"What's wrong, Jaylin. Aren't you enjoying yourself?" She took my hand and rubbed it on her pu-tain.

"Yeah, come on. Let's get this over with so I can go to sleep," I said, flipping her ass over, and taking control. I banged her insides just so I could have the pleasure of hearing her say my name. When I heard that, I cut her short and came. Then, she was all up on me trying to get close, but I wasn't having it.

"Say baby. I'm really tired. Why don't I call you tomorrow?" I said. She looked disappointed. She put her clothes back on and didn't even say goodbye. I wasn't sweating it. I got what I wanted so what the hell?

I woke up in a sweat as I dreamed about my Aunt Betty. The thought of her beating me and throwing me into a dark closet wouldn't leave my memory for shit. I prayed many nights for Mama to come back and save me, but she never came. I hoped Daddy would come and take me from that orphanage, but he never showed.

Brenda M. Hampton

I lay across my bed and busted out in tears, as I thought about my horrifying past. Every woman that had been a part of my life let me down. I finally figured out why it was so hard for me to love them. To me, they were only good for one thing and one thing only. And after what Nokea and Scorpio had done to me, wasn't no telling when I would feel any differently.

29 NOKEA

After Stephon and I cleaned up the place, as best as we could, I asked him to leave for a short while so I could be alone. He called J's Towing Service to come get his car and take it to Al's Body Shop. I was sick about what happened. I didn't intend for things to go as far as they did, and I really didn't expect Jaylin to be that upset with me about Stephon. I mean, they'd shared plenty of women before. Wasn't no biggie for them so why did he trip with me? And the baby? I wondered if he believed me when I told him the baby was his. Maybe that's why he didn't punch me in my stomach. Either way, I'd never seen him that angry with anyone. I didn't like the fact it was me who he was most upset with. I was the one who was always there for him, and for him to call me names like he did was really hurtful.

And ever since I saw him, I can't get him out of my mind. I enjoyed having sex with Stephon, but no doubt, Jaylin still had my heart. Just having him in my presence did something to me. Maybe I was wrong for sleeping with Stephon but I had needs. I'd already gone thirty whole years without sex. And nine years without having sex with the man I loved. Since Stephon was the one who was willing to take care of my needs, then I had to go with the flow. And not just my physical needs. He'd been there for me every step of the way with this pregnancy. Cooking for me, massaging my body for me, listening to the baby's heartbeat, going to the doctor with me, and feeling the baby move—everything Jaylin should be doing. It wasn't my fault he decided to be with Scorpio. I guess things didn't work out with them either. He sounded upset with everybody and I guess in his mind, he had good reason. But, when was Jaylin going to realize life doesn't revolve around him? He's got his own little messed-up world and if you aren't doing things his way, then you can forget it.

I sat around the house for hours and thought about Jaylin. I had insurance on my piano so the piano company I bought it from called to say they would replace the damaged one for a new one. I told them someone vandalized my place and smashed it. Then this guy Pat knew came over to fix my wall. Pat came with him because I didn't feel comfortable letting him in my house and I didn't know him.

When she walked in, she was stunned. Plaster was all over the floor, my table was without glass, and one of my expensive statues was without a head.

"Girl, what the hell went on up in here? I know you told me it was bad but this is ridiculous. You need to send that motherfucker a bill. He can't be coming over here tearing your shit up like this."

"Come on in the kitchen, girl. I know Jaylin was wrong for messing up my things, but if you think about it, he kind of had good reason to."

"So, if he would have punched you in your stomach, he would have been right? Is that what you're saying Nokea?"

"No. All I'm saying is maybe—just maybe—I was wrong for not telling him about the baby to begin with. And then to turn around and sleep with his cousin I...I'm not sure if that was the right thing to do."

"I can't believe after all this fool than done to you, you still sticking up for his ass. Now, you did what you had to do based on the situation he put you in. And if Stephon, or anybody for that matter, stepped in and picked up where Jaylin left off, then, hey, his loss. I'm not saying sleeping with Stephon was the best thing to do, because I think he's a bigger ho than Jaylin is. If not a bigger ho, a smoother ho. He knows how to charm a woman out of her panties just like Jaylin. The problem is both of them fine, and now you've got your work cut out for you."

"Pat, I don't care about who's the finest between them. All I care about is who's going to be there for Nokea and her baby? That's it. I want a man to love me and to be a good father to this baby. And if that's Stephon, then that's what I want. I can't see Jaylin loving me like I want him to. Right about now, he wants to kill me. I don't stand a chance with him anymore," I said, looking down at the floor.

"Nokea, forget about who loves you for a minute. Where's your heart? Who do you really want to be with? Now, I can tell you who I want you with, but you got your own mind. So, make your own decision."

"Well, who do you want me with, Pat?"

She looked at me then turned away. "Neither one. Personally, I think you were wrong for sleeping with Stephon, but since I hate Jaylin so much, I went with the flow. You need to get rid of both of them and start over. You're a beautiful person, Nokea, and you won't have a hard time finding somebody who will truly love you."

"But, it's not that easy. Sex with Stephon is great but my heart still belongs to Jaylin. I don't know what I'm going to do. I'm worse off than I was before." I put my head on the table and started to tear up again. Pat tried to console me, but even she said I messed up.

She stayed with me until Stephon came back over. When she opened the door, she gave him a look that could kill. I hurried up and walked her out the door because I didn't want her starting no mess with him over the baby.

"Look, Nokea, you don't have to push me out the door. I'm leaving. He already knows he ain't got no business over here," she said, staring him down like a bloodhound.

"Pat, I got plenty of business over here. I got a baby on the way and a woman I love. So, if that ain't enough business then I don't know what is."

"Nigga, please. Spare me the fucking lies. You know damn well that ain't your baby because if it was you wouldn't even be here. And love, don't make me sick. I think it's pathetic and absurd you call yourself in love with Nokea. Too bad she don't know any fucking better because—"

"Pat, stop! I've had enough drama already. Please don't do this, okay?" I asked politely. She threw her hands up in the air and walked out.

"Call me later, girl, love ya," she said.

I shut the door and looked at Stephon. "Tell me: Am I wrong for wanting to be happy? Can't I be with who I want to and leave it at that?" Stephon came over and held me in his arms.

"Nokea, we both knew this wasn't going to be easy. Baby, this is just the beginning. Hell, you haven't even told your parents yet. But when all is said and done, we're going to be happy together. You, her, and me," he said, rubbing my belly.

"No, it's a boy. I want a boy so I can name him—" I was about to say Jaylin but I stopped myself. "A girl will be just fine."

"No, no, now, if you want a boy then pray for one. And when he comes, we'll talk about what to name him then."

"I said a girl would be fine, Stephon. I don't ever want to think about having a boy again."

We sat on the outside deck and chilled. He wanted to make love to me but I couldn't get with it. After he jumped in the swimming pool naked, I had no choice but to join him. I wasn't even ashamed of my fat stomach because he made me feel like I was the most beautiful thing that walked the earth. He held me in the swimming pool and rubbed every part of my body with his soft hands. I hopped out, lay on a beach towel, and then looked up at the sky. Stephon jumped in the water and did all kinds of crazy flips as he tried to make me laugh. For whatever reason, Jaylin was still on my mind.

When my laughs went away, Stephon came over and laid his wet naked body beside me.

"Shorty, I know you're still in love with Jaylin but just think about what we could have for a minute. I'm not trying to make you love me but it would be nice if you would be willing to give it a try."

I turned on my side and looked Stephon face to face. "I'm trying Stephon but it's so hard. Feelings just don't go away overnight but eventually I'm hoping some day they will. So, be patient with me. I want this to work between you and I too but it's going to take some time."

He kissed me from the top of my forehead to the bottom of my feet. He made love to me like this was the beginning of something special.

I was there with him for a while, but when I closed my eyes, I saw Jaylin. I closed my eyes tighter and he went away.

30 JAYLIN

It had been almost a month since I'd last seen Mackenzie. I was devastated. Other than her, pussy was the only other thing on my mind. Since I got that from Brashaney, the rest of my time was dedicated to finding Mackenzie. I'd been to one law firm after another trying to find out what I could do. After paying big dollars for consultation after consultation, I gave up. The only thing I heard was if I wasn't her guardian, then there was little I could do.

I knew so little about Scorpio that I didn't even know where to begin to look for her. I called her house but the number had been disconnected. I even drove around Olivette today to see if I saw her car parked somewhere, but no luck.

Since Ray-Ray's bachelor party was tonight at his cousin's house, I took my ass home, showered, and changed into one of my best damn outfits. I put my black Armani wide-legged linen pants on and my black and off-white thick-stripped linen shirt with the oversized collar. Then I put on my off-white gangster hat with a black band around the middle and tilted it to the side. My Rolex was on one wrist and my thick gold diamond bracelet was on the other. I was bling-blinging and was ready to get my party on after I sprayed on some Issey Miyake. I put twenty hundred-dollar bills in my money clip and stuck it in my pocket.

I knew I'd see Stephon, but I wasn't backing down on going because he would be there. Besides, I had other friends who would surely be in attendance, so what the hell?

As I was just about ready to leave, Brashaney rang my phone. I had to answer because I didn't want to mess up the only booty I had lined up. Especially since I knew I'd probably want to get my sex on after the party tonight. The last time we got up, I went through her purse when she was asleep and peeked at her driver's license. She didn't lie about her age; she was actually twenty-seven and I felt bad not being able to trust her.

I ended the conversation with Brashaney and told her to meet me at my place around two in the morning. I told her to make sure she called before she came just in case I wasn't home. After she agreed, I jetted. I was looking good, feeling good, and smelling good so I decided to drive my Boxster for the night. Ray-Ray's bachelor party was at his cousin's mansion in Ladue and I was dying to see what it looked like. I heard it was banging but I also heard it wasn't banging better than mine.

However, when I pulled up, I knew I had some competition. I had to push an intercom button and announce who I was just for the gates to open up and let me in. Then, I drove up a long driveway lined with waterfalls and marble rock landscaping. And when I saw the house—damn. It was bad. Twice the size of mine and had big white columns in the front like the White House. When I pulled my car up, one of the valets parked it along with the other cars: Mercedes, Lexus, Lincolns, Cadillacs, Jags, BMWs—you name it, they were there. But nobody had a Boxster like mine so I was glad to see that. The lot also had its share of fucked-up cars too, so I knew it wouldn't be all good inside.

There was already about a hundred brothas outside, so I imagined what the inside would look like. As I walked past them, they checked me out from head to toe.

As soon as I hit the door, brothas were all over the place. There was a double staircase that was cluttered with people. Mesmerized, I stood in the foyer, which was covered with green, black and white marble. Shit was off the hook. Whoever told me I could compete, lied like hell.

As I walked through the place, I tried to figure out how I could be down. I was more infatuated with the house than I was with all the ladies that flounced around butt naked.

I finally stepped into the room where the party was actually happening. It was packed with fellas and the music thumped loudly. I bounced my head to the rhythm and quickly scoped one of my boys from the barbershop. He came up with a couple other fellows and asked what took so long for me to get there. Said they'd been looking for me.

"Man, I was trying to hurry but perfection takes a little more time," I said.

"I heard that, my nigga," Ricky said, giving me five. "You know you clean, though, bro. And where in the hell did you get that shirt? It's off the chain."

I usually don't tell anybody where I get my things from because I don't want nobody trying to look like me. So, I stepped away from Ricky and went to the bar to get a drink. I looked around the room to see if I could find Ray-Ray. I knew he was somewhere, but finding him would be like searching for a needle in a haystack since the place was so packed.

As I tipped the bartender, the lights flashed on and off which meant a stripper was on her way out to entertain. The floor cleared and all the brothas, including me, watched as this dark chocolate sista came in and danced her way to the middle of the floor. She danced to a slow funky song as we all watched and waited for her to take it off. She had on a red leather shorts outfit that showed the cheeks of her fat ass hanging out. Her tinted blonde hair was straight and hung down to her butt. When she sat in the chair and stretched her legs straight out in the air, motherfuckers hollered like they ain't never seen no pussy before. She grabbed this one brotha on the floor and put her shit all in his face. She tied him to a chair and pulled out some whips. Now, this shit was too damn freaky for me. Not interested in that kind of action at all.

I went back over to the bar and got another drink. A stripper who had already performed came over and stood next to me. She wiped the sweat from her forehead and she threw a towel over her shoulder.

"So, are you having a good time?" she yelled, over the music.

"Yeah, it's cool. But have you seen the groom yet?" I said, leaning down towards her.

"The last time I saw him, he was in one of the rooms upstairs." Made sense. That was probably where I should have looked for him.

I smiled. "So, what's your name?"

"My real name or my play name?"

"Whichever one you want to give me," I said, really not giving a fuck.

"It's Nicola. What's yours?"

"Jaylin," I said, looking to see what all the hype was about because the brothas hollered again.

"So, Jaylin, did you see my performance tonight?"

"No, I just got here. I must have missed you."

"Well, if you'd like, I can give you a private show in one of the rooms upstairs." I looked down at Nicola and set my drink on the bar. No doubt about it, she was fine. But since I thought about how Scorpio probably put herself out there like this, I had to turn her down. She didn't give up though. She stood next to me while we both watched Black and Lovely entertain.

When she finished, she walked out of the room with all kinds of dollars stuck in her ass, down her top, and in her hand. I slid her a hundred-dollar bill because the sista worked hard for it. She smiled and whispered she would be back. Since Nicola hadn't budged, I had no choice but to pay her some attention. I wasn't sure what she wanted from me and couldn't understand why she wasn't hounding some of the other brothas. They seemed to give her more attention than I was.

Then, finally, I saw Ray-Ray. He came down the steps with two chicks on his side and Stephon was right behind him with one.

I excused myself from Nicola and met Ray-Ray at the bottom of the steps.

"What's up playa?" I said, and then gave him five.

"Man, man, man. Where have your ass been? I've been bragging to all the ladies about my man Jaylin and you just now getting here?"

"Nigga, I've been here. I've been trying to find your ass since I got here. But you can't be found if you don't want to be," I said, looking at the two chicks. He laughed as he took his arms from around them.

"Hey, let me holla at you for a sec.," he said.

We walked into another room where just a few people were on the couch.

"Listen, I'm not going to hold you up because I know you want to get your party on like I intend to do, but Stephon told me what happened. I'm hurt man because we've been boys for too damn long. And to let some bitch come between y'all, that ain't even cool. I'm not saying y'all need to squash things tonight, all I'm saying is y'all need to get together and talk this shit out. It's crazy and I can see how much it's hurting both of y'all."

"Ray, thanks for trying but this shit goes beyond him fucking my woman. If you're worried about me tripping tonight, then don't. I don't have any intention of messing up your night."

I grabbed Ray-Ray on his shoulder and we walked back into the other room. Stephon stood next to Nicola, but when he saw her look my way, he moved away as she walked back up to me. I looked at him and he looked at me.

"Say, did I interrupt something?" I asked.

"Naw, seemed like she was hollaring at you, dog."

"Right, right. But you know if you want her, I ain't got no problem with that."

"Nope, ain't interested. Besides, I already got my shit off tonight with that sista right over there," he said, pointing to the chick he came down the steps with.

"Well, I got two questions for you: Was it good? And how much did it cost you?" He laughed.

"Aw, it was good. And so was I. So good, she gave me fifty dollars back after I was finished."

"My nigga," I said, giving him five. Stephon reached over and gave me a hug. I hugged him back, and it felt good to have my cousin back.

Nicola had worked her way over to some other brothas, as we talked about the fine-ass ladies up in the house.

"Man, I can't believe you haven't found you no shit up in here yet," Stephon said, looking at everything that walked by. "It's all kind of ass floating around here."

"Yeah, I've been checking it out. I'm just waiting for the right one. Now, there ain't no question in my mind that I'll be fucking tonight. The only question is, who's going to be the lucky woman."

After scoping the set for a while with Stephon, I thought about my conversation with Brashaney tonight. I took my cell phone out and cancelled because I knew there was no way I would be there by two. She didn't answer, so I left a message and told her I'd call her tomorrow.

When Stephon walked to the bar and got another drink, the lights flashed again. The floor cleared and the fellas made room for the next stripper. Nelly, "It's Gettin Hot In Herre," played, and I was stunned when I looked and saw Scorpio enter the room. She had on some thigh-high white leather boots with spurs and wore a cowboy hat. As she walked in and swayed her hips from side to side, the white tassels that covered her ass on her outfit also moved from side to side. Her top was a strapless bra with fringes dangling from it that covered her stomach. She strutted around the floor in circles and the men went crazy. She tossed her hat into the crowd and her curly hair fell down over her face.

Stephon looked at me and pointed.

"Is that...?"

"Yes, but don't say anything, I don't want her to see me." I ducked behind Stephon and this other dude who seemed to really be enjoying the show. I had to see for myself how nasty she could get at one of these parties that she proclaimed to be so innocent.

When the music changed, she pulled not one brotha on the floor, but three. She sat one in a chair and the other two on the floor. As they sat there eagerly waiting for her to get busy with them, she removed her top, swung it in the air, and tossed it on the floor. Then the money came in. It covered the floor, and when she slid out of her shorts and draped them across the brotha's face in the chair, I was furious. That left her standing there with a white sheer thong on that only covered the front of her up. Wasn't no need for her to have it on because you could see the smooth hairs on her pussy.

My heart raced. Stephon and the rest of the motherfuckers stood there mesmerized by the shit. And when she flipped her body over the chair and wrapped her legs around the brotha's face, with her face in his lap, I had seen enough. I put my drink down and headed for the door.

Stephon grabbed me.

"Come on now Jay. You better than that. Don't let this woman ruin your night. Besides, it ain't nothing but a show anyway." He nudged me back into the room, and I sat in the corner where I couldn't see went on. The noise was distracting because brothas screamed and hollered more for her than they did anybody. Disgusted, I knew it was a good thing I'd ended it with her before tonight. If I hadn't, I'd be up there kicking her ass right now.

After Scorpio racked up the dollars, she blew kisses at the fellas and swished her ass out of the room. I at least wanted to find out where Mackenzie was, so I told one of Ray-Ray's partners to stop her when she came out of the bathroom. I told him to tell her to come to the room at the end of the hall, and if she was willing, it was going to be worth a thousand dollars.

After I paid him a hundred dollars for doing it, he stood by the bathroom door and waited for her to come out. I ran upstairs to the room at the end of the hall and took my shirt off so she would think I was naked. Then I turned off the light, hopped in bed, and waited for her to enter.

The room had a scent like somebody had already been there fucking, but it was still a bad-ass room. It was gold and white, had mirrors on the closet doors that went from one end of the room to the other. The wallpaper was gold and white striped and the rugs matched the white curtains that draped the windows. The bed had gold satin sheets but I threw them off not knowing who had laid their ass on there tonight. I sat up with my arms folded, my legs crossed, and leaned back on the soft plush pillows as I waited for her to come. It was dark as hell but I could see a sliver of light come through the window.

When the door creaked open, I took a deep breath. She walked in and shut the door behind her. I knew it was her because I could smell her perfume.

"Excuse me, are you going to turn the light on?" she asked, still standing by the door.

"Are you going to take your clothes off for me, like the song said?" I asked in a deep voice.

"No, I'm not. I came in here to tell you I don't go out like that. If sex is what you want, I'll set you up with one of my girlfriends out there. As a matter of fact, she's waiting for you now."

"I'm not interested in her." I made my voice deeper. "I got a thousand dollars right now that got your name all over it."

"Sorry, sir, that ain't my style," she said, turning to open the door.

"I said that I'm not interested in her. I want you."

I turned the light on.

She turned around and looked at me in bed. "Jaylin, what are you doing here?"

"I came here to party. Just like everybody else," I said. She looked workable in her tight blue jeans and matching jean halter-top.

"Did you try to set me up or something?"

"No. I liked what I saw downstairs and wanted a sista to come shake a brotha down. But since you don't get down like that, then I guess I'll have to settle for your girlfriend."

She smiled. "Well, I can always make an exception for a man like you."

"Naw, naw. Don't do me any favors. I'm sure your girlfriend wouldn't mind shaking a brotha down tonight. Go ahead, call her in here so I can get this party started." Scorpio turned around and threw her backpack with her clothes in it over her shoulder.

"Well, you have a good time. I came here to do what I had to do tonight; now, I'm going home." She walked to the door.

I looked at the gap between her legs where I used to lay my dick and couldn't let her walk out. I jumped out of the bed and put my hand on the door. As I pressed my body up against hers, I moved her hair to the side and whispered in her ear.

"Don't go, baby. Make love to me. I'm sorry for not trusting you. I'm sorry for putting my hands on you. Just…just make love to me right now. I miss you beside me. I miss having your body next to mine."

She turned around and put her hand over my mouth. "Jaylin, all I want to know is, do you love me? If you miss me so much, then tell me. Do you love me?"

"Baby, you know how I feel…"

"No, no I don't. Tell me how you feel. If you can't tell me you love me then ain't no sense in me hanging around." I stepped away and looked her pretty self in the face. I touched her face and kissed her on the cheek.

"Where's Mackenzie?" I asked, as I wasn't about to tell her something I didn't mean.

"Jaylin, is it that hard for you? All I'm asking for is for you to love me, that's all."

"Scorpio, I can't. I'm sorry but I don't feel that right now. Why do you want me to lie to you? What's the big deal? My feelings don't get any stronger for you than they are right now. If this ain't enough, I'm sorry. So," I said, taking a deep breath. "Where's Mackenzie?"

"She's at my sister's house."

"Bring her over to my house tomorrow so I can see her."

"I'll try. I have a few things I have to do tomorrow, but I'll try."

"Try hard." I opened the door so I could let her out.

She walked down the steps in front of me, and brothas pulled on her like she was a piece of gold. She smiled as a couple of them stuffed money into her back pocket, then she walked out of the door.

Stephon stood in the doorway to the party room and I walked up to him. I told him to stop by tomorrow so we could talk about what's been going down between us. Then, when I saw Black & Lovely who performed earlier. I grabbed her hand and told her let's go. Maybe a little whip action is what I needed tonight. She put her drink down and didn't waste any time getting in the ride with me.

As we were leaving, I saw Stephon getting into his car with the sista he'd been with earlier. He pulled his car in front of mine and cut me off.

"Hey, man. I got something for you," he said, giving me a piece of paper. When I looked at it, it was a bill for $11,386 for the repairs to his car. "Pay the bill motherfucker, he said, patting me on the back. "Pay the bill." I ripped it up and threw it back at him.

"Nigga, please. If you don't move your car so I can go home and make love to this woman I'm gonna tear your shit up again." I laughed.

Stephon hopped back into his car and sped off. I zoomed past him on Lindbergh Boulevard and blew the horn.

I wanted to ask him about Nokea but I was staying my ass out of it. She was sadly mistaken if she thought Stephon was any better than I was. He was a charming motherfucker. I didn't have time for that shit; I was the kind of man who always told it like it was, no matter what. I guess that's why Scorpio couldn't stand me. But I wasn't changing my ways for nobody.

When I pulled into the driveway, Brashaney's car was parked in front of my house. Even though I'd told her not to come over, I guess she insisted on coming anyway. Either that or she didn't get my message. I stepped out of the car and sexy chocolate got out on her side. Brashaney walked up the driveway and looked at me like, what the hell is going on.

"Say baby. I called and left you a message. You didn't get it?"

"No, Jaylin, I didn't. So, what's up? Are you kicking it with her tonight or what?" She looked pissed.

"Well, since both of y'all here, why don't we make the best of it?" I said, thinking that a threesome would be good right about now.

Brashaney took her hand and smacked the shit out of me. I held my face and could only smile. I knew I'd played her, but, hey, at least I tried to call. She walked back to her car, threw her purse inside, and took off.

I worked sexy chocolate all night long. I put on a condom three different times but my big dick and all the pressure I put into this woman caused the damn things to break. I hated fucking condoms. I wished they'd come out with something special for a brotha packing it like me because this shit just wasn't working. After I pulled the damn thing off, she didn't know what she'd gotten herself into messing with a man like me. And when I made her come six times, I'd had enough. All the moaning and groaning, screaming and hollering, 'oh baby this is the best dick I've ever had' bullshit, worked my nerves. I rolled my happy ass over and went to sleep.

After sexy chocolate left, I laid my lazy ass around the house all day doing nothing. I waited for Scorpio to call and tell me when she would bring Mackenzie over, but it was almost three o'clock in the afternoon and she hadn't called yet. Brashaney did though. She called and cursed my ass out for playing her like I did last night. I just sat on the phone and didn't say a word. Wasn't no sense in me getting all hyped up about a bitch I really didn't care about. And after she went on and on about what a dog I was, I agreed and ended the conversation. Women are just some crazy creatures, I thought. They like too much fucking drama if you ask me. If somebody played your ass like I did last night, why would you still want to be bothered? She was actually calling here to try and fix shit. If I was such a dog, then, why waste the time? Never could figure them out, and wasn't trying to either.

I lay back on my bed with my hands folded behind my head and laughed at the situation. Then the phone rang again and it was Stephon. He asked if I wanted to catch dinner at Applebee's, or order some Chinese food from Northland Chop Suey. Since I figured our conversation would get pretty deep, I suggested he come to my place and I'd have some Chinese food delivered. He agreed and said he was on his way.

I went downstairs to the kitchen and tried to find something to snack on because I was starving. When I realized I hadn't been grocery shopping in a while, I picked up the phone and quickly ordered us some Chinese food. I ordered Stephon some Special Fried Rice with extra shrimp and bean sprouts because it was his favorite. Then ordered the same for myself minus the shrimp and sprouts. I threw in an egg roll just to be greedy.

My place seemed to be such a mess, so I called Nanny B and arranged to have her come over tomorrow. I was too tired to get down and clean the place so I asked her to do everything from washing the windows to scrubbing the floors. She gave me a price and I was all for it. Told her I'd see her at nine in the morning.

Finally, Stephon showed up as beat as I was from last night festivities.

"Damn, I thought I looked bad. What happened to your ass? Did you at least brush your fucking teeth this morning?" I said, laughing.

"Fuck you. man. I got a damn hangover. Hangover from drinking and from that pussy. Couldn't get the woman out of my place until an hour ago." He strolled in and plopped down on the couch.

"Yeah, I know what you mean. After fucking, you just want to say, 'Get your shit and go,' don't you? But you know how it is, gotta play the nice, 'Oh...I really want you to stay here with me,' role just in case you might need that ass another time."

"You got that right," Stephon said, giving me a sliding high five.

"So, uh, I hate to ask you this, but do you want something to drink?" I laughed as Stephon dropped his head.

"No, thank you! A tall cold glass of ice water will be just fine."

"Just in case you forgot, I don't serve water to my guests. So, get your ass up and go in the kitchen and get it yourself." After Stephon went to the kitchen, I went to the bathroom to take a leak. "Say man, I ordered us some Chinese food," I yelled.

"Oh, yeah?" Stephon yelled from the kitchen. "What did you order?"

"I ordered some...ahh, shit!"

"Some what?" he yelled back.

"Damn! What the fuck!" I yelled, leaning my hand up against the wall while holding my dick with my other hand.

Stephon rushed to the bathroom door. "What did you say?" He looked at me like I'd lost my mind. "Man, what the fuck you doing?"

"My dick is on fire! This motherfucker straight up feel like fire shooting out of it."

"Nigga, quit playing."

"Playing? Does this shit look like I'm...ahh, shit!" I said as it burned again.

The doorbell rang. "That's probably our food. Get the money off the table and give it to them. And don't give him a tip because he late. They told me ten minutes and it's been thirty-five."

"Man, you knew they weren't going to get here in no ten minutes."

"Well, they shouldn't be lying to people by telling them that bullshit all the time then. So, whatever you do, don't give him a tip."

Stephon laughed and went to the door. I slid my thang back into my pants, flushed the toilet, and washed my hands. I walked funny when

I entered the kitchen and Stephon took the food out of the bag. He cracked up.

"What in the fuck is so funny? I need a doctor," I said, looking for my doctor's number on the refrigerator.

"Nigga, it ain't like you gone die or nothing. I know her office closed today so you might as well wait until tomorrow. Sounds like you got a case of gonorrhea."

"Man, quit bullshitting…is that what it is? Does it have to burn like that?"

"That shit ain't nothing to play with. Happened to me a couple of times. That's why I be telling you to strap your shit up. Ain't no telling where these bitches been."

"I did! Well, I tried. I've been fucking with two gals though. Ain't no telling which one did it," I said, rubbing my hands on my precious shit.

"Nigga, you crazy. You better do more than try if you want to continue getting down like you do. It's too much shit out there now. And since motherfuckers dropping off like flies, I make sure I strap my ass up no matter what."

"But the condoms just don't fit right. They be sliding off and everything. I'm gone have to strap my shit up with a trash bag or something." We cracked up, and then chowed down on the rice.

"So, what was up with Scorpio last night? Are y'all still kicking it or what?"

"Nope. Not right now anyway. I'm sure I'll be back in them panties later."

"What happened? I mean…I didn't even know she could get down like that."

"Shit, I didn't either. That's why I kicked her ass out of here. She lied man, flat out lied about what she did for a living."

"Yeah. Ain't nothing worse than a lying-ass woman. It's alright for us to lie but women are supposed to be better than that."

"I agree. And it sure in the hell hurts when they do," I said, thinking about Nokea. "So, my brotha, how are things going with you and Nokea? She's just about ready to pop that baby out, ain't she?"

"Yeah, just about. She's getting pretty big but she looks good though. Cutest little pregnant woman I've ever seen," Stephon said, smiling.

I chewed on my food. "Tell me something, though. When was the first time you had sex with her?" Stephon was silent for a while.

"About two weeks after you did. Remember when you went over to her house— had sex with her after you had been with Felicia in your office?"

"Yeah, I remember. Remember well."

"Well, she found out about that. She was upset and came to me crying. After that, one thing led to another. And then she told me she was pregnant."

"So, you had sex with her before Aunt Betty's funeral?" I thought about our conversation at the funeral.

"Yep. And I also knew she was pregnant then."

"If we had sex with her only a few weeks apart, how do you know it's your baby and not mine. After all, she did tell me it was my baby too."

"First of all, she lied. She told you it was yours because she didn't want you to punch her stomach. How I know it's mine is she had her period after she had sex with you. And when she went to the doctor, he pin-pointed her delivery date nine months after the last time we had sex," Stephon said, not looking me in the eyes.

I took a bite of my egg roll, folded my arms, and looked at him. "So, do you love her?"

"Yeah, I can pretty much say I do. Nokea's been in my heart for a long time, Jay. I know that's not what you wanted to hear but she has. Problem was, she could never get over you. But when she did, I saw an open door and took it."

"But the door wasn't open for you yet. She was still with me— and still in love with me—when you took it upon yourself to fuck her."

"I know, but she was tired of all the bullshit. After that incident with you and Scorpio in the shower, that did it. She might have slept with you after that, but her feelings were fading."

"Man, you know better than I do a nine-year feeling don't go away just like that. If I had to place a bet on it, I'd say you were the one who approached her."

Stephon hesitated for a minute. "Actually, it worked both ways. She came to me and I was willing to comfort her."

"Well, how often do you comfort her now? I mean, since you out kicking it with other women and everything. Is she shaking a brotha down like she supposed to?"

Now, Stephon looked me straight in the eyes. "Not a day goes by I don't make love to her. Well, lately though, it's been here and there, but that's because of the baby. But I do enjoy every moment I spend with her."

My throat ached as I tried not to get upset. Hurt me like hell I'd waited nine years to make love to this woman, and now, she was giving it to my cuz every time he wanted it. I wanted to stop torturing myself with the questions, but I had a few more for Stephon.

"So, if you say you love her so much, why you cheating on her?"

"Because, I'm a man and that's what I do. These other bitches out here don't mean nothing to me. They just something to play with."

"Then why can't you be honest with her and tell her you got other people in your life. I think she's going to be more hurt by you lying to her than she was by me being honest."

"And I disagree. I think what she don't know, won't hurt. Eventually I'm going to cut the shit anyway; and when I do, I'm going to be with her and only her. So, why mess that up by bringing all this drama to the relationship?"

"Okay, man, your call. But all I ask is one thing from you."

"And what might that be?"

"Please, do whatever you can not to hurt her. She's been hurt enough by me, and personally, I think she deserves better."

Stephon chilled at my place for a while. We shot some pool and played my X-BOX on my theatre-size TV in the bonus room. He left the room a couple times and called Nokea. I don't think he told her he was at my house, but when I heard him tell her he loved her, it damn near tore me apart. Maybe asking him all those questions wasn't the right thing to do. I'd never felt jealous before when it came to him, but realistically, he had my woman. As I thought about Nokea, my heart went out to her. Stephon and I were damaging her. Now, it was all up to him to make shit right. At the rate he was going, I didn't think he was capable of doing that. I'd definitely have to sit back and watch him try.

When Stephon left, I ran to the bathroom, as I tried to hold my piss because I didn't want to go. But when I couldn't, I damn near fell to the floor and tried to stop the pain. I couldn't wait to go see the doctor tomorrow. Certainly, I had nobody to blame but my damn self for fucking around with nasty trifling-ass women.

I pulled up my pants and the doorbell rang again. Damn, can a brotha get some peace around here? I thought. But when I could see who it was through the glass, I jetted downstairs to open the door. It was Mackenzie and Scorpio. When I opened the door, Mackenzie jumped right into my arms.

"Daddy!" she yelled, as I hugged and swung her around in my arms. She gave me a big wet kiss on the cheek, and then wiped the spit off with her hand. "Why did you make me leave?"

"Mackenzie, I didn't make you leave. I had no idea your aunt was going to come get you that night."

"Well, Mommy said you made us leave, and when I asked why, she said because you were mad at us."

I put Mackenzie down and looked at Scorpio. She shut the door and looked at me like, well, you did put me out.

"Mackenzie, that isn't what happened. I'll tell you the truth one day when you're old enough to understand. But for now, please know I would never do anything to hurt you."

She smiled. "Can I go up to my room? When I left, I forgot to get something."

"Sure, baby. It's just like you left it. And you don't have to ask if you can go up to your room because it's yours. Okay?" She ran up the steps to her room.

I looked at Scorpio and wanted to kill her for lying to Mackenzie. "Why did you tell her I put her out?"

"Because you did. When you kicked me out, you kicked her out. You didn't think I would let her stay here, did you?"

"I don't know, but I'm glad you brought her over here to see me. Has she missed me?"

"Negro, I don't know what you've done to my baby. She's been crying almost every day, talking about how much she misses her daddy. Why did you tell her that bullshit anyway? You're gonna confuse her Jaylin and she don't need that right now."

"Scorpio, look. I explained to Mackenzie what type of daddy I was. She knows I'm not her biological father."

"No, she doesn't. She really thinks you're her daddy."

"Well, I'll have a talk with her later so she'll understand."

167

Scorpio walked further into the house and looked around. "Have you had company lately?"

"Why?" I asked.

"Because I want to know who's been getting what I've been thinking about every day since I left. Excuse me…I mean, since you kicked me out."

"Scorpio, get over it, would you? You know damn well that I had a good reason. Now, I was wrong for putting my hands on you but I apologized for that."

"Naw, baby, you apologized with your mouth. I was hoping you would apologize with something else." She looked down at my goods. Burning and all, that motherfucker had the nerve to get hard while she talked. And since she had to come over here looking good, I had to make sure I focused my mind on something else.

She walked up and put her arms around my neck. "You know what I want?" she said, kissing me on the lips, as I held her around her waist.

"What do you want baby?"

"I want a good fuck. Not one of those five minutes I'm-too-tired-right-now fucks, but one of those all-nighters you give me when you're really in the mood."

My dick throbbed. I wanted to strip her ass naked and wear her out right then and there. But damn, how in the hell was I going to get myself out of this one tonight? I kissed her and squeezed her ass. She took my hand and started up the steps. When we got to my room, I was able to come up with an excuse to save me for a while.

"Scorpio, you know I can't make love to you with Mackenzie still wide awake."

"Oh, I know. But I kept her up all day so she'd go to bed early tonight."

"You just knew you could bring your little sexy self over here and use a brotha for his thang when you wanted to, huh?"

"Yeah, pretty much. Especially when he be using a sista for hers when he wants to."

I hopped off the bed and felt like I didn't care about what I had. All I wanted was to feel her insides. I tried to talk about something else, but no matter how hard I tried—she kept bringing me back to having sex with her tonight.

I was glad to see Mackenzie come through the doors. But when she came in and rubbed her eyes, I knew what time it was. She yawned and walked over to the chaise to sit next to me.

"Daddy, I'm sleepy. Can I stay the night with you?"

"Of course, Mackenzie. You can spend as many nights as you want to with me."

"So, what about Mommy? Can she stay the night too?"

Scorpio interrupted. "Just one night, Mackenzie. After that, we're going back home. I'll bring you over next weekend to see Jaylin." Mackenzie leaned on me and started to cry.

"Daddy, why can't I live with you? I don't want to go to Aunt Leslie's house anymore." I held her in my arms and wiped her tears. I knew how she felt; it was the same way I felt when I had to go live with my Aunt Betty. I carried Mackenzie to her room and told Scorpio we'd have to talk when I came back. I read her a bedtime story and she was asleep in less than ten minutes. I was so glad she was back in my life and I didn't know what to do. I for damn sure wasn't letting her go again.

Scorpio had already taken her clothes off and was under the covers. She had the blankets up to her neck and was all smiles. I sat down on the bed and pulled the covers off her just to get a good look at what I couldn't have. I rubbed my hand on her breasts and slid my hand down her stomach. Then I gently rubbed her hairs; they felt so smooth that I rolled my fingers around her insides. Touching her excited the fuck out of me.

"Baby, I can't...I can't make love to you tonight," I said.

"And why not, Jaylin?" I turned my head and thought about telling her the truth, but I couldn't. "Is this why you can't make love to me?" she said, picking up the card on my nightstand that sexy chocolate gave me. "Did you have sex with her last night?"

I took the card out of Scorpio's hand and looked at it. I laid it back on my nightstand and massaged my chin for a while.

"Yeah, baby. I did. I, uh, brought her here last night."

"You did, huh? Do you want to tell me about what happened? Or should I call her so she can tell me like she told me this morning after she left." Damn, I was busted. Didn't even dawn on me that she knew Scorpio. "Yeah, that's right. She told me how you fucked her so good and made her come six times. Said you banged her on the floor and in the shower. And then told me how good your dick tasted. When she gave me the exact measurements, I had to hang up on her. But the killing part about it was she said another bitch was waiting for you when you got here. When she described her, it didn't sound like anybody I'd ever seen you with, so I guess she's a NEW BITCH, huh?"

I couldn't do nothing but sit there and listen. Seemed like if I tried to open my mouth, she already had the answer. "You really don't waste no time do you?" she said. "Kicked my ass out just to let somebody else in. You're pathetic, Jaylin, and you seriously need to cut the bullshit before it's too late." Scorpio pulled the covers back over her and turned away from me.

I went downstairs and lay on the couch so I didn't have to hear anymore of the drama. I knew the shit wasn't right but I was my own man. I didn't have any ties anywhere and was free to do whatever I wanted. But when I thought about it more, I realized Scorpio was probably hurting the same way I was when I found out about Stephon sleeping with Nokea. I thought about what I could do to make it up to her.

I sat on the examination table and waited for my doctor to come back in with the results. She was a beautiful classy-ass forty-seven-year-old lady, and if she wasn't married I would have tried years ago to knock her. When she walked in, she gave me a funny look. She tilted her glasses down and rolled her eyes.

"Now, Jaylin, you know better. How many times have I told you to use a condom? You're a grown man and shouldn't be as naive when it comes to sex as these younger men are."

"Doc, I'm still a young man," I joked. "I'm only thirty-one."

"Well, you'll be thirty-two in a couple of weeks. You need to start being responsible for your actions. So, how many girlfriends you got now?" she asked.

"None."

"Aw, you got some. You wouldn't be all messed up down there if you didn't." She laughed.

"Doc, I've been waiting on you. Waiting for you to tell your husband you're marrying a young man like me."

"Jaylin, please. I wouldn't trade my husband in for something like you to save my soul. You need to get your mind out of the gutter and start putting it to work like you did when you landed your job. Leave all these fast-tail women alone and start taking care of yourself. This time, I'm happy to say it's only gonorrhea that you have. Next time it might be something else. And you know what I mean," she said, taking her glasses off.

"I got you doc. But you act like a brotha forever coming up in here with this shit. This was my first time, and as many…"

"Go ahead, say it. As many women as you've slept with you could have had something along time ago, right? But, having unprotected sex one time is too many, Jaylin. And who says you don't have anything else? Gonorrhea is just the first sign. If you've been messing around for a long time without using protection, I suggest you get an AIDS test done. Today."

"Are you serious? You know I ain't got no damn AIDS."

"I'm just trying to be on the safe side. Go get yourself tested and when your results come back, we'll talk about it then."

She gave me a shot and a prescription. When she said I couldn't have sex for a week, I damn near went crazy.

"One whole week? Why a whole week?"

"See, you should be ashamed of yourself. Get your butt out of here and go take that test like I told you to," she said, hitting me on the butt with a towel.

"Now, you know that turns me on," I said, holding my ass.

"Jaylin go! Get out of here before I have you arrested for statutory rape."

We laughed and I left.

I went down the hall and took the AIDS test. They told me they would send the results to me by mail.

By the time I got home, Nanny B was there cleaning up the place—with the help of Scorpio and Mackenzie. I didn't do shit. I watched as all three of them worked hard at getting my place spotless.

31 FELICIA

Jaylin didn't have to worry about me calling his ass anytime soon. After he choked and damn near killed me, I'd had enough. I haven't called him since then, nor do I intend to.

Damion was back in my life though. No matter how hard I tried to pretend Paul had set it out for me, I couldn't. Dick just couldn't do the job I wanted it to do. And after I made it perfectly clear to Damion that I wasn't going to put up with his baby mama's drama, he promised me there would be no more confrontations.

When Friday night came, I didn't feel like being bothered with Paul or Damion. I took a hot shower and decided to go to St. Louis Nites on Broadway. The women at work bragged about how they be kicking it, and this one lady named Shirley invited me to her birthday party there tonight. It was time for me to get out since I hadn't been out in a while.

I put my braids in a bun and let two single ones dangle on the sides of my face. Then I slid into my satin coal-black mini-dress with a v-dip in the back. I added silver accessories and put on my high-heeled black satin sandals that tied up just below my knees. My eyebrows were a little bushy so I quickly arched them, then put on my new Oh Baby lip-gloss I picked up at the MAC counter. I looked too good and couldn't even stand myself.

I hopped into my Lexus and jetted down Broadway to St. Louis Nites. It was so packed that I had a hard time finding a parking spot. When I did, I looked in the mirror and slid some more lip-gloss on so I didn't have to keep running to the ladies' room to put more on. As soon as I got out of the car, I noticed another club directly next to St. Louis Nites, the Spot. I stopped in for a few minutes to see what was happening there first. When I noticed a large number of younger sistas and brothas, I decided this wasn't the place for me. There were several nice looking young brothas I wouldn't mind taking home, showing them a thing or two, but I left. As I headed to St. Louis Nites, this attractive older man with gray hair stopped me.

"Say, beautiful, are you coming in?" he asked, looking me up and down.

"Yes, I'm supposed to meet some of my girlfriends from work."

"Then you don't mind if I escort you in, do you? I have an EGE-VIP card so you don't have to pay. And when we get inside, if you'd like a drink, let me know." He walked to the door with me. I was fucking flattered as I entered the club with this man. He had clout, and, I could tell money. Not only that, he must have had every woman up in there before, because when we walked in the door, the eyes started to roll. I went right over to the bar with him, told him my name, and got my drink. After that, I planned to stay away from him for the rest of the night. I had enough drama already and definitely wasn't looking for more.

I found my girlfriends in the Party Room sitting at some tables that were reserved for Shirley's party. When they saw me, the fakeness began. They really didn't expect me to come and were surprised to see me there.

"Felicia!" Shirley said, running up and giving me a hug like we were the best of friends. "I'm so glad you came. And your dress, girl, where did you get it? It is nice." I hugged her back and didn't tell her shit. She introduced me to some of her other fake-ass friends and they all looked at me with jealousy in their eyes. I smiled and pranced my ass over to the buffet table to get some chicken wings.

After I sat at a table and talked to this brotha whose breath smelled like garbage, I went back out to the dance area to look for a dance partner. Since the DJ played "Air-Force-Ones" by Nelly, I was ready to get my party on.

The floor was crowded, hot, and musty. Somebody had definitely forgotten their deodorant before they came, but the brotha I danced with had his shit together. He broke it down to the floor, and I tried to keep up with him. I could tell he was a little younger than I was, but what the hell? If he was setting it out like that on the dance floor, no telling how good he was in the bedroom.

We laughed with each other as we left the dance floor. I danced so well that several men grabbed on me for another dance. After I declined, my dance partner asked if I wanted something to drink. I told him a Sour Apple Martini would be fine. When he walked over to the bar, my eyes followed his ass because I damn sure thought about taking him home with me tonight. However, when I looked up and saw Stephon at a table with some of his boys from the shop, my plans changed. He looked down right workable—and so did several of his friends.

I went to the ladies' room to check myself and made sure everything was still in place. Then, I freshened my make-up and hiked my dress just a tad bit higher. When I came out of the bathroom I headed straight to the table where Stephon sat. I swayed my hips from side to side and worked my ass so they'd be sure to notice when I walked by. I saw them checking me out from a distance, but I continued to look forward as if I wasn't paying them any attention. As I neared the table, one of Stephon's friends grabbed my hand.

"Say, baby, why you moving so fast? Why don't you have a seat and holla at a brotha for a minute?" I smiled; my plan was already working well. I eased myself between Stephon and his friend and sat down.

"What's up, Felicia?" Stephon said, smiling at me with his pearly whites.

"Hey, Stephon," I said, and quickly turned to talk to his friend.

His friend looked at my breasts and licked his lips. "So, uh, what did your mama name such a pretty woman like you?"

"Well, my mama wasn't the one who named me, my father was. My name is Felicia. Felicia Davenport."

"Felicia, huh? I got one question for you Felicia. How does a woman get as fine as you? You are definitely a sight for sore eyes."

He put it on too damn thick for me, and I tuned him out. I tried to figure out how I could kick up a conversation with Stephon, who sat next to me and smelled like Gucci Envy. When he got up to dance with this other chick, I gazed at his tall nicely cut body that showed through his light blue silk shirt and pants. The front of his shirt unbuttoned just enough where you could see the thickness of his chest. And his light-blue round glasses that covered his hazel eyes had me melting like butter. Brotha had it going on and it was hard for me, along with many other females, to keep our eyes off of him.

The brotha I danced with earlier came over to the table and handed me my drink.

"I was looking for you. Why did you leave?" he asked. As I put the drink on the table, I noticed the crookedness of his teeth.

"Sorry, my man came in," I said, rubbing my hand Stephon partner's back. "I'll pay you for the drink...if you'd like." Cheap motherfucker stood and waited for me to give him the money. I reached into my purse and gave him ten dollars. He snatched it and walked away.

After he left, Stephon came back to the table with this light-skinned bitch who wasn't giving him any room to breathe. There wasn't any room for her to sit so she stood behind him and talked. I could tell he wasn't interested because he conversed with other women as she stood talking to him. She finally got the picture and walked away.

And when she did, I picked up where she left off.

"So, how's things been going, Stephon?" I crossed my legs so he could check out my sexy thighs. And that he did. Looked at them like he wanted to see what was between them.

"It's going pretty good, Felicia. Can't complain."

The DJ was right on time with a slow song. I interrupted as Stephon talked to one of his boys.

"Say, Stephon, would you like to dance?" I already pulled the chair back because I knew he wasn't going to turn me down. He didn't say yes or no. He just got up and followed me to the dance floor, as I strutted with a sexy walk. When he put his arms around me and leaned his head down close to my shoulder, I took his hand and slid it over my ass.

"Felicia, what you doing?" he said, grinning, and keeping his hand where I'd put it.

"What do you mean, what am I doing? I like for a man to have his hands on my ass when we're slow dancing. Not on my back." He slid his other hand down and cuffed my ass with it.

"Is that better?" He pulled my body close to his.

"Yes. A whole lot better." I felt his thang rub up against me.

"So, what are you doing out? I didn't even know you still hung out at places like this."

"I don't. I came tonight because it's one of my co-worker's birthday. And now that I'm here, I'm so glad I came."

"And why is that? Would it have anything to do with me?" he whispered.

"As a matter of fact, it does. I got a feeling something good is going to happen to me tonight."

"Oh, yeah? Something good like what?"

"Something good like my place or yours," I said, moving my body slowly to his rhythm.

"Felicia, are you trying to get me in bed with you?"

"Stephon, I don't try at anything I do. I only succeed. So, like I said, my place or yours?" Stephon quit dancing before the music stopped and looked at me.

"Meet me outside in five minutes. I have to take care of something before I leave so just give me five minutes.

I walked off the floor and went back to the table to get my purse. His friend asked where I was going, but I kept on walking.

I was outside talking to a police officer when Stephon walked out. "Come on," he said, grabbing my hand and walking me to his car.

When we got in, he sat for a minute before he started the engine. "Are you having second thoughts or something?" I asked, rubbing his bald head.

"Nope. Just thinking about something."

He backed up.

"May I ask what?"

"No, you may not. And put your seat belt on. I don't like people riding with me without their seat belt on."

I buckled my seat belt just so I didn't have to hear his mouth. "I guess since you're driving, we're going to your place, huh?"

"Yes. Do you have a problem with that?"

"No, I didn't know if you wanted to take me there since Nokea might decide to show up."

"Felicia, if you came with me tonight to talk about Nokea or Jaylin, I can drop you right back off at the club. I don't play games like that, baby, alright?" he said, sternly.

"Stephon, I didn't come with you to talk about them. I just asked you a question. And since you don't want to answer it, then so be it. Ain't no trip."

We were quiet the rest of the way to his house. By the time we got there, I'd almost fallen asleep from boredom. I hoped his sex was good since he seemed to have no conversation.

As soon as we got inside, he went directly to his phone and checked his messages. I stood by the door until he gave me the go-ahead to have a seat. When he came back, he'd already taken his shirt off and walked towards me.

"Come on, let's go downstairs," he ordered. I walked behind him as he led me to the basement. He had the damn hook up downstairs. Looked a whole lot better than his upper level did. Had a leather beige sofa that circled the room, huge beveled-glass mirrors that covered the walls, a diamond-shaped bar that sat in the middle of the floor with wine glasses that hung down above it, and beige leather bar stools surrounded the bar. The floor had shiny beige, black and white tile that looked like it had never been stepped on before. And his entertainment center covered one complete wall itself. Jaylin's name was written all over his basement; I knew he had to be responsible for financing this son of a bitch because there was no way Stephon could afford to live like this.

Stephon went over to the bar, while I took a seat on his plush sofa that was amazingly comfortable. When he walked over to me, he didn't waste any time. He sat a bottle of Cristal on the floor next to him and kneeled in front of me. He rubbed his hands on my hips and slid them up the sides of my dress raising it up a bit.

"Felicia, I don't want you having no regrets after I fuck you," he said, already pulling my dress over my head.

"No regrets for me." I started to unbuckle his pants. "And definitely no complaints," I said as I got a glimpse of what was seconds away from going inside me.

After he took the rest of my clothes off, he picked up the bottle of Cristal and poured it all over my body. I trembled as he had the pleasure of slurping it up. It burned a little between my legs but he had no problem cooling it off with his tongue. Then he stood up and flipped me upside down so he could get a better taste of me. I wrapped my legs around his head so I wouldn't fall. He held me tight around my back as I worked his goodness on the other end. My hair fell down, after I ran my fingers through it and felt the excitement from him working me so well. He backed up to the couch and lay back with my legs still straddled across his face. After he fondled me with his fingers, I slid my body down and sat on top of his goodness. I put my pussy to work on him, as he tightened up and held onto my ass.

"Felicia! Slow down, baby. I ain't ready to come yet."

He moaned, as I showed him something Nokea probably didn't know how to. Then he squeezed my hips tightly and eased himself in deeper so I could feel the full effect of him. I was in another world with him, as we seemed to click so damn well together. Almost better than Jaylin and me—but right now, Jaylin was the last thing on my mind.

Stephon and I finished up in the middle of the bar. He had emptied the second bottle of Cristal on his body, and this time, the pleasure was all mine. I hopped down off the bar and plopped my naked body on the couch.

"I had no idea you had it in you Stephon. I mean, I've always noticed how nice looking you were but I guess I couldn't see past Jaylin." I said, lying on the couch next to him, while rubbing my hands up and down on his chest.

"Well, I knew it was good because Jaylin told me it was. But he didn't tell me you could work it like that."

"I only work it like that when I have to. Besides, it was hard for me to keep up with you. You're packing a load down there, aren't you?"

He laughed. "Something like that. But I'm sure you'll be good company for it."

"So, does this mean this isn't a one-night stand? I know you told me not to ask about Nokea, but won't this interfere with your relationship with her?"

"Nope. Because what she don't know won't hurt her. Besides, I'd like to keep this on the down low as much as I can. Jaylin and I kind of just got close again after what happened with me and Nokea, and I don't want to do anything to mess up our relationship again."

"Stephon, please. If Jaylin finds out you and I are sleeping together, he'd laugh. He doesn't give a fuck about me. He could care less. I was really surprised to find out you and him went at it over Nokea. Her friend Pat told one of my girlfriends at work what happened and she told me. I knew he liked Nokea, but I thought I'd never see Jaylin fighting over a woman."

"Well, he's happy now, Felicia. He's doing what he wants to right now, and so am I."

He rose up.

"Where are you going?" I asked not wanting him to leave my side. He turned on his CD player and sung a song by Luther Vandross. He moved from side to side with his hands on his chest like he was slow dancing with himself. His eyes were closed as he sang: "Let me hold you tight, if only for one night." I laughed, as his voice didn't sound anything like Luther.

He smiled and held his arms out for me. There was no way I could resist holding a sexy naked body like his. This motherfucker had charmed the hell out of me and had me leaving with a serious smile on my face.

32 NOKEA

I was so ready to have this baby. My doctor had me on bed rest early because my blood pressure was high. I tried to remain calm and focus on the positive things, but I was so worried about Jaylin finding out the truth. Stephon told me about their conversation and I felt bad that he had to lie to Jaylin about us having sex two weeks after I did with him. But, I guess everything was for the best.

Jaylin's birthday was just around the corner, and no matter what, I always spent it with him. Even when he was in the orphanage. My mother and I went to see him and took him some toys both years he was there. As we got older, we met each year at Café Lapadero where we laughed and talked about the crazy college life. When I turned twenty-one, he was all mine. I always went out of my way for his birthday, just to let him know that somebody still cared about him.

This year would be different. I wanted to do something nice for him, but things were going so well with Stephon and I that I didn't want to go behind his back and cater to Jaylin. Stephon was a charm. Was just what I needed during my pregnancy and he satisfied all of my physical and mental needs. Problem was, I still didn't love him. Couldn't kick these damn feelings I still had for Jaylin. And every time Stephon left, I cried. He had no clue how I felt and I hoped to overcome my misery, soon.

I sat around the house and wondered if Jaylin would show up at Café Lapadero on his birthday. Then I thought about calling him to make sure he would be there. Finally, I decided to just show up without calling.

The morning of his birthday, I searched my closet for the nicest maternity outfit I had. I decided on a peach outfit with big white blooming flowers on it. The pants were linen and loose enough for me to get my fat butt into. I couldn't get my hair to act like I wanted it to so I put on a white straw hat that covered it up.

We usually met up around one, and I got there an hour early so I could make sure we had a seat just in case he showed up. The sun shined brightly and there was a nice comforting breeze, so I asked the waiter if he could seat me outside. I asked him for an ice-cold glass of water with a lemon and some rolls. I hadn't eaten anything all day because I was so nervous.

I pulled out the *Black Expressions* card I had bought him and signed the inside. I still had thirty minutes, so when the waiter came over again, I went ahead and ordered a salad. I didn't want to sit there doing nothing and looking stupid.

By quarter after one, my stomach felt queasy. After another fifteen minutes had gone by, I felt like a complete fool. Why would I think Jaylin would put forth any effort to meet with me? Especially on his birthday. He probably had plans with his other woman. Plans to make love to her and make her smile like he'd done to me over the years. Stupid me, I thought. Always setting myself up for disappointment.

Damn near in tears, I stood up and dug in my purse to pay the waiter. I wiped my eyes and hurried to get the hell out of there.

The wind picked up and blew my hat off my head. I quickly turned around to pick it up, and when I did, Jaylin stood behind me with my hat in his hand.

"Were you getting ready to leave?" he asked, handing my hat back to me.

"Yes," I said, still wiping my eyes.

"Why are you crying?" He put his hand on my cheek, as I sat down in the chair and laughed.

"No reason. Since I've been pregnant I get emotional all the time for no reason."

"I wouldn't know nothing about that." He pulled back a chair and sat next to me.

He looked amazing. Tan was in full effect and his tailored suit had me screaming naughty things silently to myself. No doubt, life seemed to treat him well, as it always seemed to. I wasn't sure how good I looked; I'd gained so much weight since the last time I'd seen him.

"So, were you getting tired of waiting for me?" he asked.

"Yes. I was about to leave. I...I didn't think you were going to come."

"I always come, don't I? No matter what I always come," he said, looking at my stomach like he was just as hurt as I was.

"Well, thank you. You don't know what it means to have you in my presence right now."

181

"No, no I don't know. I really didn't think you were going to show. That's why I took my time."

"Really? I've been here. Been here since noon." I was unable to look him in the eyes. He continued to look at me, and then he grabbed my chin and made me look up at him. My eyes watered.

"What's wrong, Nokea? Why do you keep crying? I thought you'd be happy to see me."

"I am. I didn't think it would be this hard for me see…seeing you again. The last time we spoke you were pretty upset with me. And—"

"And, I'm sorry. I should have never come to your place and disrespected you like that. I was wrong. That's what I wanted to come here and tell you today. I'm sorry for everything I ever done to you. I fucked up and now I have to move on and stop thinking about what could have been."

"Do you ever think just maybe there might be a chance for us down the road? I mean, right now you're happy, I'm happy but…but is there a chance we can be happy together?"

"Honestly, Nokea, I don't think so. You have my cousin's baby on the way and you shared something with him I will never be able to forget. And as much as I thought that maybe someday we would be, that dream ended when you got pregnant. I'm not saying I don't still have feelings for you, all I'm saying is I got to take my feelings elsewhere."

My throat ached; that was definitely not what I wanted to hear. I dug in my purse and pushed his birthday card to him. "I wanted to do something else special for you but I decided to keep it simple."

He picked it up, read it, and smiled as he closed it. Then I reached into my purse and pulled out the Teddy bear he'd given me on my birthday. The front of the shirt still said, *Happy Birthday Nokea Yours forever, Jaylin.* And I had printed on the back, *My heart belongs to you forever, Love Nokea.* He smiled again and held the bear in his hand.

There was silence. "I guess sometimes people who love each other just can't be together," he said, looking at the back of the Teddy bear.

I closed my eyes and fought back my tears with everything I had. "Yes they can. Love can conquer anything. If you love me, we can make this work, Jaylin." I reached my hand out to touch his on the table. He took a deep breath and moved his hands.

"Nokea, it'll never work out. There's too much damage that's been done. And I'm not talking about with just you and Stephon. I'm talking about all the damage I've done to you. You deserve better. Much better than I can offer you." He stood up and reached into his pocket. He tossed a fifty-dollar bill on the table and put his Teddy bear under his arm. "Listen, I'm not going to be able to stay for lunch. I have some business to take care of. This should take care of lunch and then some. Good luck, baby. And I wish you and Stephon all the best." He leaned down and gave me a kiss. I closed my eyes and held his face, as he floated his tongue around in my mouth for a few seconds. He backed up as he felt me getting deeper into it. I took his glasses off and held them in my hands so I could look into his eyes.

"I love you," I said.

"I know." He took his glasses out of my hand and walked away.

I was crushed. After I left, I sat in my car and cried like a baby. For the first time, reality kicked in. I'd have to let go. I'd have to definitely find a way to get rid of these feelings I had for Jaylin. Not being able to be with him drove me crazy.

When I got home, Stephon was there. He was in the baby's room putting up some wallpaper I'd picked out at Babies R Us. I felt guilty as I stood in the doorway and watched him go out of his way for a baby that wasn't even his.

He climbed down the ladder and came over to give me a kiss. "Hey, baby, are you okay? You don't look so good. Why don't you go lay down for a minute? I'm just about finished anyway."

"I'm fine. I went to the mall with Mama this afternoon and she had me doing a lot of walking."

"Aw, so, what do you think? It looks good, don't it?" he said, looking around at the wallpaper.

"Yeah. It looks perfect. Just how I imagined it—" I held my stomach, as I started to feel pain.

"Nokea, why don't you go lay down for a while? I'll cook us some dinner in a little bit. Let me tidy up in here, okay?"

"Alright. I think I will go lay down for a minute."

I felt a little faint walking into my bedroom. I lay across my bed and let out some more tears as I thought about Jaylin. I held my stomach as another pain started to come, then I yelled for Stephon to come help me. If it was contractions, the baby was early. I wasn't due for another three weeks.

As I curled up on the bed and held my stomach, Stephon ran into the room.

"Nokea! Are you okay?" he said, bending down on the bed to hold me.

"Stephon, I think I'm in labor—"

"Well, come on. Let me get your things for the hospital and get the car." He rushed around the room. "I'll come back and get you in a minute."

"Hurry!" I yelled, as I continued to hold my stomach.

Stephon zoomed around the house and gathered my things. Then he came back into the room, picked me up, and carried me to the car. I couldn't tell who was the most nervous, him or me. He kept asking me the same questions over and over: How am I doing? Can I feel the baby yet? And by the time we finally got to St. John's Mercy Medical Center on New Ballas Road, I actually could.

The emergency room crew rushed me to the delivery room and called my doctor to come immediately. I asked Stephon to call my parents to let them know. But when I told him to call Pat, he looked at me like I was crazy. After I begged him, he said he would.

After he called everyone, he came back in the room with me and held my hand. He kissed it, as I lay there in so much pain. My doctor asked me to push and I gave it everything I had—but I couldn't force this baby out for anything in the world. Stephon bent down and tried to coax me, and after he squeezed my hand tighter and yelled at me, I pushed harder and the baby came out.

It was a boy. A six-pound-five-ounce baby boy. After the nurses cleaned him up, they put him in my arms. He was handsome. Had a head full of curly coal-black hair, was light-skinned, and when he forced his eyes open they were a beautiful gray like Jaylin's. Looked just like him.

After I held him for a while, Stephon picked him up and held him in his arms. He smiled and rubbed his little hands with his finger.

"You did good, Shorty. I'm really proud of you," he said, bending down giving me a kiss.

"Thanks, baby. Thanks for being there for me. I don't know what I would have done without you," I said, feeling exhausted.

Stephon gave the baby back to the nurses. They cleaned me up and took me to the private room I'd arranged for.

Soon, Mama and Daddy rushed in and couldn't wait to see the baby. I told them the nurses would bring the baby to me in a few minutes.

Stephon gazed out of the window like he was in deep thought. Daddy walked over to him and shook his hand.

"Man, thanks. Thank you for being there for my baby. I was a little worried about her but I'm glad her and the baby have you."

"You're welcome, Mr. Brooks. You don't have to thank me; I wouldn't have had it any other way."

I was relieved it was all over and couldn't wait for them to bring my baby in to see me.

After hours of visitors and playing around with the baby, I was completely exhausted. I was still in a little pain and asked everybody to clear out. Stephon walked Mama and Daddy to the car, but Pat hung around so we could talk.

"Girl, you got yourself a fine young man there. He's got to be the cutest little baby I've ever seen."

"Isn't he? I feel so blessed to have a healthy beautiful baby. Especially since he came early."

"You mean, especially since he came on Jaylin's birthday. Ain't that something? When Stephon called me, I damn near died because I remember you said you were going to see him today. So, how did that go? Did he even show up?"

"It was okay. He came, but he was late. Bottom line, he said in so many words he loved me but we could never be together," I said, feeling hurt again.

"Well, Nokea, just move on. Stop trying to chase him. If he hasn't come back to you in all this time then let it go. I hate to see you keep torturing yourself like this."

"I know. The baby is born now, so it's time. I think I'll be much better anyway knowing I have him in my life."

"Well, good." Pat gave me a kiss on the cheek. "Get some rest and I'll call you later."

As she headed out, Stephon came in with a balloon and some flowers he'd picked up at the gift shop. "Take care of her for me," Pat said, stopping him at the door. "She's a good woman and she deserves a good man in her life."

"I got her back," Stephon said.

After she left, he put the flowers and balloon on my windowsill. I smiled and scooted over so he could sit next to me. He rubbed my hair back with his hand.

"I know...it looks a mess, doesn't it?"

"Naw, Shorty, you look beautiful. I can't believe you're a mother now. You're going to be a good mother. I know you will. Your mama and daddy did a good job raising you," he said, sadly, as if he thought about his mother.

"And you're going to be a good father. My baby is going to have a daddy in his life that he can be proud of. Thing is, I don't know what to call him. Would you help me name him?" Stephon walked over to the baby and picked him up again. He brought him over to the bed and sat next to me. He stared at the baby for a minute and then looked at me.

"He really doesn't look like you, you know?" he said.

"Yes he does. He's got my nose."

"No, no he doesn't. Actually he has my aunt's nose. He looks like his daddy. Don't you little man?" He rubbed his nose up against the baby's nose. "You look just like your daddy. I say we name him after his daddy. Why don't you call him Jaylin?" I looked at Stephon and was shocked as hell.

"Stephon, I don't think that's a good idea. I mean, if we're going to raise him together—"

"Yes, we're going to raise him together but ain't nothing wrong with me naming my child after my favorite cousin, is it?"

"No, I guess not..."

We both held little Jaylin in our arms for a while. After he went to sleep, Stephon called the nurse to come get him. He climbed in bed next to me and stared me in the eyes.

"I love you, Shorty. And every chance I get, I'm going to make you the happiest woman in the world. Your worries are over. So, no more tears, no more arguing, and no more disappointments." He held me in his arms. I took a deep breath and kissed him on the cheek.

"You are so wonderful. Why couldn't you have come into my life before Jaylin? This would be a lot easier for me if you had. I just don't know when or how I'm going to be able to move on."

Stephon climbed out of the bed and stood next to me. "You're going to move on right now. It's time. I have always been in your life since you and I were kids. Unfortunately, you just recently started to notice. Life is so unpredictable and sometimes we have to go wherever it takes us. I never thought in a million years I would be here with you. Loving you like no other man in this world can love you. And asking you to...to be my wife." He reached into his pocket and pulled out a small black box. I was too nervous to open it so he opened it for me. I looked at it and blinked my eyes so I wouldn't cry. "Shorty, will you marry me? I don't want to waste any more time being without your love." He took the ring out of the box and waited for an answer. Must have paid a fortune for it because the diamond was huge.

"When Stephon? When do you want to do this?"

"Whenever you want to, baby. I want to give you time to get things situated with the baby, and also time to let the news settle in with your parents. After that, I want you to be my wife. And I'm not taking no for an answer." I took the ring out of Stephon's hand and slid it on my finger. I looked at it and smiled, as it weighed my finger down. I took his hand and pulled him on the bed next to me.

"If I never loved you before, I love you now. There is no way I'm going to let you walk out of my life when you've been so good to me. Six months, Stephon. In six months, you'll have your wife." I kissed him on the lips.

Stephon stayed in the room with me all night. He fell asleep in the bed next to me. Feeling some slight pain, I eased out of bed and sat in a chair by the window. I raised my hand several times and looked at my ring. I was happy. All of this started to make sense to me. I stared up at the sky and thanked the Lord for my healthy baby boy, and my new handsome fiancé.

33 JAYLIN

Meeting with Nokea was one of the toughest things I had to do in my life. Some old feelings I had for her rekindled and surprised the fuck out of me. She looked beautiful though. And a part of me really wished she were having my baby. But since Mackenzie was the only kid I cared about, that was enough for me. Her and Scorpio had moved back in. I didn't care what it took to keep Mackenzie in my life and I was never going to let her out of my sight again.

When I got back from meeting with Nokea, Scorpio and Mackenzie were in the kitchen baking me a Black Forest cake for my birthday. My favorite. It didn't look too bad either.

I sat on a stool in the kitchen, as my mind drifted back to my day with Nokea.

"Baby, you seem kind of preoccupied today," Scorpio said. "Does your birthday always get you down? You know, since you're getting older and everything." She laughed.

"Don't go calling me old until this motherfucker here can't rise anymore," I said, grabbing my thang.

"Jaylin, watch it. Mackenzie in here."

"I'm sorry," I said. I walked over to Mackenzie, standing by the counter and putting more icing on the cake, as if it didn't already have enough.

"Daddy, do you like it?" she asked, licking the icing off the spatula.

"Like it, I love it. And since you made it, I really love it."

"Well, I really didn't make it," she whispered. "Mommy did." Now one thing I like is an honest woman. She wasn't taking credit for what she didn't do. I kissed Mackenzie on the cheek and put just a dab of spit on it so I could wipe it off. She smiled.

After Mackenzie put the finishing touches on the cake, her and Scorpio stuck some candles in it and sung "Happy Birthday" to me. It was so sweet, I damn near wanted to cry. Later that day, they took me to Morton's Steak House in Clayton and we ate up some shit.

On the way back home, my cell phone rang off the hook. I answered and it was Stephon. I hadn't heard from him all day, which was quite unusual since it was my birthday.

"Say, man, Happy Birthday. Sorry I just got around to calling, but I had a busy day," he said, sounding like he was out of breath.

"Well, I'm glad you found time in your busy schedule to call a brotha."

"Listen, what's on your agenda next weekend? I have something really important I want to share with you but it'll have to wait until then."

"Nothing. Nothing much. I signed Mackenzie up for ballet classes but that don't start until nine a.m. After that, I don't have any plans."

"Good, good. Then I'll see you Saturday afternoon. I'll call before I come to make sure you're there because it's imperative that we talk."

"If it's that important, why don't you meet me at my house tonight. I'm on my way there now."

"Naw, it's got to wait until the weekend. Besides, I want you to enjoy the rest of your birthday with your fine-ass woman tonight."

"Alright, man, if you insist. I'll be by the shop this week anyway to get my hair cut so I'll see you before then."

"Okay, that's cool."

He wished me Happy Birthday again then hung up.

By the time we got home, Mackenzie was sound asleep. I carried her to her room and kissed her for at least the hundredth time today. I really appreciated her and Scorpio as they tried to make sure I had a good birthday. I shut Mackenzie's bedroom door, and Scorpio stood downstairs in the foyer and looked upstairs at me.

"Oh, Jaylin," she said, smiling and motioning with her finger for me to come to her. I smiled because I knew what time it was. She was butt-ball naked and headed towards the Jacuzzi. By the time we got outside, I had dropped my shit off in the living room. And since I'd kept sex between us on the down low because of my burning ordeal, I was ready to tear into her. And that, I did. Loving was so good, made me wanna fuck all night long. And at the rate she went, she was definitely up for the long haul. I couldn't find it in my heart to kick her out again, no matter what.

I'd hired a private detective to keep an eye on her, though. I had to know for myself if she was still lying to me about stripping. I knew that if she was, it was all about the money. Had nothing to do with trying to get her fuck on with somebody, because I was doing that and doing it well. It was strictly about making sure she kept some money in her pocket. And the best way she knew how to do it was by showing men her sexy body. She promised me that she would leave all that bullshit behind. According to her, her main focus was finishing school.

But last week, she came in at two in the morning. She claimed her and her sister went out with some of their girlfriends, but I wasn't no fool. I'd been a playa for many years and definitely knew the game. Knew it well.

After I finished making love to her, we went to the kitchen and warmed up our leftovers from Morton's. Scorpio stood her naked body in front of mine and stuffed some potatoes in my mouth with a fork. I rolled the potatoes around in my mouth and opened it wider for some more.

"Damn, I didn't know your mouth could get that wide," she said, holding back on giving me some more. I slid her closer between my legs and held her ass with both of my hands.

"Where do you see us in five years?" I asked. She laid the fork on the plate and gave me her full attention.

"I see us standing here in the kitchen doing the same thing we're doing right now. I see me loving you more and more each day. And maybe, just maybe, some more kids in our future." I nodded and thought about it for a while.

"Do you ever think you'll get tired of making love to me? Not only that, do you think you'll always be willing to put up with my sometimes fucked-up ways? I can be a motherfucker when I want to, you know."

"Oh, trust me, I know. Probably better than anybody does because I'm the one who lives with you. But it's okay, baby. I know how to deal with your mood swings. I just get out of your way when you don't want to be bothered. Eventually you come around, don't you? Anyway, why are you asking me about the future? Are you planning on keeping me forever?" She rubbed her fingers through my hair like she always does. I took her hand and kissed it.

"Baby, I have a serious problem with loving women. I told you this before and I don't want it to damage our relationship. It's not that I don't love being with you, but something inside just won't let me get too attached. And every time I feel as if I'm getting too close, I back off. I go find myself another lady to occupy my time…to take away some of these feelings I have for you."

"But, in due time Jaylin that will change. Those days I was away from you were hell for me. But it took that for me to realize I couldn't lie to you if I wanted to be with you forever. I had to do whatever it took to get you to trust me again. So, now, I'm working on proving to you that you can trust me. And once you realize you can, then all of this is going to change. You'll be able to love me like I want you to. You'll see." I turned Scorpio around and pressed her butt against my thighs.

"I'm tired, baby. I'm truly burned out. It's time for me to get back to business. I've focused too much of my time elsewhere. After tonight, I don't know how much time I can offer you. I mean, I still want us to be together but my work is going to take priority over everything. I'm losing money that I can't afford to lose anymore. And since I'm a brotha who likes the finer things in life, I know what I have to do to make sure that continues."

"Jaylin, by all means, handle your business. You've been more than a blessing to Mackenzie and me, and there's no way I'm going to stop you from doing what you need to do to better yourself. All I ask is that you don't forget about us. Maybe some day I'll be able to handle it if you do, but Mackenzie won't. She's so crazy about you it scares me. I really think she wants to be with you more than she does me. But you do have a way with the women so I know exactly where she's coming from."

"I will never forget about you and Mackenzie. Especially, her. She's made me realize so many things over these past months; and most of all—she's shown me how to love somebody. In a different way, of course. And for me, that's a big step. I don't think I've ever loved anybody in my entire life except for her and…" I stopped.

"Her and who Jaylin?"

"My mother. Her and my mother," I said, clearing my shit up.

"Well, I'm at least glad you love a part of me. That makes me feel special right there. And I know if you can love my daughter the way you do, then I know you will eventually find a way to love me too."

"Maybe so," I said, kissing her on the neck and getting ready to stick my thang where it belonged. Scorpio and I got down in the kitchen, but I cut it short because I had to get up early and get back to work.

Shit was crazy back at work. The market had dropped to a five-year low and everybody lost money—including me. Roy tried to keep up with all my accounts, but the way things were, we were all lucky to still have jobs.

No sooner had I plopped down in my seat, Schmidt rang my phone.

"Jaylin, welcome back. Hope you're ready to do some work around here today because you have it cut out for you." I laughed and hung up on his ass. That's what I always did when I felt pressured. Just laughed and did what worked best for me.

My first call was to Higgins. Even though I spoke to him occasionally from home, I wasn't really able to handle my business with him like I was at the office. He was cool. He understood the ups and downs of the market, and didn't blame me at all for losing thousands of dollars in his investments. My suggestion to him was to buy while the market was low and wait to see what happens. Didn't expect much to happen any time soon, but a year or two from now, we could all be set. He went with the flow and so did his buddies.

Roy had seen how well my plan worked for me and he got on the phone and started to do the same. We called people we hadn't talked to in years and tried to get them to invest. Drove around visiting companies that didn't have pension or any type of retirement plans set up and talked to them about investing.

By day's end, we were exhausted. Schmidt came in my office and congratulated both of us. He told me he was glad to have me back, and frankly, I was glad to be back. Not once did I think about my crazy life outside of work. Because that's truly what it was—after my conversation with Scorpio, and seeing Nokea. I knew I had love for Nokea. I knew she was the one who'd kept me going all these years. And as much as Scorpio fulfilled all my other needs, my heart was empty because Nokea hadn't been there to fill it for a long time. But wasn't't a damn thing I could do about it. I was hurt too bad by Nokea being with Stephon, but I just had to play it cool and focus on the good things I had in my life. Like Mackenzie and my job, my wealth, and even my woman's pussy. For that was getting better and better each day. Just wasn't filling that emptiness up inside of me. For now, anyway.

Things started to calm down by the end of the week. Everybody went with the flow of the market and waited for something positive to happen. Angela and Roy became my right-hand team. They had things under control and made sure I hadn't felt much pressure. It didn't dawn on me that the reason they were so close was because Roy was banging her ass.

When I left the office on Friday, I had to go back and get my keys because I forgot them. And when I passed by Roy's office, the lights were out. I knocked and could hear a bunch of rambling going on. The only thing I could do was smile and think, I had been there and definitely done that before. Roy didn't know what he was getting himself into. And to think Roy and her husband were supposed to be friends fucked me up.

Made me think about who I truly considered to be a friend of mine. I really didn't have many to begin with, because it was too many brothas hating when I inherited my grandfather's estate and started making money years ago. I had to leave motherfuckers I'd known for years behind. Not because I was big-balling, but because they tried to take me for everything I had. If not that, but when they came to my house, shit always came up missing. I learned my lesson early and decided to limit myself to just a few friends. Actually, Stephon was the only person I really needed.

When I pulled in the driveway, Scorpio's car was gone as usual. Sometimes she was there when I got home, but usually she wasn't. When I met up with the private detective yesterday, he said she was definitely still in school. Also confirmed there was nothing going on with her and old man Jackson. But he did tell me she still stripped at parties. Showed me pictures of her entering and leaving mothefuckers' cribs— and even tried to defend her by saying she always left alone. I paid him for his time and thanked him for what he called "easy work."

The thing about it was, I didn't even trip. Pretended like I didn't know nothing about it. And for damn sure didn't ask her any questions when she came in last night. She always gave me excuses anyway like, she went somewhere to study, or she went out with her sister. Explanations sounded pretty good. And if I was a brotha who didn't know any better, I'd probably believed her. Sad thing about it was she thought I was stupid enough to believe it. Puzzled the hell out of me, but what the fuck? Arguing about it wasn't even worth my time.

The only reason I kept my mouth shut was because of Mackenzie. I told Scorpio I wanted to adopt her, and without any hesitation, she agreed. Once everything was settled with the courts, I would do what I had to do to have shit Jaylin's way. I didn't hate Scorpio for what she did because after all, money was the name of her game. I knew people out there who would do anything for money, no matter who got hurt. But she was a sista who could have had it all. Didn't even have to go out like she did. Looks, charm, personality, and ambition could have gotten her anything she wanted. And she wasn't even smart enough to realize that. That's the reason why I couldn't love her like she wanted me to. Besides, there was no way to forgive a woman who lied to me as much as she did.

Mackenzie always waited for me when I came through the door. I sat her on my lap in the living room, as I rummaged through my mail. I had gotten the results from my AIDS test back. I took a deep breath and slowly opened the envelope. I unfolded the letter, and when I saw the word "negative" I jumped for joy. Mackenzie jumped with me. She didn't even know what I was happy about; she was just happy because I was. Now, that's the kind of love I need in my life, I thought, as I swung her around the living room.

I paid Nanny B for watching Mackenzie and called Stephon to make sure he still planned to come over tomorrow. When a very familiar voice answered his phone, I was shocked.

"Felicia?" I said.

"Hold on," she said, handing the phone to Stephon.

"Man, was that Felicia who answered your phone?"

"Yeah, what's up?" he said, sounding like he was asleep.

"I just called to see if it was still on for tomorrow. But, uh…what is Felicia doing answering your phone?"

"I was asleep. She wasn't supposed to answer it. If Nokea had called, I would have been fucked."

"Yeah, you pretty much would have been. But are you fucking Felicia? When did this shit take place?"

"Man, I don't know. It's been a while. I was going to tell you but I didn't want you tripping like you did when you found out about Nokea."

"Man…whatever, whatever. That's your prerogative, so, hey, go for what you know. It ain't nothing but some pussy anyway." I heard Felicia in the background moaning.

"Right, right. But, uh…I'll give you a holla tomorrow. This one here just can't seem to get enough."

"Tell me about it. I definitely know how that is."

I hung up and didn't even trip; wasn't even worth me stressing over. I threw Mackenzie over my shoulder and carried her up to my room. When I put her down, she laughed so hard that spit dripped down her face.

"Mackenzie, that's nasty," I said, tickling her.

"Daddy, stop tickling me," she said, grabbing her stomach. "Stop before I tickle you back."

"Okay, give it your best shot." I flexed my muscles and held my six-pack in. She ran her hands across my stomach and tried to tickle me. When I didn't laugh, she stopped. Then she sat on the edge of my bed and pouted. "Mackenzie, what did I tell you about pouting? What's wrong with you now?" I asked.

"When I tickled you, you wouldn't laugh. Mommy said when you stopped laughing and smiling it was time for us to leave. I don't want to leave Daddy. I want to live with you forever, and ever, and ever." Her eyes were watery.

"Mackenzie, how many times have I told you you're here to stay? Wherever I go, you go. I don't care what your mommy says to you. You're my little girl and I'm never going to let you leave this house again until you get married."

"Like you and Mommy. She said you were going to marry her."

"No, no, Mackenzie. I told you that you'd be the first to know when I decided to get married. And right now, Daddy ain't ready for no wife."

"But I'm ready for a husband. Can my husband come live here with us too?"

I laughed. "Baby, you're much too little to be talking about having a husband. Daddy's going to have to screen these young men out here for his baby." I hugged her. "When the time comes, he'd better have it going on like your daddy does, and able to buy a beautiful home for you so you can live there with him."

Just then Scorpio walked in. "Or be able to afford one yourself," she said, taking her jacket off and laying it on the bed. That still bugged the hell out of me, and after I gave her a crazy look, she grabbed it and hung it up in the closet. Mackenzie ran up and gave her a hug. She walked out of the room with Mackenzie, and I went into the bathroom and shut the door.

I ran some steaming hot bath water and hung my clothes up neatly in the small closet in the bathroom. I slid my body deep down in the tub and closed my eyes. Scorpio knocked on the door and cracked it open so she could see me.

"Hey, you got a minute?" she said, walking into the bathroom. I continued to close my eyes.

"Always. I always got a minute for you."

"Jaylin, why do you be telling Mackenzie all that crazy stuff? I want her to grow up being independent. I don't want her to think the only way she can make it is if a man takes care of her. You're giving her the wrong impression about life." I kept my eyes closed and tried to prevent myself from going off on her. When I opened them, I took a deep breath and looked at her.

"Scorpio, almost everything you tell Mackenzie has been a lie. They might be small lies to us, but in her mind, they're big lies. If anyone is giving her the wrong impression about life, it's you, not me. I make a decent living. You don't. Well, in your mind it's decent. But I tell you what: I'm going to make damn sure, whether you like it or not, she don't have to go through life shaking her ass just for a fucking dollar. Now, if you got a problem with that, that's too bad. I'm not going to sit here and convince somebody who thinks I'm too damn stupid to realize she's still taking her clothes off for money." I closed my eyes again.

She got up and walked out. I could see her in the mirror, as she sat on the bed and started to tear up. I wasn't in no mood to comfort her. After a few minutes, she took her clothes off and came back in the bathroom.

"Can I join you?" she said, putting on a fake smile.

"I'd rather you didn't. I'd like to enjoy my bath alone if you don't mind."

"Sure." She grabbed a towel and walked back into the bedroom. Then, she lay across the bed and turned on the TV.

I stayed in the tub for a while then got out and flaunted my big dick in front of her. I walked into the closet and pretended to look for something. I stood right in the doorway and wiped myself off with a towel. Then I grabbed the *St. Louis American Newspaper* off the nightstand and pimped my ass out of the door. I lit up a Black and Mild and laid my naked body on the floor with my feet propped up on my leather sofa in the bonus room. I opened the newspaper and started to read.

Scorpio came in and took the newspaper out of my hand. She straddled my chest then sat on top of it. I got a glimpse of her good stuff, as every bit of it stared me in the face. She rubbed her clitoris and allowed her fingers to find a way inside of her. As her juices flowed, she placed her fingers on my lips because she knew that was definitely how to turn me on. I sucked her fingers into my mouth and continued to lye there and watch. If anything, I knew she was seriously trying to fuck with my mind. And just for the hell of it, I took my fingers and gently rubbed against her walls. But when she turned around and put her ass in my face, how could I resist? I took a few puffs from the Black and Mild, and blew the smoke out of my mouth. Afterwards, I scooted her down on my face so I could lick her at the right angle. She knew I was weak when it came to fucking her. And when I realized she knew that, I stopped the action. I moved her over to the side and stood up.

"Jaylin, why did you stop? Don't you want to fuck me?" she said, kneeling down in front of me.

I rubbed my hand across her face. "Baby, sex doesn't solve everything. I'm not saying that I don't want to have sex with you. All I'm saying is it's not going to keep us together. I find it funny how easy you can make me love your pussy; question is, can you make me love you? For that's, the only thing that counts." I picked up my paper, grabbed my Black and Mild, and went to go sleep in one of the guestrooms.

Scorpio didn't bother me for the rest of the night. I actually got up in the middle of the night to make sure she hadn't left with Mackenzie. When I saw both of them still there, I went back into the guestroom and went to sleep.

Mackenzie and I rushed to get her to ballet class on time. I bought her pink shoes instead of purple, and she made a big deal about it and cried. We had to stop by the store to exchange them before we went to ballet class. I made it perfectly clear to her there would be no more bullshit from her. And even though she cried again, I felt good about standing my ground for the first time.

After seeing her twirl around the floor, I couldn't do nothing but smile. I stood and watched as she took charge and learned everything that the instructors taught her. I was proud of my baby girl and I didn't care what anybody said.

After the class, we stopped at McDonalds on Olive Street Road. She took about ten minutes deciding what she wanted only to play with the damn toy that was inside of the Happy Meal. Didn't eat a thing. When I tried to make her eat it, she did her normal routine and pouted. When I reminded her about our conversation and told her I would give her hamburger to Barbie, she ate it.

When we arrived home, I was surprised to see Scorpio's car still in the driveway. Usually on Saturday morning she'd find somewhere to go, like to the gym or to Chesterfield Mall to spend my damn money. But I guess that since I'd gotten a little tight with the money, she had fewer options.

She must have heard us pull up because she came outside and asked how Mackenzie's ballet class went. I felt like if she really wanted to know, then she would have gotten her ass out of bed and gone with us. But what the hell? As long as Mackenzie had me, she really didn't need Scorpio.

I went into my office to turn on my computer. My intentions were to catch up on some work before Stephon came over, so I closed the door so I wouldn't be interrupted. No sooner had I taken my coat off, I saw him pull in the driveway. He was outside talking to Scorpio—probably trying to coax her ass in the bedroom too. I did promise him a while back that as soon as I was finished with her, he could have her. Again, it didn't matter to me either way.

They were outside for a while, so I pulled my curtain slightly over to the side to see what took them so long. Scorpio had what looked to be a baby's pumpkin seat in her hand, and Mackenzie jumped up and tried to look at the baby.

I guess Nokea finally had it. I sat nervous about seeing it. And Stephon, of course, couldn't wait to bring it over here and throw it in my face. As I heard them come through the front door, I sat at my desk and pretended to be occupied. Scorpio peeked in and told me Stephon was here to see me. When I told her to let him in, he walked into my office with the baby in his arms. I was crushed. Couldn't even get up enough nerve to look at the baby. Frankly, didn't know how to respond.

"Say, man, I know I'm a little bit early but I figured you and Mackenzie was probably back from her ballet class," he said.

"So, I see you got yourself a son there, huh? Can't help but notice all the blue and white he got on."

"Yeah, I got myself a son," he said, trying to get comfortable in a chair with the baby.

"How's Nokea? I didn't think she was due so soon. I just saw her last weekend on my birthday and she didn't look as if she was ready yet." I knew Stephon had no idea we'd seen each other on my birthday.

"So, you saw her last week? What did she say?"

"Nothing much. She just wished me a Happy Birthday and we talked, that's all."

"Okay. But, uh, she's doing pretty good. She hasn't been getting much sleep because of the baby, but her parents and I been trying to help out."

"So, I take it you had a night off last night since you were at your place with Felicia."

"Aw...yeah, that. Well, a, Felicia and me, we cool. But I didn't come here to talk to you about her. You and I have shared plenty of women in the past—seventeen of them to be exact—and we never made it a big issue, so, I don't want to do it now."

"I'm with that. And actually, it was eighteen to be exact. I counted them myself just last night."

"Well, eighteen then. I'm just glad we don't have a problem keeping it in the family."

"Naw, no problem. But there was one exception. One I sure regret not keeping to myself," I said, trying to lay it on the table.

"I know, Jay, but things happen. I couldn't control my feelings for her and I really thought you had moved on with Scorpio. So, what I'm about to tell you, I want you to listen and listen good. If you find yourself getting upset with me, just know I didn't come here to fight with you again. I think it's time this came out in the open so we both can get on with our lives."

"That's all I'm trying to do. But every day, it's something new. I don't know how much of this back-stabbing-playa-hating bullshit I can take".

"It ain't even like that, but first, I'll start from the beginning. As you know, when we were growing up, I always liked Nokea. You never paid her any attention and I think that's why she liked you so much. When y'all started dating, I was really disappointed. And then when you kept fucking around on her, seeing all these other different women, man, it hurt. All I wanted to do was see her happy. Year after year, same ole shit. And each time y'all got into it, she came to me for comfort. This past year was the first time she ever said it was over between y'all and I truly felt it was time for her to move on."

Stephon moved around in the chair and tried to get more comfortable. He could see the fury burning in my eyes. "So, anyway, I stepped up," he said. "I tried to show Nokea what a good man could really be like. But she still wouldn't love me like she loved you. No matter how hard I tried. So, a part of me felt like if I saw other women, maybe her feelings would change. Maybe she did want a bad boy in her life. She doesn't really know about the other women in my life, but I think she suspects something. And just that small suspicion is bringing her closer to me. Making her want to be with me more and more. I know it sounds crazy but it's the truth. She seems to like me more because she thinks I'm a challenge for her now." Stephon took a deep breath. "When I told you I made love to her a few weeks after you did, I lied. When I told you we'd had sex before my mother's funeral, I lied about that too. I lied to you because I wanted this baby to be mine. I wanted Nokea to be happy and I wanted him to be raised by me. I know it was wrong, my brotha, but I felt like at the time, it was the best thing to do."

He stood up and walked the baby over to me. He took him off his shoulder and laid him in my arms. "This is your baby, Jay. I took it upon myself to name him Jaylin because he looks just like his daddy."

I held my arms out as Stephon gave the baby to me. I pulled the blankets back so I could get a good look at him. I rubbed his soft curly black hair and held his fingers with my hand. He squirmed around a bit and started to open his eyes. And when he did, they were mine. I could see myself written all over this baby. Wasn't no denying him. I looked at Stephon as a tear rolled down my face. I hadn't cried in a while, but having my son in my arms just did something to me.

"Did anybody ever think about what I wanted? This could have changed things for me a long time ago. But it was never about me. And by all means, I appreciate you stepping in and taking over when I didn't have my head on straight but...but this is something we could have worked through together. You all I got, man. And I thought our bond was much stronger than that," I said, softly.

"It is. That's why I couldn't go another day without telling you. It's been killing me not being able to, but I did what I thought was best." Stephon looked just as hurt as I was.

"So, when was he born? She had to just have had him."

"He's a week old today. She had him on your birthday. I guess after seeing you last week, it was too much for her. Because, by the time she came home, she was already in pain."

I smiled. "On my birthday, huh? She had him on my motherfucking birthday." I sat and thought about how God had a way of working things out for the best. "So, now what Stephon? You seem to be the man with all the answers. What do you want me to do?"

He hesitated for a moment. "I've asked Nokea to marry me. She accepted, and in less than six months we're going to be married. I don't want to keep you from seeing your son, but I want to be a part of his life too. He will definitely know who his father is and I will never do anything to keep him from you."

I could have damn near died. "So, now you're going to marry her? Just like that. Walk her down the aisle knowing damn well that she still loves me. Man, that's crazy. How can you be with a woman knowing how she truly feels? Don't make any sense and it damn sure ain't going to help this fucked-up situation."

"Well, it makes sense to Nokea and me. She's different, cuz. Ever since she's had the baby. She wants a family. She wants to set the same good examples her parents set for her. And personally, I think she is starting to love me. I didn't expect you to be happy for us...but I would like for you to be my best man. I really wouldn't have it no other way." I stood up and put the baby on my shoulder. Did the best I could anyway because I really didn't know how to hold him.

"Stephon, you have got to be out of your fucking mind," I said, not knowing any other way to put it. "You expect me to stand there and watch you marry the woman I love. Man, please. I'll be there because you asked me to, but I won't be a part of something so ridiculous." I stood by the window and looked at Scorpio and Mackenzie outside washing the cars.

"Jay, man, don't be like that. We can put this behind us, today. We can accept this situation for what it is and move on. Please man; be there for me. You don't have to give me an answer today but think about it." He picked the baby's pumpkin seat up. "We gotta go. I told Nokea I was taking him to the barbershop to brag on him. She's going to be looking for us so I'd better go."

I closed my eyes and kissed my son on the forehead. I gave him to Stephon and watched him lay him down in the pumpkin seat. Motherfucker had my son and my woman and wasn't a damn thing I could do about it. It was actually the first time in my life I wasn't in control. He gave me a hug and got ready to walk out of my office with my baby.

"Don't forget, Jay, think about it. Call me when you've made your mind up."

"I already gave you my answer, Stephon. Ain't much to think about, but you can do me a favor. Tell Nokea to call me. I want to talk to her and make sure this is what she wants to do."

"No problem. Will do. I'll ask her to call you later." He walked out and knew damn well that he wasn't going to tell Nokea shit. I looked out of the window and watched him put my baby in the car.

I couldn't blame anyone but myself for fucking Nokea over like I did. I never thought my mistakes would have cost me my son and the only woman I'd ever loved. But no question about it, what goes around definitely comes around, and I started to feel the effects of every bit of it.

I sat in my office all day long with the door locked. Scorpio hollered in and told me her and Mackenzie would be at her sister's house for a while. I guess she figured I needed time to myself since I'd refused to come out of my office when she asked me to.

It had gotten dark outside, and still, I didn't move. I didn't turn on any lights, just sat there thinking. I called on Mama and she encouraged me to go get my son. Said she was finally proud of me for realizing the mistakes I'd made. Claimed it was not always about me, even though I wanted it to be, and yelled at me for not respecting her wishes by being with Nokea. When I tried to touch her again, I woke up. It was another dream, but it seemed so damn real.

I got up in the dark and lay on the couch in my office. I rested my fist on my head and the tears started to roll down my face. I put my hand on my chest and let out a loud cry. I was hurting and no one was there to stop my pain. No one was there to hug me, and right about now I needed that more than anything in the world.

Shortly after soaking in my misery, there was a light knock at the door. "Daddy, are you in there? Come out. You haven't played with me all day."

I smiled as I felt a sudden sense of relief. I walked to the door, opened it, and locked it back when Mackenzie came in. I sat back on the couch in the dark because I definitely didn't want Mackenzie to see I'd been crying.

"Daddy, why are you in the dark?" she whispered, as she hopped up on the couch and turned on the lamp next to it.

"Because, Mackenzie, I'm thinking." I held my head down. She got off the couch and stood in front of me. Then she lifted my head like I did hers when felt down.

"Have you been crying?" she asked. "It looks like you've been crying." She wiped her hands on my face. "Don't cry. I'll take care of you." I busted out in more tears. She held me and we rocked back and forth together.

"I love you, Mackenzie," I said, holding her tight.

"I love you too, Daddy. But, I'm hungry. Would you make me some of those pancakes you made me last week?"

"Sure, baby. Anything you want."

I walked her into the kitchen. Scorpio came in and sat on one of the stools. Mackenzie didn't waste no time telling her I'd been crying, and she looked at me with sympathy in her eyes.

"I know. I know that was your baby Stephon had today. I want you to know that I will be here for you if you need me. Whatever you decide to do, I'll back you all the way. Even if that means you want me to move out. I talked to my sister about moving back in with her and she said it would be okay—"

"Scorpio, I don't know what I'm going to do. But I haven't asked you to move anywhere. Don't go making plans to move out just yet, alright? Besides, I need you right now. Need you more than I ever have before. You and Mackenzie both." Scorpio walked over and gave me a hug.

"I love you," she whispered. "More than you will ever know."

34 FELICIA

Stephon and I fucked every chance we got. He crept into my place and I crept into his. But when he told me he had proposed to Nokea, I was devastated. It didn't stop him from putting it on me, though. I put it on him pretty thick and tried to get him to change his mind, but after a while, I didn't see that happening. No matter how hard I worked my thang on him, he stood his ground. I thought about calling the bitch up and telling her the news about her so-called fiancé, but knowing her, she'd probably try to kill her damn self. And I didn't want to be responsible for nobody taking his or her damn life.

She was a fool though: a prime example of every stupid bitch who puts all her fucking trust in one damn man. I knew better. And even though I kicked Paul and Damion aside for Stephon, the door was always open so they could come back. I made sure of that because I kept our conversations going, the dinners going—and even the money. Anything I needed, they gave. But me, I'd cut off all the sex. Wasn't no need for me to be fucking three men when Stephon tore it up like he did. Pertaining to sex, no question about it, he was definitely better than Jaylin.

When Stephon and I got together, we were like two dogs in heat. He couldn't stay away from me for two days so I didn't know how he thought this marriage thing would work itself out. If it did, he knew damn well that as soon as the honeymoon was over, he'd climb right back into my bed. When I brought that to his attention, he laughed. Laughed because he knew I wasn't lying. He knew Nokea couldn't satisfy his physical needs like I could. So, I knew for sure, if I wasn't a pain in her side now, I'd sure as hell be one in the future. The Jaylin drama was over for us, but her husband drama had just begun.

I'd called ole Jaylin a few times to try and explain the Stephon situation, but he didn't give a fuck. I knew he wouldn't, but to hear him say it kind of fucked me up. He kept it real short, and when I asked if I could cook him dinner for old time's sake, he hung up on me. I was a little hurt but I wasn't expecting him to embrace me with kindness. After all, I knew Stephon probably shared the details about our relationship with him anyway.

Stephon promised to be here no later than nine o'clock. But when he didn't show until eleven-thirty that night, I was pissed. I had put the food back in the refrigerator and sat on the couch with my arms folded, as he tried to explain why he was so late.

"Look, Felicia, I told you I had to work late tonight. A couple of fellas called the shop and told me they needed their haircut before going to this concert tonight. Since I need the money, I stayed and cut it for them."

"Well, you could have called. I cooked all this food for you and you didn't even have the decency to call and tell me you were going to be late. And when I paged you, you didn't even call back."

"I don't know what else to tell you. I'm answering to you like you're my fucking woman or something. Let's get an understanding, now, before this shit starts to get out of hand. I don't answer to no motherfucker! I've told you where I've been out of the kindness of my heart. But if you don't believe me, that's your problem, not mine." He stood up and got ready to leave.

I grabbed his hand, as I didn't want his sexy ass to leave without screwing me.

"Stephon, I'm sorry. You're right. You don't owe me an explanation. I appreciate what you told me, but I get upset when I think about you being with someone else."

"Well, ain't no need for you to think about it. I am with someone else. And not just Nokea. So, make your mind up because I'm not going to be dealing with this bullshit every time I come over here. Either you're with it, or you're not. If you decide to deal with it, then I don't want to hear anything else about it, okay?"

"No trip. But don't get upset with me when I get back to business with some other people who I've put on the back burner for you."

"I never asked you to put anybody on the back burner for me. You did that yourself. So, don't be mad at me about your own decision."

"I'm not, I thought it would make things easier for you and I, that's all."

"Naw, baby," he said, standing and unbuttoning his pants. "Do what you want and with who you want. I ain't got no control over it."

Stephon took the rest of his clothes off and undressed me as well. He fucked me good. So good that I realized even though his mouth said he had no control, his dick showed me he did.

After he left at three in the morning, I put some clothes on and took a late night drive down by the St. Louis Riverfront. I parked close to the river and laid a blanket on the ground so I could sit and think for a while. For a sista to have it going on like I did, I was a bit disappointed in myself for settling for less when it came to men. I knew I could have always had one to call my own, but couldn't figure out why I always had to have somebody else's man. Paul was the only man I ever had that I could call my own and I treated him like garbage. I knew if he and I got together, there would be nothing in the world I couldn't have—with the exception of a big dick. But a part of me knew that wasn't what it was all about. Paul had hinted several times about us getting married, so going forward, I was going to focus on trying to make it happen. I knew Stephon's good loving would set me back a few times, but since he had plans to move on with Nokea, it was high time I moved on as well.

35 NOKEA

Nobody in the world was happier than I was. I still had my Jaylin withdrawals, but slowly but surely those were fading away. My baby showed me how important it was for me to be there for him. I loved him more than life itself and hadn't let anyone or anything stand in the way of our happiness.

Not even Stephon. I could feel something wasn't right with him, and when Pat told me she saw him at the Old Spaghetti Factory on Laclede's Landing with this other chick, it confirmed my suspicions. I didn't question him about it or anything; I'd had enough of dealing with unfaithful men and really didn't have time to give it my attention. The only person who needed that kind of attention from me was little Jaylin.

I still planned to marry Stephon because I knew that sooner or later he would get his mess together. And even though he cheated, what man wasn't? To me, it's in their nature. And no matter how hard they tried not to, they just couldn't be right even if their lives depended on it. As long as he gave little Jaylin and me what we needed, I really didn't care.

When the phone rang, I was rocking LJ to sleep. I hurried to it because Mama was supposed to come over and watch him while I went to the gym, but she was late. It was Jaylin. I was surprised to hear from him, but also, it was good to hear his voice. He asked if he could come over, but when I told him I thought that might not be a good idea, he begged me to come to his place. He said it was important that we talked, and since I knew Stephon had told him about the engagement, I figured I had to at least tell him the news myself.

I put on a sexy outfit to make sure I looked better than the last time I'd seen Jaylin. My weight was back to normal so I wasn't too worried about it. When Mama came over, she said it didn't look like I was going to the gym. But when I told her I had plans to see Jaylin, she smiled and told me she loved me.

I was nervous about going to see him. Every time we got together something always seemed to go wrong. This time, I kept my head up and prayed for God to give me strength.

I rang his doorbell and waited for him to answer. He ran and opened the door quickly. I stepped inside and felt more nervous because he definitely wasn't smiling.

"Have a seat, Nokea," he said, walking me into the living room. "Can I get you anything?"

"Yes. Some water. My throat is a little dry." I tested him because I knew Jaylin never served his guests water. He smiled and walked into the kitchen. Then came back with a glass of water in his hand.

"Here," he said. "Take your time though because you won't be getting any refills."

"And why not?" I said, laughing.

"Because, I ran out. Besides, there's something in that water I don't want anyone to have but you."

"Oh, yeah, and what's that?" I said, holding the glass up to my lips.

"It's called love. And since I never knew how to love anyone before, it was hard for me to do. Today, I can only thank God for putting people in my life to show me how. There are so many things I want to tell you—but first, I want to tell you I love you. I don't know what that means to you but it means a whole hell of a lot to me."

Jaylin sat next to me on the couch. I uncrossed my legs and put the glass of water on the table. He quickly grabbed a coaster and put it underneath the glass.

"I want my son, Nokea. I want him in my life twenty-four-seven. Not only that, I want my woman back."

"But, Jaylin, what about your other women? What about Stephon? I can't turn my back on him after all he's done for me. I'm finally happy and he's part of the reason why. Things can't just happen when you want them to."

"I know, I know, but there aren't any more women. The only person I've been chilling with for a while is Scorpio. But, we decided that she move out. I bought her a condo, had my interior decorator hook it up for her, and we're trying to move on. We do get together at times, though. As for her daughter, who I love with all my heart, she comes to see me twice during the week and spends the night here on the weekends. Right now, I'm going through the channels to adopt her. But it's still not enough. Especially since I know I have a son now." Jaylin was almost in tears. "Come on, let me show you something."

208

He grabbed my hand and walked me up the steps. He showed me the guestroom he'd converted into a baby's room. It was to die for—better than the room I had for the baby at home. It was blue, yellow and white. The walls were painted with white clouds and had yellow birds drawn on them like they flew around the room. The crib was round and had sheer blue material above it that draped to the floor. It was white and matched the dresser and the changing table that had light blue handles on them. The closet was filled with baby clothes: T-shirts, pants, jogging suits, and tennis shoes. Like LJ was really going to be able to wear all these things. So damn infatuated with the room, I walked around almost in tears. And when I looked in the baby's bed and saw the Teddy bear, I damn near lost it.

Jaylin came over and held me in his arms.

"I feel you, baby. I know exactly how you feel." I saw a tear fall down his face. "Do you still love me?" he asked, backing away from me.

"Jaylin, I can't answer that. I'm confused right now. I don't know how I feel." He pulled me closer to him.

"Let me make love to you today. I know it hasn't been that long since you've had the baby but I promise you I'll be gentle. I promise it will be everything you always wanted it to be. And if it's not, then you leave here and go marry Stephon. I won't interfere with your relationship with him any more."

"Jaylin, I do still love you. But, I don't know if making love to you is going to solve my problems. I don't know if it's going to answer all these questions I have. In fact, I think it's going to complicate things more if I do..."

He put his fingers over my lips then he picked me up and carried me to his bedroom. He laid me on the bed and pulled his shirt over his head. He eased between my legs, and came up closer to me.

"Don't think about anything else right now but me," he said, knowing that I started to think about him being in this bed with Scorpio, Felicia, and who knows who else. "Clear your mind right now, and think about me making love to you."

I closed my eyes as Jaylin undressed me. And as I cleared my mind, I helped him remove his pants. He closed his eyes and laid his head on my chest for a minute like he was in deep thought. Then he opened them and went to work on me.

As his hands massaged my breasts, I leaned my head back and thought about how good they felt on my body. He gently circled his tongue around my nipples and they gave him their full attention. As he went down and kissed my belly, I ran my fingers through his soft curly hair. He couldn't wait to taste my insides and I couldn't wait for him to either. As I trembled and thought about how good he made me feel, I put my hand between my legs to stop him; that wasn't how I anticipated on coming. He smiled because he knew exactly what I wanted, and when he went inside, I could have cried. He stroked me gently and the feel of him was better than it had ever been before. I wrapped my legs around his back as he rubbed his soft hands up and down them. I hadn't thought about ending this anytime soon and neither was he.

After a while, he slowed down a bit and I unwrapped my legs from around his waist. He kissed me and nibbled on my ear.

"That tickles," I said, moving my head so he would stop.

"Turn over so I can love you from behind," he whispered.

His wish was my command. I turned over on my stomach and he laid his body on top of me. He held himself up with his strong arms and rolled his tongue down my back. After he kissed my butt cheeks and massaged them with his hands, he then reached around and fondled my insides while inserting himself back inside me. No doubt, my insides burned for him. The only thing I could do is lay my head down on his pillow and prevent myself from trying to pull my hair out.

Soon, we released our energy together, and he continued to kiss the back of my neck.

"I love you, I love you, I love you," he repeated.

"I love you too. But, what now, Jaylin? Do we now just say to hell with everybody who's been there for us? Do I go home and tell my parents I've changed my mind? I'm not marrying Stephon?" Jaylin was quiet for a minute. He brushed his lips across the back of my head and kissed it.

"You don't tell anybody anything," he whispered. "You go home and hold my son in your arms and think about what's best for him. You think about who you want in your future. Think about where your heart truly is and where it's always been. And when you get your answer, you come over here again so I can make love to you like I just did and we can talk about putting our relationship back together. If there is any doubt in your mind, I want you to be honest with yourself. I don't want you to have any regrets, and would rather you stay with Stephon if you think I can't be everything you want me to be. The last time I told you to go home and think about it, I didn't give you time to think. I decided for you. This time, I'm not. If you want to be with me, I'm here. I'm not going anywhere until I hear from you."

We got out of bed and took a shower. As he washed me, the thought of him being with Scorpio was in my mind. And when I washed him, I knew the thought of me being with Stephon had crossed his as well. Trying to clear my thoughts, I asked Jaylin to make love to me again and he did.

Afterwards, Jaylin sat in the bed and watched *The Steve Harvey Show*. I put my clothes on and got ready to go. He said Scorpio was on her way to bring Mackenzie over for the night, so I hurried as fast as I could. The last person I wanted to see was her. She had a way of making me feel insecure—I really felt none of this would have happened if she had never met Jaylin. But the more I thought about it someone else probably would have interfered.

Jaylin walked me to the door and kissed me goodbye. No sooner had I got in my car, Scorpio pulled up. She really was an attractive woman and I knew Jaylin had to have a difficult time keeping his hands off her. And as much as he claimed to love me now, a part of me knew she would remain in the picture no matter what.

I watched as her daughter ran up to Jaylin and he picked her up. He was all smiles and so was she. As he waved goodbye to me, she waved with him. I waved back and hurt badly inside. I really knew that no matter how hard I tried, this just wasn't going to work out. As I drove away, Luther sang on the radio "I'd Rather." On the way home, I listened as he said "he'd rather have bad times with the one he loved than good times with someone else." I didn't quite understand why, but I definitely understood where he came from.

36 JAYLIN

I could see the hurt on Scorpio's face when Nokea pulled off. And when she went up to my room and saw the bed all messed up, she sat on the chaise and looked at me with disappointment in her eyes.

"So, is it over between us Jaylin? Is this as far as we go?" she asked. I went over to the bed and sat in front of her. I took her hands and rubbed them in mine.

"For the most part, it is. But I don't want you to ever think you didn't mean anything to me. These past months with you have been the most exciting time in my life. You've taught me a lot. More than I thought you would when I met you. I was in it for one thing and you knew it. Never in my wildest dreams did I think I would come out of this with a daughter who I love with all of my heart—and with so much respect for you. So, don't walk away from this feeling empty-handed. If there's anything, and I mean anything, I can do for you, I will."

Scorpio wiped a tear from her cheek and looked at me. "Jaylin, I never wanted anything from you but for you to love me. I was so sure I did everything to make you do that. But, I'm not giving up on you that easily. I was always taught to fight for what I wanted and I intend to do just that."

"Baby, but I'm in love with someone else. I don't know what good fighting is going to do you when my heart is with her. I'm just telling you this because I don't want to see you continuing to hurt yourself over something that will never be. Besides, I want my little girl growing up with a mother who is sure of herself. One who knows she can't fight a battle that can't be won. Don't make her suffer through watching us tear each other apart because we can't get along, okay?" I handed Scorpio the Kleenex box on my nightstand and she wiped her eyes again.

"So, what about just last week? You made love to me like you wanted to be with me forever. You can't tell me you were thinking about her when that was happening. You seemed to be right there with me. Am I wrong?"

"No, I was there. I'm always there but...but there comes a time when sex just ain't everything. I know coming from a man you might not believe that but I'm at a point in my life when I want more than just

212

sex. And everything else I want aside from sex, I can't get from you. Not to say you're not good enough, but there's some things that, over time, I know only Nokea can give me—"

"See, Jaylin, this is all messed up because I know you. You're saying these things today, but tomorrow, you'll have a new attitude. You'll come over to my place and strip me naked. Convince me to make love to you and be right back there again two days later. In the meantime, what do you want me to do? I can't resist. I can tell you no all I want, but we both know I'm going to give in to you. And when I do, I'm continuing to set myself up for disappointment after disappointment."

"I'm not going to deny what you're saying because you're right. But I'm going to need you to stand your ground. Tomorrow might be different for me. I probably will be knocking at your door some lonely nights, but be woman enough to stop me. Especially since I've told you where things stand. The harder you make things for me, the easier you're going to make things for yourself. I have a sexual passion for you that I've never had for any other woman. Including Nokea. But the love I have for her goes deeper than that. And that passion is going to bring me back to you over and over again. Until you say no. When you say no, then I won't have a choice but to move on."

Scorpio went into the bathroom and splashed some water on her face. She looked at the shower that still dripped from my recent encounter with Nokea. I didn't like myself right about now because I'd for damn sure hurt too many women. I always thought it was about me, not realizing they had needs and feelings too.

I tried to make Scorpio laugh before she left and dressed up like a Barbie doll because Mackenzie had asked me to. Scorpio seemed out of it, though. If anything, I knew how badly she was hurt. When she got ready to leave, I hugged her and patted her ass.

"If you decide to give yourself to someone else, don't let him get it from behind because that's my place," I said, laughing. She found no humor in what I said and didn't crack a smile.

"See, Jaylin. That's what I'm talking about. Don't be saying or doing shit like that," she said, pointing her finger at me.

"I just wanted to see what you were going to tell me, that's all." We laughed and she walked out of the door.

Brenda M. Hampton

The next several weeks were hell. I was sure I'd hear from Nokea but she never called. Didn't come by either. I promised myself I would give her time to think about what she wanted to do. However, when Stephon called and asked again about being his best man, I knew the wedding was still on. Still hurt, I continued to turn him down. Told him it wasn't in my best interests to be there for him like that. And when he said they'd made plans for their honeymoon, I was crushed. I continued our conversation like I wasn't even tripping. Certainly, after our conversation was finished, I got right back on the phone and called Scorpio. She'd made herself available to me whenever I called. And when she did try to tell me no, I went to her place anyway. I had a key to let myself in and fucked her like fucking was going out of style. Couldn't help myself.

And to think Nokea didn't even have the decency to call and tell me she'd made her decision, really fucked me up. Tore me apart. I couldn't concentrate on anything but the last time we were together. How deep my love was for her. She had to know it. If not, she had to feel it.

I went into my son's room and looked around. He was almost two months now and didn't even know I existed. He'd never spent one fucking night with me, and if it were left up to Stephon and Nokea, he never would. Stephon promised he wouldn't keep him from knowing who his real father was, but every time I talked about bringing LJ over to see me, Stephon always made excuses. If he did bring him by, they only stayed for a few minutes then he said they had to go. The only reason I wasn't trying to see him more was because I promised Nokea I wouldn't interfere after she made her decision. I just truly wished it had been different.

37 JAYLIN

A week before the wedding, I had mentally prepared myself for it. Everything else in my life went smoothly. The market was on its way back up and my adoption of Mackenzie had gone every bit of my way. I spent every moment I had with her, and tried to ease some of the pain I felt. Without a doubt, she helped me cope very well. I'd even changed the baby's room back into a guestroom. Gave all his clothes to charity and sold his furniture to my neighbor who was pregnant.

Nokea, never did call and I made no attempts to call her. It was obvious who she wanted to be with so I left things as they were. Scorpio didn't lie though; she wasn't giving up on me and did everything in her power to win me over. Even had Mackenzie begging me to get back together with her. And even though Nokea had moved on with her life, I still wasn't ready for the type of relationship Scorpio wanted with me.

Fucked me up, though, because according to Stephon, he still saw Felicia and screwed around with his ex-girlfriend. And if that wasn't bad enough, he planned to get up on this new chick that started working with him several weeks ago. So, Nokea really had her work cut out for her if she planned on marrying him.

Me, I pretty much chilled. I was down to fucking Scorpio about twice a week and that was it. For me, that was good considering the fact it used to be twice a day. I'd met a few other ladies from time to time, but wasn't nothing but phone conversations going on. I hadn't invited anyone over yet until I knew for myself this marriage was actually going to happen.

The night of Stephon's bachelor party was like any other night to me. He'd invited me and so did our other boys, but I made it clear to him that I didn't want to have anything to do with his marriage to Nokea. He called in the middle of it and told me what went down. Sounded pretty interesting when he talked titties and ass, but I wasn't in the mood. I told him to knock one out for me and hung up.

I lay my head back on the pillow, tired from flipping from channel to channel, when the phone rang. When I heard Nokea's voice, I quickly sat up on my bed.

"Jaylin, I'm sorry I haven't called you until now but I felt this was the only way for me to figure out what I really wanted to do. I had to give Stephon at least six months to show me if he really cared for me. And even though I know there's a possibility he's sleeping with someone else, I truly don't believe it's going to be any different with you. You told me if I had any doubts, to marry him...so that's what I'm going to do." I was quiet because I'd finally heard it straight from her mouth. I cleared my throat, as it ached so badly.

"So, have you prepared yourself for the storm? It's headed your way. And it's nothing like what I did to you. It's worse." She didn't respond. "My storm is over. I'm not saying I've been celibate, but it's been different since I've been in love with you." I could hear her crying on the other end of the phone. "Stop torturing yourself and let this happen with us. I won't get another chance to ask you before the wedding tomorrow, but think about it. Close your pretty eyes tonight and think about us—" She hung up the damn phone on me. And when I sat for a moment and thought about why, she called back.

"Hey," she said, sniffling. "I love you."

"Right back at you," I said.

She hung up again.

After talking to Nokea, I turned on the radio to listen to Doc Wynter from Majic 104.9 and the Quiet Storm. I turned off the lights and lay there with my eyes closed and with one hand resting on my chest. I hoped that Nokea realized how much love I have for her. As Gerald Levert sang "Made To Love Ya" the words to the song took effect and tears fell. My heart felt like somebody squeezed in it their hands and wouldn't let go. And the harder I cried, the tighter the grip got. I reached into my drawer, pulled out a picture of Nokea, and laid it in bed next to me. I couldn't really see her picture in the dark but I rolled my fingertips around it thinking that I could feel her, and wished I could have her in my bed forever. I hoped that tomorrow she'd do the right thing.

As I fell off into a deep sleep, Mama stared down at me and smiled. She told me to go get my woman, my son, and told me to never lose them again. When I reached out to touch her, Aunt Betty touched my hand and told me it was too late for me. Said that Stephon was the one for Nokea and I didn't deserve her. As I started to dispute that with her, they both faded and I woke up.

The sunlight beamed through my room and I sat up on the edge of the bed with my face resting in my hands. A few more tears fell but I wiped them and got out of bed to prepare myself for a long day.

I was running late for the wedding messing around with Mackenzie. She acted like she was the one getting married, and looked like a little princess. We dressed alike in our cream outfits; mine a suit and hers a dress. We accented the cream with royal blue because that's what she wanted. But when I tied the bow around her waistline, she insisted it didn't look right. She pouted all the way there because I wouldn't stop by the store and get her a new color. Once again, I reminded her of our previous conversation and she perked up.

Mackenzie and I sat in the last pew of the church because I really didn't want to be seen. However, Stephon saw me and came over and sat next to me.

"Thanks, man. Thanks for coming. I know how hard this is for you but you always had my back when I needed you to—even when you refused to be my best man. It was foolish of me to ask knowing how you felt. I just hope after today, this will all be over."

"Me too," I said not being able to look at him.

"I want my cousin back. I miss kicking it with you dog. Talking about the ladies and shit. You can't tell me you don't miss the same."

"Of course I do," I said as a sharp pain hit me in the heart. "After today, I'll be alright. I came here not only for you but for me as well. I need closure. I need to put this shit behind me and get on with my fucking life. And after I see for myself, today, how happy you and Nokea are going to be, then I'll be able to do that. So, go do your thang, man, don't let me stop you."

"Thanks, bro. You don't know what it means for me to have your support."

"Always my brotha, always," I said, then watched Stephon as he walked and stood in front of the altar.

I looked at the front pew and saw Nokea's mother holding my baby. I wanted to walk down there and hold him, but the last person her mother wanted to see right about now was me. So, Mackenzie held her arm around mine and held it tight. She could feel the tension I was under and was my support system.

I took a deep breath as the music played and the bridesmaids started making their way down the aisle. When the Maid of Honor came in, I knew it was just about Nokea's time. The slower she walked, the better off I was. But seemed like shit moved fast and purposely did so. Then, the song played: "Here Comes The Motherfucking Bride." I dropped my head and couldn't even stand up and watch her as she walked down the aisle. Mackenzie stood up because everybody else was, and claimed the bride was the most beautiful thing she'd ever seen. As I held back my tears, I stood up as well. And when Nokea turned the corner right by my pew, she looked at me with her eyes filled with water. I nodded and gave her the go-ahead. She slightly nodded back.

As she got closer and closer to the altar, I looked at Stephon. He was all smiles. Definitely knew he was getting a jewel. And he'd promised me he would make her happy.

When Nokea made it to the altar, everybody took a seat. The minister prepared for the exchanging of vows. But before he did, he asked if there was anyone who knew any reason why these two should not be joined together in holy matrimony. "Speak now, or forever hold your peace," he said. I dropped my head again, covered my face with my hands, and then watched my legs as they trembled. I knew damn well that this was something I couldn't let happen. It was obvious to me that Nokea loved me, so I felt if I put her on the spot, she'd have to come to her senses and do the right thing.

I took a deep breath and stood up. I stepped out into the aisle and didn't give a fuck who looked at me. Mackenzie grabbed the back of my jacket and asked where I was going. I bent down, touched her soft little face, and then gave her a kiss.

"I always told you, you'd be the first to know baby. Daddy's going to get married."

I proceeded down the aisle and I could feel Mackenzie walking behind me. Everybody watched as I made my way to the altar. I stood there and held my hands behind my back with the entire church in disbelief. I cleared my throat and looked directly at the minister.

"I, uh..." I cleared my throat again. "I don't mean you any disrespect, sir, but I have love for this woman who stands before you today." I held my hand out for Nokea to take it. I looked her directly in the eyes. "If love for me is not a good reason to stop this wedding, then I don't know what is." I continued to hold my hand out for Nokea. Stephon's mouth was wide open and her father looked like he wanted to tear me apart. Nokea, though, she smiled as she dropped her bouquet on the floor.

Later that night, I smiled as I stood on my balcony and drank a glass of wine. I looked up at the stars as a south wind blew, and lifted my glass to Mama. Nokea's decision had made me realize how important it was for me to have someone in my life to love. I tilted my wineglass upside down, poured the wine out over the balcony, and thought about where I'd go from here. Going forward, it would be "MY WAY OR NO WAY."

Printed in the United States
49757LVS00006B/1-24